SECRETS OF
Truth & *Beauty*

by **MEGAN FRAZER**

Disney • HYPERION BOOKS
New York

MAKE YOUR OWN KIND OF MUSIC
Words and Music by Barry Mann and Cynthia Weil
© 1969 (Renewed 1994) SCREEN GEMS-EMI MUSIC INC.
All Rights Reserved   International Copyright Secured   Used by Permission

First edition
1 3 5 7 9 10 8 6 4 2
This book is set in 11-point Sabon.

Printed in the United States of America

Library of Congress Cataloging-in-Publication Data on file.

ISBN 978-1-4231-1711-7
Reinforced binding

Visit www.hyperionteens.com

For NCB

With you, all things are possible

Chapter One

It started with Mr. Fitz.

Mr. Fitz was a great teacher. Really. He wanted to inspire us, challenge us, and make us into better people. I think he found his calling while watching one of those movies about a heroic educator going into an inner-city school and turning kids around. But instead of saving at-risk teens, he ended up teaching at small, swanky Portland Academy, where half the kids were bound for the Ivy League, just out of inertia. Nonetheless, he was always trying to come up with new and exciting ways to get us involved in literature; so after we read *I Know Why the Caged Bird Sings*, we had to do our own autobiographies. It couldn't be a simple narrative, even though that was good enough for Maya

Angelou. No, we had to do a multimedia presentation.

"Try to organize your presentations around a theme. Think of the moments that have shaped you and made you who you are." It was late in the period, and Mr. Fitz was developing sweat stains under his arms.

Melissa rolled her eyes at me. Like we really wanted to watch seventeen multimedia presentations about our classmates.

"Really look into yourself: who are you? What do you stand for? Capture that using all the senses."

"Even smell?" Dennis Epstein asked. Our desks were in a circle, and he was a few seats away from me. His hair fell down in long bangs over his face and into his eyes. Some days he wore dark eyeliner, but today his eyes were clean.

"Even smell," Mr. Fitz said.

Dennis leaned back in his chair. If I were to tell the truth, I'd have to admit that I found Dennis Epstein attractive. Sure, he tried too hard to look like a rock star, but he could almost pull it off. Almost. "So, this should be like a scratch-and-sniff presentation?" he asked. I smiled even though it was kind of a dumb joke.

Mr. Fitz turned from the board, where he had written the word AUTOBIOGRAPHY in all caps with a blue dry-erase pen. "No, Dennis, this should not be a scratch-and-sniff presentation. But how else could you evoke scent?" He looked out over the class. I guess I hadn't completely wiped the grin off my face, because he called on me. "Dara?"

Dennis looked toward me, smirking. *Say something funny*, I thought. *Say something clever.* But I said, "With the words you use."

"Right!" Mr. Fitz grinned. "Fresh cut grass. Burning sugar. These don't just tell us how something smelled, they set the tone."

I glanced at Dennis, who'd gone back to looking totally bored. He almost always had that expression on his face. Even when I'd seen him in town with friends—usually emaciated hipster girls I didn't recognize—he'd seemed bored. Not surprisingly, he'd pretended not to see me.

"Let's brainstorm," Mr. Fitz said. "Take a few minutes to write down some ideas for your project." He leaned against his desk.

I stared at my notebook page. I, too, wrote AUTOBIOGRAPHY at the top. That was all. I hadn't done anything yet worth writing about or had anything tragic or exciting happen to me. None of us had. It was almost insulting to Maya Angelou to ask us to write autobiographies like hers.

Next to me, Melissa was filling her page. She swung her foot, and her frayed Free People flip-flop threatened to fall off. I knew she spent a lot of money to look poor, though she would have called her look "boho." I tried to peek over at her paper—some of her stories were my stories too—but her curly hair fell down like a curtain. Everyone was bent over, writing, writing, writing. Did they really have so much to say?

Even Katie North had a full paragraph. Now *Katie*, unlike Melissa, spent a lot of money to look rich. She wore jeans from companies that didn't even make them in my size, and tiny tank tops that pushed the boundaries of our lax school dress code. If I had worn them, I probably would have been called up to the office for showing too much cleavage. Slim as she was, she got away with it.

Dennis tapped his felt-tip pen against his notebook and stretched his long, thin legs out in front of him. His narrow pants barely reached the tops of his Converse All Stars, and his ribs showed through his vintage T-shirt, which was so thin it looked as if one more wash would tear it apart completely. I could tell from the way he was scribbling things in short spurts that he was writing lyrics. I had no idea whether his band, The Raging Tongues, was actually good, but he definitely had the look: gaunt, pale, a little sickly. Did he work at it, I wondered, or was he one of those lucky guys with a ridiculously fast metabolism?

It made me sad to look at him. It didn't help that just then my skirt was digging into my waist, which was very annoying since it was relatively new and in a size larger than I normally bought.

"All right, people," Mr. Fitz said. "Let's share. Dennis, what olfactory sensations did you hope to portray?"

Dennis tucked his pen behind his ear. "Well, Mr. Fitz, I have a really good idea that I'm working through, but I don't really want to share it, 'cause someone else might try to steal it." Steal an autobiography? Was he serious?

"A bold statement. At least tell us what scent you were so keen on including."

He stretched his hands out in front of him. "Vinyl."

I wondered if Dennis had ever actually listened to music on vinyl. My dad kept an old record player, and when I was younger, we had listened to show tunes, jazz standards, and opera together. He once had his collection appraised and found that it was worth thousands of dollars, not that he'd ever sell.

"Good." Mr. Fitz clasped his hands in front of him. "Who else?"

We all looked down at our desks.

"Avoiding eye contact will not keep you from getting picked," Mr. Fitz said. "Kathryn, what have you got?"

Katie North twirled her pen around her fingers like a baton. Her face was so vacant, I didn't think she had heard him. But then she said, "I don't get it, Mr. Fitz, are we supposed to do our whole life or just part of it?"

"Good question. I'm looking for a part that represents the whole." He picked up the dry-erase pen. "What's the literary term for this part-whole relationship?" He paused for a moment, waiting for someone to answer. "Dara?"

I thought about pretending I didn't know, but both Mr. Fitz and I knew that I did; it had been a key part of my final paper last year. "Synecdoche," I said. Part of me was proud for knowing something that no one else did, but I was also embarrassed, because it was obviously the kind of thing you only know if you spend way too much time reading.

"Perfect. So, Dara, what are your thoughts?"

"Thoughts?" I asked, blushing. It seemed unfair that my reward for knowing the answer was having to spill my project ideas.

"Have you come up with some potential topics?"

I scribbled a spiral onto the paper in front of me. "I'm not really sure yet . . . but I guess I was thinking I might do something about being an only child that my parents had late in life, or something."

Melissa wrote *Yawn* on her paper, and pushed it over to me. I shrugged. It was the first thing that had popped into my head. My parents were a good twenty years older than all my friends' parents. There was a long story behind this fact, but Melissa didn't know that. I had never told her.

Mr. Fitz said, "That could work. You'll probably need to find more of a focus, though."

"Weren't you in some beauty pageant?" Dennis asked.

I felt my cheeks grow warm. How did he know that? He hadn't gone to the Lower School; he had transferred in for ninth grade. Only a handful of the people in that room, Melissa among them, knew me back in those days. The whole class stared at me.

"She was Little Miss Maine," Melissa said, grinning.

"It's no big deal," I said.

"That's what I'd do my project on if I were you," Dennis said. "Those things are creepy as hell."

"It's really not that interesting," I said quickly. "I just sang and tap-danced."

"And won," Melissa added. She leaned over her desk, excited to talk me up. I wished she'd just s*hut up*, because I knew what everyone in the class was thinking.

"You won Little Miss Maine?" Katie asked. She looked amused, like she had just caught me in a lie and was ready to pounce. "The beauty pageant?"

"Actually, it's a talent pageant." A subtle difference to be sure, but one I felt compelled to point out. Anyway, screw her, she hadn't known me back then. She didn't know how cute I had been.

"Wow," Katie said. For a second, she almost seemed impressed. "I think it would be really interesting if you did your project about the pageant, and you know, what happened *after*."

She might as well have punched me. Melissa was ready to jump out of her seat and throttle Katie, although, really, Melissa had given Katie her ammunition.

No one said anything. There's that expression about the elephant in the room—this big, glaring, obvious thing that no one is talking about. Not for the first time in my life, I felt like the elephant.

Here's what happened after the pageant: I got fat. Not immediately after—the weight came slowly. But I'd been skinny and cute then, and now I wasn't, and Katie just had to point that out in front of the whole class.

My mom said the weight gain was a reaction to the pageant. I was uncomfortable being judged on my appearance, and rebelled by sabotaging my looks. Whatever. It just sort of happened, right around the time I turned eleven. First the hips came, and then the boobs. And then the little paunch around my stomach. Then on one horrible shopping trip right before seventh grade, I discovered that I was too big for regular girls' sizes. I panicked in the dressing room, staring at my tear-streaked reflection in the mirror for a long time before I finally emerged. My mom didn't even have to ask what was wrong; we silently walked over to the adjacent women's store.

Mr. Fitz was nodding, oblivious to Katie's insult. "The pageant seems like intriguing material. What do you think, Dara?"

I heard someone snicker. "I don't know," I said. I did know: I had no interest in doing my project on the Little Miss Maine pageant. Couldn't Mr. Fitz see how mortifying this was?

"It sounds very interesting to me," he said. "Great audio visual potential."

I frowned and spiraled my pen harder into my paper, desperate for us to move on to embarrassing someone else. But Tina Baxter raised her hand. She and her boyfriend, Dimitri, who sat next to her and never spoke, were the lone emo-goths at Portland Academy. "Didn't you feel, like, so, I don't know, cattlelike for having all those men judge you?"

Cattlelike. I couldn't tell if Tina had meant something by that or not. "Most judges are women," I said. But I wasn't answering her question, and we both knew it. "I didn't really think about it that way. I just liked singing and dancing and having people clap for me."

Tina raised a single pierced eyebrow. Thankfully, Mr. Fitz moved on. "Well, now Dara has some ideas. Who's next?"

So everyone, Mr. Fitz included, wanted to see me do my presentation on being in a pageant and getting fat? Was it really so fascinating? The thing was, if this could have been an anonymous project, I actually did have something important and interesting I might have explored. But it was too personal, and too messy, as real-life stories tend to be.

Chapter Two

After class, Melissa looped her bony arm through mine as if nothing had happened, and we made our way downstairs to the cafeteria. "Ah, do I detect the fine odor of day-old chicken?" she asked as we pushed through the door to the dining hall.

I tipped my head back and inhaled dramatically, as if I were stepping outside on the first warm day of spring to smell the lilacs. "Accompanied by soggy green beans and salty rice pilaf."

"Lovely," she said.

"Perfect," I agreed.

Melissa skipped off to make herself a peanut butter and jelly sandwich, her gold lamé headband glinting in the fluorescent lighting. I went to the salad bar and filled my plate. I was tempted to try the new dijon ranch, but I realized that if I was going to pour pure fat on my salad, I might as well have gotten the fried chicken (not like I'd ever eat fried chicken in front of my classmates). Instead, I grabbed the bottle of balsamic vinegar and doused my vegetables. Madame Bovary had drunk straight vinegar in order to lose weight. Probably an odd thing to know, but it was the type of trivia that stuck in my head. I tried it once, just to see what it was like, and the taste alone made me gag.

I saw Melissa and her boyfriend, Jeremy, sit down at our regular table, and walked over to them. I took a seat with my back to the wall and slid forward, so just the edge of my butt was on the seat, and my thighs didn't spread out across the bench.

Jeremy had gone for the fried chicken, which he surrounded with rice and french fries. "That's going to kill you someday," Melissa said, taking a self-righteous bite of her peanut butter and jelly.

"It's good," he replied. "I don't know why you guys complain about the food so much." I glanced down at my lunch. It had actually been a good day at the salad bar: fresh field greens and ripe grape tomatoes as opposed to the limp iceberg lettuce and pale beefsteaks they sometimes served. And at public schools they probably didn't even have salad bars. Still, it was hard to get too excited about it.

Jeremy dug into his lunch, taking huge bites that somehow didn't look piggish. He was cute and sloppy in an alt-rock sort of way: today he wore a faded blue T-shirt with a green hoodie over it, despite the warm weather. He still had mild bedhead, and as always, he looked slightly amused. He and

Melissa sat side-by-side with their bodies pressed together, a magazine-perfect vision of teenage coupledom.

I snuck a glance over at Dennis Epstein. I got the feeling he was looking at me while he spoke to his friends, and it was making me nervous. Was he talking about me? Was that a good thing? I'm no lip-reader, but I'm pretty sure he said the words "beauty pageant." All the girls giggled. I looked down at my plate and willed myself not to blush or get angry. Melissa would notice and ask me what was wrong, and then we'd have to go into what happened in class.

Thankfully, just then Simon, Claire, and Toby joined us.

"So," Melissa said in greeting. "Tomorrow night. You guys in?" My stomach did a little flip.

"Absolutely," Toby said.

The plan was to try to go see a band at Geno's, an over twenty-one show. Claire raised her eyebrows at Melissa, and Melissa answered with a subtle wink. I wasn't sure what this little dialogue meant, but I assumed it had to do with Claire's goal to hook up with Toby by the end of the school year. Then Melissa turned to me with her sweet-as-you-please look. "Can you be the driver, Dara? You always drink less than us anyway."

I did not, in fact, drink less than Claire or Melissa. They were just so tiny that they got hammered after two beers. "Actually . . ." I began. "Actually, I'm not sure if I can make it."

"Big plans?" Melissa asked with a hint of sarcasm.

"No, it's just . . ." I let my voice trail off. I couldn't think of an excuse that didn't sound lame.

"What's the worst that could happen?" Jeremy asked. "They tell us no and we go get pizza or something."

That wasn't the worst, though. The worst would be if everyone else got in and then the bouncer eyed me and said, "Sorry, lady, we're at capacity." A close second: Claire and Toby finally get together, and the two pairs spend the evening in blissed-out coupledom, while I'm ignored, not drinking because I have to drive my friends home. Another option: we all get in, and the twenty-somethings hit on Melissa and Claire, but not on me. This was the most likely scenario, as it was what happened whenever we went out together. They'd spend the night flirting, while I'd try to feign interest in the bowling scorecard or a pamphlet on organically harvested coffee. Another evening of that just didn't seem fun. In fact, the whole thing seemed completely not worth the effort.

I poked at a tomato. "This weekend is really bad for me. This autobiography thing is going to take a lot of work."

"You throw a couple of pictures of you in the pageant into a PowerPoint, what's so hard about that?" Melissa never really believed that I had to work for my good grades.

"I need to get an A on this or I won't have a flat A in the class, and in the spring of junior year, that's bad."

Melissa shook her head, making her curls bounce, and it was clear why so many people found it hard to say no to her—she was adorable. "It's a show. You like music. They're supposed to be like Modest Mouse, only cuter. And anyway, you love going to see live bands, even when they're crappy."

"I'm sorry," I said. "I'm out."

Melissa didn't reply. She was angry, but there wasn't anything I could do about that. I had made my decision.

Chapter Three

I got home from school at 3:00, thankful to have a couple of hours to myself. I dropped my bag at the foot of the stairs and went into my mom's office, leaving the door open in case she or my dad got home early. That way I could scuttle out and they wouldn't know I'd been poking around.

Mom worked for an investment firm as a wealth and asset manager—she helped rich people get even richer. She had a huge office downtown that over-looked the port. But she was always working, so she also had a home office with a beautiful set of cherry furniture. She kept all of our family documents there, in a small file cabinet next to her desk. I slid open the second drawer and flipped to the back where I found the folder labeled "Rachel."

Every family has secrets, or so I've heard. They never seem very interesting unless they are your own.

When I was seven, my parents took me to Disney World so that I could meet Grumpy. My father had told me I was so sweet, so lovely, that even Grumpy couldn't be grumpy around me. I was there to cure him! We spent the first day going from ride to ride, scattershot, each attraction more enticing than the last. They took my picture with every costumed character that happened by. At the end of that first day, though, we still hadn't seen Grumpy.

"You can see him tomorrow," Dad promised.

I sat down on the preternaturally clean sidewalk and threw my first temper tantrum. Dad brought me an ice-cream cone, which I pushed back at him and mashed into his jeans. He went in search of Grumpy. He found Goofy, Daisy, Sleepy, but no Grumpy. I clenched my fists and wailed, surrounded by a small cast of Disney characters. Mom leaned her head into mine. "Oh, Rachel, please calm down," she said. "Please, my love, please."

I howled that my name was not Rachel, and I wanted to see Grumpy. Sleepy was dispatched. He hustled faster than Sleepy had a right to move and returned with Grumpy. We still have the picture, in a frame in the living room, of a tear-stained, pink-faced me giving Grumpy a death grip of a hug.

I put the memory of Mom calling me Rachel away, and didn't revisit it until I was nine. I was in her office, working on an earlier school autobiography project, "The Artist's Journey" (the benefit of going to private schools: it's all about you, you, you). We had to find a drawing we had done in our preschool years and create a new version of it. My parents had gone out, and my babysitter was asleep on the couch in the living room, so I started looking in the family file drawer on my own. I found a folder marked "Dara's B.C.," and pulled out a heavy, yellowed piece of paper with my little feet stamped onto it: my birth certificate.

Then I noticed, toward the back of the drawer, a file marked "Rachel's B.C." My stomach tightened. I got the feeling that what I saw wouldn't be good, wouldn't fit into the life I knew. But now that I'd found it, I had to look. So I pulled it out.

The birth certificate was for Rachel Cohen.

I had a sister.

A sister my parents had never mentioned.

There are some dreams that are so real, you confuse them with real life, even though the things that are happening don't make much sense. That's what this felt like. None of it made sense, none of it could be true, and yet the details were so vibrant, it had to be.

I waited up for them that night, perched on the sofa in the front sitting room. My skin was cold. I had looked at myself in the mirror and seen dark circles like moons under my eyes.

They came through the door laughing, and stopped short when they saw me waiting in the dark. "Dara?" Mom asked. "What's wrong?" When I didn't answer, she did the swoop. It's an action that only moms seem capable of: she traveled from the door to my side in under a nanosecond. "Dara? Honey?"

I pushed the birth certificate between the sofa cushions behind me. "I don't feel good," I said.

She placed the back of her hand on my forehead. "You're clammy. Come on, let's get you up to bed." I was still little then, and she was able to carry me upstairs.

The next morning I stayed in bed, still pretending to be sick. It was like if I got up and went about my normal life, then it was real: my parents had kept a huge secret from me.

I heard them downstairs arguing, but I couldn't make out the words. Then they came upstairs and sat at the foot of my bed. Mom's lips were pressed together in a straight, gray line. Dad had found the birth certificate in the cushions while he was cleaning.

"She's your sister," Mom said. "She ran away before you were born." She looked at Dad, cueing him to take over the story.

He held my hand as he spoke. "She's living in Massachusetts now, at least that was the last we heard. On a farm. She's made a new life for herself, and doesn't want us to be a part of it."

My sister didn't want me in her life? That seemed impossible. "We have to call her and tell her to come back," I said.

"She doesn't want to, honey," Mom replied.

That didn't make any sense. I couldn't imagine wanting to be anywhere else. Surely, my sister must want the same.

"There's no reason for you to worry, sweetheart," Dad said. "This is all in the past now."

But they were both looking at me with anxious expressions. I sat there with my mouth open, ready to speak, questions racing through my head. *When did she . . . How did you . . . Why didn't you . . . ?* But I could tell that they didn't really want me to ask. I closed my mouth and didn't say anything.

"Good," Mom said. Her face relaxed a little. "After breakfast, we can work on your art project."

We went back to the drawer, and I chose a crude crayon drawing of me, Mom, and Dad in front of our house. I drew a new family portrait. This time I included Rachel. I drew her just as I had drawn myself, only taller. Mom said I couldn't turn that picture in; she made me do a new one. She pulled out a picture I had drawn of a monster with green skin and oversized teeth—my tribute to *Where the Wild Things Are.* "Everyone is going to be drawing family portraits," she said. "Why don't you draw a new monster?"

"I'm not into monsters anymore," I told her. She held on to both of my family portraits, and it was clear that she wasn't going to give them back to me. So I abandoned that idea and instead drew a picture of Hogwarts, my latest literary obsession.

For a while after that, I made attempts to ask my parents questions about her. Once, when my grandmother was in the hospital and my mom and I were driving down to see her, I began to worry about Rachel. Had anyone told her Bubby was sick? "Do you have Rachel's phone number?" I asked.

She concentrated on the dashboard. "No," she said. "Not anymore. She didn't tell us when it changed."

17

"But you did before? Did you ever call and ask her to come home?"

"Of course, honey. But she didn't want to. She was very troubled, Dara, and she made it clear that she didn't want us in her life." She was distracted and aloof for the rest of the ride, but I'd needed to hear that they would have called her if they could.

I missed Rachel without ever having met her. I day-dreamed about her a lot, picturing her as my twin, though I knew she was much older. Then I started addressing my diary entries to her, just as Anne Frank had written to Kitty. I didn't ask how she was or anything like a real letter; they were typical diary entries about where I had gone that day, and why I was annoyed with Mom, and that kind of thing. Still, on lonelier days, I imagined her coming home; I'd give her the diary so she would know what she'd missed.

One night when I was about twelve, Mom came into my room while I was writing in the diary. "Who's Rachel?" she asked, reading over my shoulder.

I wondered for a moment if I had somehow made the whole thing up. If maybe Rachel had never existed. Then I looked up at Mom and saw her lips pressed together. "My sister," I said.

Mom sat down on the edge of the bed without touching me. "You shouldn't do that," she said. Her voice was quiet and low. Not threatening, but there was anger in it. "It's morbid, Dara."

"She's not dead," I replied.

Mom pressed her fingers against the corners of her eyes

and pulled back toward the temples. "I know you want to meet your sister, but she doesn't want to meet you. I'm sorry. It's not your fault. Believe me, it's not your fault." Her lips were pursed, as if she had a bad taste in her mouth. "Rachel's just messed up inside. She was very cruel to us, Dara, and tried to make us unhappy."

I didn't answer.

"If there was any way to make it work, don't you think we would?"

"Yes," I whispered. I wasn't sure, but I stopped addressing my diary to Rachel.

I opened up Rachel's file. Though it had been a while since I'd last looked in it, I knew every detail of the contents. There was a class picture from kindergarten. I was pretty sure I knew which one she was: a small girl with olive-toned skin and her hair in two braids. Her report cards were stacked in order. She hadn't done as well as I had: mostly B's and C's with the occasional A and even a couple of D's. There was a certificate from a class spelling bee, and an award from the art department at Deering High. I was surprised she'd gone to the public school; my parents were both snobs about education, and that's why I had gone to Portland Academy since kindergarten.

It was all artifacts, like in a police record or a medical file—it was hard to believe whoever had collected these things had any relationship with my sister. This made me even more desperate to meet her. I'd had this hope that I could still do my project on her, but it wouldn't really be much of a project: a bunch of pictures, a story I didn't know beyond the fact that my parents thought she was a horrible person. I slid the folder neatly back into the drawer, making sure Mom wouldn't be able to tell I'd been in there.

It was stupid that I had to sneak around like this just to learn more about my own sister. And on top of that, I had to do this lame autobiography project, basically find the metaphor that represented my life, and I couldn't think of an alternative more interesting than Little Miss Maine. Well, if that's what they wanted, then that's what they would get. I'd just slap those pictures together, like Melissa had said, and be done with the whole stupid thing.

Chapter Four

When my mom got home, I went back down to her office. She was sitting behind her desk, leaning over a file folder, and, I noticed, had gotten herself a small tray of sushi from Whole Foods. She held a tuna roll between her long, thin fingers, and pursed her lips while she read. When she turned the page, her Cartier watch slipped down her slim wrist toward her elbow. I tapped the door frame. She looked up and gave me a nonplussed once-over. "Ready for bed so soon?" she asked sarcastically. "Has it been that taxing of a day?"

Hello to you too. I had only changed into pajamas to keep my school clothes nice. Before I could say this, she asked, "Did you find the Middlebury brochure?"

I rubbed my socked foot against my calf. "Uh-huh." She had left it on my bed.

"I'd really like to get a trip in this summer. I talked to Phyllis, and she and Robyn have already visited seven schools."

We had visited only Bowdoin and Bates, each less than an hour away, and I dreaded the thought of another visit with Mom. At Bowdoin the guide had been Kim, a peppy political science major who walked really fast and told us she was on the student council, a member of the swim team, and she was organizing a trip of students to go to Guatemala to build shelters during spring break. My mom thought she was fabulous and asked her all sorts of obnoxious questions that were either not-so-subtle jabs at me ("All of those activities and you still find time to stay fit? Dara's already winded just walking across the campus!") or attempts to control the tour, as though I couldn't speak for myself ("I've read so many good things about your English department. Dara was hoping she could drop in on a lecture.") The thing I really wanted to see, though, was their theater, which I'd read was an acoustic masterpiece. Opera singer Placido Domingo had recently performed there. But in the end, we breezed by Memorial Hall, which housed Pickard Theater, because I felt too humiliated and infantilized at that point to ask to go inside.

After that day, I had no desire to visit schools with my mother. But when Melissa and Jeremy planned a trip to Boston to see Harvard and Wellesley, Mom wouldn't let me go. She said it was "a dangerous city" and she didn't trust Jeremy as a driver, and anyway she wanted to take me to

Harvard so we could visit with one of her old college friends. Normally my mom and dad tried to be mostly laissez-faire, like my friends' parents—no curfews, no limits on movie ratings, etc.—but all of a sudden I couldn't even go to *Boston*. I knew it was because she wanted to micromanage the whole college application process.

"Fine," I said. "I'm looking for my pageant pictures."

"Why on earth do you want to look at those?"

"It's for a class project. We need to do an autobiography."

"And you want to do it on the pageants?" She pushed her reading glasses up on top of her head, her brow furrowed as she chose her words. "Dara, those pageants were a long time ago. Are you sure you want to share those with your classmates?"

I felt my ears turn red. It might have been easier if she'd just said it: *You're fat now. You're going to make a fool of yourself.*

"We need to do something with audio and visual components."

"How about your trip to Europe last year? You took a ton of pictures of that."

Half the class had been on that trip. I couldn't do my project on it. Plus I'd been a tourist. That made it completely un-autobiographical. "Mr. Fitz thought it was a good idea."

"Fine," she said, giving up on me. "I have no idea where those pictures are. Ask your father."

I found Dad in the kitchen making a ham-and-cheese sandwich, humming "The Girl from Ipanema." He looked up at me, surprised. He always seemed confused when I walked into a room, as if he had forgotten he had a daughter. He recovered gamely, though. "Hey, Dara Dear," he said, tucking the sandwich into a plastic bag. "What happened in school today?"

"Nothing much," I replied.

He nodded and said, "Mmm-hm," perfectly satisfied by this answer.

"How was your day?" I asked automatically.

"Good," he replied. "I think we're going to get the Matisse after all."

"Nice," I said. "What changed the owner's mind?"

"She died," he replied.

"That'll do it. Hey, do you know where the pageant pictures are?"

Dad laughed, which at least showed he was listening to me. "Why do you need those?"

"School project," I said.

"I think they're in the den in Bubby's old secretary maybe." He looked down at his watch. "I can't really help you look right now. I'm meeting with an art dealer at Fore Street."

It was one of the fanciest restaurants in town. I pointed to his sandwich. "What's that for?"

"Pre-dinner." He chuckled and patted his round belly. "See you later, pumpkin."

After he left, I opened the refrigerator. Almost all we had were condiments. Margarine, mustard, fat-free cream cheese, a block of low-fat Swiss, a take-out container of steamed vegetables. We were out of the Lean Cuisine dinners Mom stocked the freezer with for me. Dad had finished the ham, which he'd probably bought for himself. None of our food was any good, which is why Mom always picked something up on the way home, and Dad tried to meet people for dinner. I was the only one who was stuck with the crap food that seemed created to make you not want it. The least Mom could have done was pick up some sushi for me; sushi was healthy. Obviously she thought that if I actually liked the way my food tasted, I would overeat. Screw her, I thought. I'll get my own sushi.

Twenty minutes later I was walking through the automatic doors of Whole Foods, but I didn't make it to the sushi. As soon as I entered, the smell of fresh bread assaulted me. And right next to the bread, innocently stacked, were cupcakes. Plump chocolate cupcakes with creamy white frosting. I bought a four-pack, intending to eat one and leave the rest on the kitchen counter for my dad. Mom would love that.

But after my first cupcake, devoured discreetly at a table near the café, my stomach growled for more. I knew I should go buy something healthy like carrot sticks and a low-fat yogurt to complete my dinner, but there was no way I was going through the checkout twice. I had another delicious confection right in front of me. After my third cupcake, my gums were starting to hurt from the sugar. I stared at the last lonely one, its frosting smeared. If I took it home, I'd have to hide it in my room. And then I'd probably eat it for breakfast and ruin my resolve for the rest of the day. So on my way out, I chucked the package in the trash, feeling sad because it had been such a foolish waste.

Chapter Five

When I got home, I went into the den to hunt for the pageant photos and DVD, but I got distracted by a ridiculous E! True Hollywood Story about boy bands of the nineties. The hysteria was dumbfounding. They weren't that talented, and some of them weren't even that cute. Still, watching it was like eating cupcakes. Hard to stop, and when it was over, I felt gross and tired and I didn't get to my project until the next morning.

Dad was right. All of my childhood photo albums were packed into my grandmother's antique secretary desk. I sat for a long time, poring over pictures from my elementary school days. There were pictures of me dressed up for dance recitals, my makeup heavy and gaudy. In one I stood in my bathing suit in front of a friend's pool, posing with one hand behind my head, the other on my hip. My body was lithe and long. But as I turned the pages and grew older in the pictures, I saw myself getting chunky. In a photo from a family trip to Cape Cod, my cheeks were puffy and my knees were starting to dimple. In another, the shirt I wore for PA's annual holiday concert looked about a size too small, the buttons around my waist strained.

It was around that time that Mom took me to the doctor. I remember standing on the cold linoleum floor in my bare feet, wearing only my underwear. The doctor looked at my height and weight record, then looked at me, frowning. "You aren't obese," she said. "Yet." Perfect. Not obese yet, but definitely fat. It's hard to deny something when a doctor tells you. She passed Mom a pamphlet on childhood diabetes. Mom looked surprised and disappointed, as if she were hoping I had some medical condition that explained the weight gain, something that could be fixed. On the ride home, she stared straight ahead and didn't talk to me.

The casual photos of me sort of dwindled off at that point, and I could understand why. In the photos from my bat mitzvah I looked bad, and my smiles were forced. Those were the diet years. It was eighth grade, the other girls were still thin, and I fought my weight every day, crying almost every night. I cut all the tags off my clothes, as if that could hide the fact that I was plus-sized. Then one day I came into my homeroom and someone had written "Dara Cohen is fat" on the chalkboard. When Melissa saw it, she ran up and erased it, but the letters were still there, just faded. My boyfriend, Tim, had dumped me at the beginning of the year, saying that we were "you know, not right for each other." I knew he was embarrassed to be seen with a girl who outweighed him by twenty pounds.

I couldn't stand to see myself in the mirror, so I stopped going to dance class. Mom was really mad about it. I remember one night at dinner she said to me, "You can't quit now, Dara. We've invested too much." She looked to Dad for backup, but by this point he had almost completely disengaged from my life, so he just shrugged and said, "It's her life. Let her do what she wants to do." Later that evening I overheard her arguing with him about it. "But Phil, she's *ballooning*."

By the time of my bat mitzvah, all I had were Melissa and my grades. I looked back down at the photos and realized that almost all of them were of relatives, and Mom had taken all the ones of me from the neck up. I slammed the album shut and found the one with the pageant photos. There I was, shiny in my top hat and tails. I was seven, which is usually an awkward age for girls. They aren't baby-cute anymore, but they aren't pretty yet. I had managed to be both. My hair was curled into bouncy spirals. My cheeks were rosy, and my smile took up my whole face.

The pageant thing was my dad's idea. He loved music of any kind, but his favorite was classic rock and roll, and he always sang in the car. One day I started singing along. He pulled the car over to the side of the road and turned around to look at five-year-old me belting out Bruce Springsteen. It's not like those home videos they show of Christina Aguilera, all tiny and cute, and then she opens her mouth and it sounds like a soul diva has possessed her body. I wasn't *that* good. But I was close.

Soon, he signed me up for tap lessons, and he would play the piano while I sang and danced to ragtime tunes, entertaining Mom. But as I got better, Dad got more and more eager to show me off. I think he thought I might actually have fame potential. Then he read an ad for a local "talent" pageant, and signed me up. I wore little black pants and a black jacket, and Dad helped me glue rhinestones onto the lapel—a big "D" for Dara. I sang "A-Tisket, A-Tasket," in the style of Ella Fitzgerald, while tap dancing.

I won that one, which meant that I got to go on to the Little Miss Cumberland County pageant. I got a top hat and worked it into my increasingly complex dance routine. Mom started to complain about how much time I was spending rehearsing, but Dad ignored her and spent hours of his own time coaching me. The other girls did clumsy pop dances or gymnastics. My well-rehearsed, well-performed song and dance earned me another win and brought me to Little Miss Maine.

The state competition was a whole different world. These girls had professional-looking hair and makeup, all done by their moms, who, even then, I could tell had gone through about six or seven plastic surgery procedures. I had thought my top hat and tails were adorable, but I looked like a gnome next to my body-glittered competition. When Dad sensed my misgivings, he just chucked me under the chin and said, "We know what matters, don't we, Dara Dear?"

I didn't believe him. They all looked like models. It was the first time I remember feeling not pretty enough. But I was good. I knew that then. And I guess being good was good enough, because I won.

On the next page of the album was the official picture of me in my tiara. I loved that tiara. I adored wearing it out to public appearances, and even donned it around the house. I couldn't have explained it then, but it wasn't just because it was pretty and sparkled. I was proud of what it represented. I had won Little Miss Maine, not by looking like a miniclone of an adult pageant winner, but by being me.

Upstairs, I popped the DVD out of its case and slid it into my computer. Dad had filmed most of it, so it was shaky and jumped around when he turned the camera off and started it up again. I watched myself in the Cumberland County pageant, singing on a stage in a hotel ballroom with gilded chandeliers. The sound quality wasn't that great, but still my voice came on strong.

The camera panned over to Mom, who looked happier than she'd been before the pageant, when, I remembered, she'd told Dad I was going to get "warped." On camera, she was smiling, leaning forward slightly as she watched me perform. Dad stage-whispered, "Here's Dara's lovely mother." She rolled her eyes and Dad swung the camera back up to me.

When I sang, I tilted my head back and puffed my chest out. I strutted like a little rooster, but gorgeous. I waved my hands from side to side like an old 1920s flapper, then slipped into a Charleston. The grin across my face was enormous. Smiling back at myself, I remembered what it felt like on the stage, in charge, in control. I could never see the audience because of the lights, but I could feel them. In the video, I could hear their oohs and ahs.

I fast-forwarded through the footage until we were back-stage at Little Miss Maine. It was right before the bathing suit competition, and I was wearing a bright yellow one-piece. Two-pieces weren't allowed, but some of the girls were walking around in suits that were cut out around the belly, sucking in their tummies so their ribs showed. Dad zoomed in on me just as I started chewing my fingernail. "You nervous, Dara Dear?" he asked. I nodded. He said, "Well this is the silly part. Just go out and be your silly old self."

I repeated a tongue twister he had taught me, "Silly sally swiftly shooed seven silly sheep." This set me to giggling, and I twirled away from the camera, and then back.

Then it was Mom's voice. "Dara," she said, her hand coming into the frame and reaching toward my hair. "Hold still." She pushed a bobby pin closer to my head, holding down a flyaway strand. I squirmed away from her. "Your strap is twisted in the back," she said. I turned around so she could fix it, hopping from foot to foot; then I accidentally stomped on her toe. "Ow! Dara, control yourself," she hissed. "Are you trying to look ridiculous? Doesn't this matter to you?" I nodded exaggeratedly. "Aye, aye, captain!"

Mom wiped her forehead, looking nervous and out of place in her tailored suit and pearls. In the background, you could see the other moms fussing with curling irons and blow dryers, obsessing over their daughters' makeup. When Dennis had said that pageants were creepy as hell, I knew this was what he meant: the freaky pageant moms, the sexy outfits, and the obsession with appearance. I knew I could do something ironic that Dennis and everyone else would think was funny. Maybe I could do something about the contrast between me and my dorky enthusiasm and the other girls, who were dressed up like little sex objects—kind of like in the movie *Little Miss Sunshine.*

I opened a program that would convert the DVD into a file I could import into my editing program. When that was done, I selected the backstage clip and dropped it into its own bin, and started playing with the audio. I filtered out some of the ambient noise, and when I did, a mother's voice became clear: "Suck in, Brandy," she said. "Your belly is sticking out. Look at her posture. She doesn't look very pretty, does she?" Brandy quietly murmured, "No."

My stomach turned. There was material that was definitely ripe for commentary. I continued to watch the footage with the editing program, so I could cut out the parts I wanted as I went along and add them to my project.

The bathing suit portion was followed by the talent competition—a long series of sexy dance routines. I fast-forwarded through the other girls; they became a whirl of sequins.

Then it was me. I walked to the middle of the stage and struck my pose—but the music didn't start. Dad zoomed in on a man offstage shuffling through a stack of CDs, searching for mine. Little me looked out at the audience and shrugged. "It seems," I said, "that we are having technical difficulties."

The audience chuckled, and Mom said, "This is ridiculous. Why can't the idiot find her music?" I rewound and watched that little snippet again. I loved the way she said "This is ridiculous." I clipped out just the audio track of it.

Onstage the seven-year-old me kept talking. "So I guess I'll tell you a little bit about the song I'm gonna sing." I put one hand on my hip. "It's called 'A-Tisket, A-Tasket.' Most people know it as a jazz song that Ella Fitzgerald sang, but it started out as a nursery rhyme. I don't know about you, but I'd rather sing it than rhyme it." This made the audience chuckle a little bit more.

"All right," the man at the desk called.

"Sounds like we're set," I said. "But before I begin, I just want to say, Don't ask me what a tisket or a tasket is, 'cause I don't know." The audience was clapping before I even began singing.

I reveled in the performance, grinning the whole time. My voice faltered a little bit as I tried to reach some of the high notes, but it was still impressive. I growled out the lower notes like I'd been singing in speakeasies for years.

In the last clip, I won my tiara. The runners-up wilted and cried. When my name was called, I strode up to the pageant master, an orangey-tan middle-aged woman, who beamed as she placed the tiara on my head. "How does it feel, Dara?" she asked.

I replied, "It's a whole lot lighter than I thought." The audience laughed. I could hear Mom next to the camera, her laughter crackling over the sound of the audience. "She's charming, isn't she?" she asked.

"Yes, she is," my dad agreed.

I felt a residual glow of the pride my parents had in me. You could hear it in their laughter as I walked down the runway. Then I lifted my arm to wave, pulling my dress taut against my belly, and Mom breathed in sharply. "You're going to have to lay off the ice-cream dates, Phil," she said. "She's getting round."

I paused the video and peered at myself. It's true; when I moved in certain ways, you could see a little pooch, but nothing major. It was only noticeable in contrast to the other girls' sucked-in tummies. I couldn't believe it! She couldn't give me a chance to be a princess for a moment, not even when I was cute and tiny and had just won the whole pageant. All she could see was that I wasn't skinny—she was just as bad as the other pageant moms. Worse. She was a snob *and* a hypocrite.

I realized I had gotten so caught up in reliving the pageant that I had forgotten about my project. I went back and cobbled together some of the footage—me singing, winning the tiara—but it wasn't funny anymore. Mom had ruined it. It was like it didn't matter how good you were at anything; people were always going to judge you based on how you looked. What was the saying? You could never be too rich or too thin. The second part really seemed to be true—at least everyone believed it was.

That was it. That was my project. If Katie could call me out in class, then I could call her out in my presentation.

After the happy pageant clips, I added some that were not so sunny: the mother telling her daughter to suck in; my own mom noting, just as I was crowned, that I needed to lay off the ice cream. Next, I put in an interstitial, like in old silent movies, that said "What Happened After . . ." Then I went back to the photo album and took out all of my class pictures from kindergarten to eighth grade. I scanned them in and strung them together so that each one faded into the next. As the weight piled onto me, my mom's voice said, "This is ridiculous." I froze on the last one and put in the pageant mom's words: "She doesn't look very pretty, does she?" My mom's quote served as the reply: "She's getting round."

I went online and found a bunch of pictures of gaunt, angular models. With these I made a quick montage of scary-skinny women interspersed with pictures from my bat mitzvah, and added my mom's backstage scolding as a voiceover: "Dara, control yourself. Are you trying to look ridiculous? Doesn't this matter to you?"

Next to last came the picture of me in my tiara, smiling so big the camera's flash glinted off my teeth. "She's charming, isn't she?" Mom asked as the picture dissolved into a close-up of one of the models, whose cheeks were sunken and her eyes empty and dead-looking. "Yes," my child-self answered.

When I watched it all together, the transitions were a little choppy, but it just added to the effect. The first part was what people were expecting, and the second part made them think. I decided to call it "(Re)Think Thin." I watched it one more time. A smile spread across my face. Mr. Fitz refused to give A-pluses on principle, but this was an A-plus project. It belonged in an art museum, in the modern wing. It was like an installation piece, an avant-garde commentary on our culture's obsession with weight. I loved it.

Chapter Six

Our presentations were due the last Wednesday and Thursday of classes, before the three-day weekend they gave us to study for exams. Mine was on Wednesday. I woke up that morning and decided to dress the part of an artiste: black A-line skirt, black T-shirt. The T-shirt, however, was clearly too tight and showed the outline of my belly button, so I ended up wearing a black silk blouse that looked a little more DAR than hipster. Oh well. My makeup looked great. I wore dark eyeliner with gray shadow and deep red lipstick, and before I went into class I pulled my hair back into a low bun.

The first few projects were what I expected: obnoxious PowerPoint presentations of baby pictures, soccer game pictures, prom pictures, etc., etc., all set to pop music that normally I didn't mind, but in this context made me want to retch. Katie's was all about her horse. She had won some sort of New England amateur dressage competition the year before, which was good I guess, but no Little Miss Maine.

When Dimitri went, I glanced at Melissa and raised my eyebrows. I had heard him speak on literally three occasions in the entire time he'd been at PA. He didn't even say anything before he started his presentation. He'd filmed black for three minutes. Three minutes. It was ballsy, I have to admit, but also totally boring. I looked over at Mr. Fitz. He bit his lower lip, and I figured he was trying to decide if he should stop it. Then three slides came up, filling the screen, one after another: *You don't know me. You won't know me. You can't know me.*

"That was a unique take on the assignment. . . ." Mr. Fitz said. Next to me, Melissa snickered. "Although you could argue that the purpose of the assignment was for you to let us know you," he added.

Dimitri shrugged and walked back to his seat. What a jerk.

Dennis went next. His "great" idea was to make a self-portrait in the form of an album. The first slide looked like a record cover. It said, SONGS OF MYSELF: SIX ORIGINAL INSTRUMENTAL COMPOSITIONS BY DENNIS EPSTEIN. PERFORMED BY THE SAME. We hadn't studied Walt Whitman, and it was possible Dennis didn't even know he had ripped off the title.

Each short song was introduced by a title screen and accompanied by a montage of photos and video clips. In the song "Wicked Molybdenum," the video showed him scowling at a girl I didn't recognize; she looked almost comatose, draped over a drum kit. For "Fractured Sadness" he had photographed himself leaning against a brick wall, looking down to the side. He was even skinnier than I had realized. And so it went through "Joy to the Nihilist," "Body of (Un)Knowledge" (which offered a close-up of his emaciated bare chest), "Sinful Singularities," and "Baby, Good, Ain't I?"

When he was finished, he got a huge round of applause. I wondered if everyone else had seen the same thing I had, but then I realized that they had *seen* it, while I had listened. The songs were uninspired and whiny, but it didn't matter because on tape he looked like a rock star.

Melissa was the only other person who saw how ridiculous it was. She could barely keep herself from giggling out loud. She shook next to me and bit her finger to stop herself.

So of course Mr. Fitz asked her to go next. Like me, she had done a video. It was a monologue, really, but she had done it several times, with herself at different distances and angles from the camera, and then edited it all together. So the monologue was seamless, but the camera work jumped around in a really cool way. "Hey," she said. "This is Melissa. Now, I know that materialism is a bad thing, but no matter who you are, and what you do, your objects say a lot about you. What you keep close to you reveals your values. That's the basis for archeology, right? So here are a few of my favorite objects." She held up each object as she spoke about it: her copy of Gandhi's *Non-Violent Resistance*, a box of candy hearts from Valentine's Day, her ticket stub from a trip to Mexico with Habitat for Humanity, the keys to her car, the stuffed rabbit she'd had since birth. She concluded with the statement, "Now, Mr. Fitz always tells us that it's not the author's job to explain what he or she meant, but for us to figure it out from what's written. So I leave it to you to figure out who I am from all of these objects. Thanks, and peace."

"Nice work," Mr. Fitz told her. "Dara, why don't you follow your sidekick?"

At the front of the room, I brought up my video. Although I was proud of my presentation, and certain it would be one of the best so far, I was nervous. I was making a statement about my weight, something I'd never done before. "The name of my presentation," I said as dramatically as I could, while still sounding artiste-blasé, "is (Re)Think Thin." I made brackets with my hands for the "Re" part. Mr. Fitz smiled, and I pressed PLAY.

The opening clips of me singing made people smile, except for Katie, who chewed on the end of her pen, trying to look bored. I watched her face as the content got darker. Her expressions were subtle, but I could tell I was getting through to her. Then the words WHAT HAPPENED AFTER . . . came up, and she froze. Ha! The second half of the presentation made everyone squirm, which I took as a good sign. Dennis even rubbed his temples.

When it was over, the room was silent. I looked to Melissa. Her eyes were moist and she was sucking on her bottom lip. "What?" I mouthed. She shrugged and looked down at her desk. Katie finally broke the spell. "Jesus, Dara, I didn't mean it like that."

"Yes you did," Tina Baxter shot back. "And she called you out on it. What, did the last part hit a little too close to home?"

Katie raised both eyebrows and said, "What's *that* supposed to mean?"

"I've seen you after lunch."

"Girls," Mr. Fitz said. "Enough."

Katie and Tina glowered at each other.

I looked over at Mr. Fitz. "At least it was provocative."

"Yes, well, let's move on to the next presentation."

I didn't understand his reaction. It was good. My presentation was good. It had made people think, which is exactly what Maya Angelou had done, not incidentally.

Melissa didn't say anything about the presentation during lunch. She prattled on to Jeremy about her summer trip to Belgium, practically ignoring me. She was freaking me out. When I was about halfway through my salad, Mr. Fitz came into the cafeteria and waved at me, then gestured for me to follow him out into the hall. I could feel everyone staring at me as I dumped my tray and walked toward the doors.

"Sorry to interrupt you, Dara," he said when I joined him in the hallway. "I've just spoken to Mrs. Arendt about your presentation, and I think it might be good for you to talk to her."

Oh crap. Mrs. Arendt was the school counselor. "Really?"

"She'd like to see you now. She'll write you a pass."

"Oh," I said. "Okay." Although it was not okay. At all.

I turned and walked away from him down the hall. I

rounded a corner, then paused for a moment in front of Mrs. Arendt's door. What the hell had happened?

I knocked, and Mrs. Arendt opened the door almost instantly, then sat me down on a cream-colored couch in her office. In contrast to the fluorescent-lit classrooms, this room was filled with soft lamplight, and classical music played from a mysterious source.

"Dara Cohen," she said. "We've never met before."

"No," I replied.

"It's not a bad thing, meeting with me. It doesn't mean you're in trouble."

"Okay."

"Let's talk about why you're here." She tucked her shoulder-length hair behind her ears.

"I'm not really sure."

"You're not in trouble," she told me. "Mr. Fitz just had some questions about your presentation. Why don't you tell me about it?"

"It's about how people think there's no such thing as too thin, and that you can't be beautiful if you're not thin." I paused and then corrected myself. "Considered beautiful, I mean. By society."

She nodded. "Sounds interesting. Can I see it?"

"It's in my school folder on the computer," I told her.

"Go right ahead and bring it up," she said.

I started the presentation on her laptop and went back to the couch. There was a small coffee table covered with various toys: a magnetic base with lots of little metal pieces to make sculptures out of, two stuffed animals, a stress ball, a Rubik's Cube. When the video was over, she walked over and sat down next to me. "How long have you been feeling this way?"

"What way?" I asked. I wasn't trying to be difficult. I really didn't understand where this was going.

"Angry."

"I'm not angry."

"You're not angry at your parents?"

I grimaced when I realized what she was talking about: my mom's voiceover. She thought the whole thing was about my mom. "No, you don't understand," I said. "I just used her voice because it was the audio I had. I was trying to make a larger point."

She nodded as if she understood, but then she said, "I'm sensing quite a bit of resentment, Dara. And unhappiness in general."

I was too stunned to protest.

"If there are"—she paused to find the right word—"*pressures* at home, it can be useful to talk about them as a family."

I coughed, my throat suddenly parched. "My mom does annoy me sometimes. But whose doesn't?" I chuckled lamely. "Really, everything's fine."

She just stared at me, waiting for me to say more. When I didn't, she stood up. "There's no need to be defensive, Dara. You're not in trouble. But I'd still like to call your parents in. I just think it would be good for them to see the project."

My heart began to race. "I don't think that's necessary," I said, trying to stay calm.

She picked up the school directory and flipped through it. Then she dialed. I thought about diving across the room and pushing the disconnect button. She should not call my parents. They would definitely not understand. "Hello, this is Mrs. Arendt, the school counselor at Portland Academy . . . Well, I have Dara here with me . . . She's fine . . . No cause for alarm, but I'd like you to come in, along with your husband."

I stared at her computer. Could I get rid of the project? It would be worse if they saw it, rather than just heard about it. As if she could read my mind, she stepped closer to her desk and said, "It has to do with her autobiography project . . . It brought up some concerns . . . Yes . . . Right, then, I'll see you soon . . . Good-bye."

She put down the phone. "I'd like to go talk to Mrs. Whiteside for a moment," she said.

I watched her leave the room. When the door closed, I scurried over to the computer. She had locked it. Could I guess her password? My fingers hovered over the keyboard for a few seconds before I realized I was being ridiculous. I went back to the couch and slumped down, feeling trapped.

About forty-five minutes later, Mrs. Arendt led my parents into the office and shut the door behind her. "Have a seat," she told them.

I instinctively slid forward on the couch as Dad sat down next to me. He was wearing one of his nicest suits, and his tie was loose, as if he'd been tugging on it. I hoped his stressed-out appearance had nothing to do with the Matisse he'd been trying to acquire for months. . . . Had this pulled him away from negotiations? "Hi, Dad."

"Hello, Dara," he said, barely looking at me.

Mom frowned at my outfit. I cringed. "You okay?" she asked brusquely.

I nodded, although really I was sweating and my stomach was reaching panic levels. I knew it was only a matter of moments before they hated me.

Mom turned to face Mrs. Arendt, in full bulldog mode. "I understand that we are here because of something in Dara's English project. I have watched Dara work very hard on this assignment, and I cannot fathom what it contained that would warrant calling my husband and me away from work."

Dad interjected, "I don't see why we *both* need to be here."

He sounded so annoyed and put out. It hurt worse than outright scolding. He rubbed his chin, where a hint of gray stubble was emerging. He was old, I realized. Too old to remember high school. I had hoped he might at least see the artistic merit in my presentation, but now I realized it would just seem like angsty crap to him.

Mrs. Arendt smiled patronizingly from behind her desk. "No need for alarm. I just thought it would be good for you to see the project."

Mom exchanged a look with Dad. He shrugged as if to say, "Let's get through this as quickly as possible."

She turned back to Mrs. Arendt. "Please. Show us."

Mrs. Arendt pulled it up on her laptop and turned it toward them. The three of them watched my video while I watched their faces. Dad looked bemused at the beginning, and Mom revealed nothing—until she heard her own voiceover. Then the color drained from her face while Dad's face turned red.

The video ended, and Mrs. Arendt cleared her throat.

"Can we have a minute alone?" Mom asked, preempting her from speaking. "As a family?"

"Of course," Mrs. Arendt said.

When she left, I picked up one of the stress balls from the table and began to squeeze.

"If you were unhappy," Mom said, "you should have told us. We could have dealt with it privately."

"Where did you get those audio clips?" Dad asked.

"From the pageant DVD," I said softly.

"You used your mother's words out of context, Dara. Don't you realize how immature that is?"

"Not all of them! And I wasn't even using most of them as Mom. I was just using them as commentary. They weren't even all her." My voice was rising in pitch, and I struggled to control it. "I was just using those words to show how people in our culture react to weight, that's all."

"This is slander, Dara, don't you see that?" Mom asked.

"I'm sorry," I said, sounding whiny in my own ears. "I really am, but that wasn't what I was trying to do. I had an important message, don't *you* see that?"

"That it's okay to be fat?" she shot back. "I'm sorry," she added quickly.

I looked down at my hands, tears stinging my eyes. Of course I already knew how she felt, but she had never come right out and said it: it was not okay to be fat. It was not okay to be like me.

"I clearly didn't take you that far out of context," I said angrily.

Mom rolled her eyes. "Dara, that is just delusional."

"So you think I'm fat *and* crazy?"

"Enough!" Dad shouted. He looked disgusted and tired. Then he sighed and muttered, "Why me?"

I realized what he was thinking, and it felt like a blow to the chest. He thought I was another screwup, like Rachel.

I squeezed the ball harder. Mom glared at the floor, tugging at her hoop earring. Dad traced the corner edge of Mrs. Arendt's desk with his finger.

There was a knock on the door, and Mrs. Arendt poked her head in. "Everything okay in here?"

Mom nodded. "Yes, thank you. And thank you for bringing this to our attention."

Mrs. Arendt stepped back into the room. "You're welcome."

"We didn't realize how depressed and angry Dara has been about her weight. We think she should start seeing a therapist."

Therapy? I wasn't crazy. I wasn't even that depressed. And I was sorry I had hurt them, but really, they were reacting like children.

"I think therapy would be good for Dara. It might also be wise to consider family—"

Mom cut her off. "Given the amount of stress Dara is clearly under, I also think it best that she postpone her exams until later this summer when she's had a chance to reflect and get back on track."

"But that will just make the exams—" I started to protest, but Mom shot me a look and I closed my mouth.

"And of course she'll redo the autobiography project."

"No way," I said. "No, I did the project, and I did it well." They ignored me.

"Are these terms acceptable?" Mom asked.

Terms. As if I were a used car or something. I kept squeezing the ball.

"Yes, I think that's a good start," Mrs. Arendt said. "But as I was saying, I think fam—"

I gave out a startled squawk as, all of a sudden, the ball popped, and goo and little rubber beads spilled out all over my fingers.

"Oh, Dara," Mom said. "Now this?"

Dad stood up and tried to find some paper towels. He found a cloth napkin by Mrs. Arendt's tea set and began to mop up the goo on the floor. Mrs. Arendt went into the hall and came back with her hands full of brown paper towels from the bathroom, and Mom wiped off my hands and shoes. They dumped the paper towels in the trash can, and Dad threw the napkin in too. Then all three of them turned to look at me and realized I was crying.

Chapter Seven

I drove myself home, which was dangerous since I couldn't get the tears to stop. I'm not normally a crier, but then, things like this didn't normally happen. They hadn't said a word to me as we walked out of the school to the parking lot. Mom was seething. Dad didn't even say good-bye before he got into his BMW and drove back to the museum.

I had never seen them so angry. I felt sick. This hadn't been some stunt for attention; I wasn't like Rachel, who supposedly tried to hurt them. But now they were basically proving the point they'd accused me of making in my project: they were ashamed of the way I'd turned out—fat and immature and embarrassing. Another screwed-up teenager, like Rachel.

I needed to talk to her. I needed to find out what had happened and whether she really was as crazy and horrible as they claimed. Because I knew I wasn't crazy, and yet they were making me feel like I was a psycho. After today's disaster, I could definitely imagine my parents throwing up their hands and letting her go without much of a fight. They lacked the understanding gene. They didn't even try. And I could definitely see why Rachel might have gone a little crazy living with them.

Mom pulled into the driveway just before I did. She didn't wait for me, and closed the front door behind her. I stood for a moment on the step, heart pounding, before I let myself in.

"Well," she said. "That was something."

I just went upstairs and shut myself in my room, crawled under the covers, and curled up into a little ball. Maybe I *was* crazy. Maybe I had been off all along and hadn't even known it, that's how bad I was. People were careful with me and didn't let on that I was one of the special kids.

But obviously that wasn't true. There was nothing wrong with me, unless being fat really was a despicable sin, as my mother had implied. I didn't exercise enough, sure, but my mind was fine. I knew my mind was fine. If my parents thought I was messed up, well then that made two messed-up daughters in a row. Not a stellar record on their part.

If I could find Rachel, I could go see her. It's not like they could stop me. They wouldn't help me, though. Dad said she'd gone to Massachusetts, and I'd Googled her before. "Rachel Cohen Massachusetts" gave me like 544,000 results.

There was one person who might know—and might be

willing to tell me. My uncle. Uncle Barrett was a perennial bachelor living in a loft apartment in New York City with mirrors on his bedroom ceiling. He and Mom didn't get along so well, and I hadn't seen him in years. The breaking point, actually, was the Thanksgiving after I had found out about Rachel. I had heard them arguing about her in the kitchen. Uncle Barrett told Mom, "I can't believe you lied to her."

"You don't know what you're talking about, so stay out of it."

"You don't want to have your whole family back together?"

My mom said something that shut him up, but I couldn't hear it. The argument continued silently for the rest of that night, and he left the next morning.

We were still in touch, though. He called sometimes, and we e-mailed. He was one of my Facebook friends. I flipped open my computer and sent him an e-mail:

From: daracohen47@gmail.com

To: barrettw@verizon.net

Hey Uncle B,

Some crazy stuff is going down here. Nothing to be too worried about, but it's got me thinking—I'd like to get in touch with my sister. Do you know where she is?

Love,

Dara

Uncle Barrett was always on his BlackBerry, and he

e-mailed me back almost immediately.

I Googled "Rachel Cohen Massachusetts Lilith farm." Nothing. Maybe he was wrong? I compiled a list of biblical women and continued the search. Finally I came upon the site for Jezebel Goat Farm, makers of fine small-batch goat cheese, located in Hollis, Massachusetts. There were no pictures of Rachel, only of the goats. There was, however, a phone number. I dug my phone out of my backpack and flipped it open. I snapped it closed. It was almost ten—far too late to be calling a long-lost sister.

I wrote the phone number down on a piece of paper and then cleared the history on my computer. I folded the paper in half and stuck it inside an old children's book, *The Velveteen Rabbit*, in my bookshelf.

With that taken care of, I felt calmer. Just as I was getting into bed, my phone buzzed on the nightstand. It was Melissa. "Hey," I said.

"Hey," she replied. "So the rumor is you've been expelled. Tell me it's not true."

"My parents are pulling me out. Just for the end of the year."

"That sucks," she said. "Are you okay?"

"Yeah, I'm fine." I wanted to know what she really thought of my project, but she hadn't mentioned it. Was it that bad? Did she think I was crazy too? We were both silent for a while, until finally I blurted out, "I have a sister."

"What's that? Like a mentor?" she asked.

"No, an actual sister. As in, my-parents-had-another-child-and-never-told-me-about-it sister." I left out the part about knowing for years and never telling her, my best friend.

"Oh my God. How did you find out?"

"I found her birth certificate."

"That's messed up."

"Tell me about it." I wrapped my fingers in my sheet. "I'm thinking about maybe going to visit her."

"You think that's a good idea?"

I didn't know if it was a good idea, I just knew I had to do it. "Yes."

"Where is she?"

"Massachusetts, I think."

"What's her name?"

"Rachel."

"Cool. How long are you going to stay?"

"I don't know," I replied. "I haven't called her yet." Melissa was silent.

"I'm sorry," she said after a minute. "I'm just kind of stunned. They can't take you away from me."

"I know," I said. I was stunned too. And exhausted. "Well, I should probably get to bed."

"Call me tomorrow, okay?"

"Okay."

"Good night."

"Good night."

My abrupt transformation from average high school student to emotionally damaged exile had, for once, rendered Melissa at a loss for words.

Chapter Eight

I woke up the next morning a little before 8:00 and lay there for a minute before it all came crashing back down on me.

I waited until both my parents had left for work, then got out of bed and went to my desk. It was now 8:15. That wasn't too early to call someone on a weekday.

As I punched in the numbers, my thumb slipped, and I had to start over again. What was I going to say to her? *Hello, I am your long-lost sister. Can I come live with you?* I closed the phone.

I felt like throwing up. I licked my lips, which were still dry and gross from sleeping.

What's the worst she could do? I asked myself. I knew the answer. She could say no. But I wouldn't just be a burden to her. I could help out at the farm. I wasn't sure precisely how, but there had to be something I could do.

I picked up my hoodie from the floor and wrapped it around me, suddenly chilled. I opened up my phone again and dialed.

It rang once. Twice. Halfway through the third ring, someone picked up. "Hello?" a voice asked. A male voice. He sounded like a teenager. Rachel was thirty-four. Was that old enough to have a teenage son? I was too nervous to do the math. "Hello?"

"I'm sorry," I said. "I think I have the wrong number."

"But you didn't even say who you were looking for," he replied.

I sat down on my bed. "I know, it's just—"

"Who do you want to talk to?"

"Rachel Cohen."

"See?" he said. "You do have the right number. Hold on." He called out, "Rachel, phone."

My stomach flipped.

I heard some rustling, and then a female voice said, "Who is it?"

"I don't know," the boy replied. "She seems a little confused."

Perfect. Just how I wanted to be introduced to my sister.

"Hello?" the female voice—Rachel—said. The line was a little fuzzy. I pushed my phone harder against my ear.

"Hi," I said.

"Can I help you?" she asked. She had a deep, kind voice. That's what saved me. I wanted to hang up. I wanted to snap the phone shut and forget I had ever tried to get in touch with her, but her voice made me go on.

"This is Dara," I said. "Dara Cohen."

Rachel didn't say anything for a moment. I heard her breathe in sharply, and then nothing. Finally she said, "Oh."

"Yeah," I said.

She gave a nervous laugh. "Well, that was one thing I wasn't expecting to have happen this morning."

"Sorry," I said.

"No, it's fine. It's good." She kind of giggled. "How are you?"

"Good," I said. "Well, okay, I guess."

"Is everything all right?" she asked, concern edging her voice.

"Yeah. It's just that, well, I was hoping maybe we could meet. I mean, I would like to meet you."

"Of course." She said it just like that, without hesitation.

I tugged on the string of my hood. "And also, maybe stay with you for a little bit. I was thinking I could work on your farm for a few weeks. If you needed help, I mean."

"Is everything really okay?"

I started to chew on the plastic-covered edge of the string. Without spitting it out, I said, "Yes. There's some stuff going on here, and with school, and it made me, I mean, I realized it would be good to meet you."

"Okay," she said. There was a pause. I took the string out of my mouth. "Do Mom and Dad know you're calling me?"

"No."

There was another pause. "You're going to tell them that you're coming, though, right?"

"Sure. Of course."

"I would love for you to come here. I just want to make sure that you—" She hesitated. "I wouldn't want it to mess things up for you at home."

How could things get any more messed up? I didn't tell her this, though. Instead I said, "I'm going to try to take my car, but I may need to take a bus."

"That's fine. When do you want to come?"

"As soon as possible," I said. "Tomorrow, maybe."

Amazingly, she didn't hedge at all. "Great. I'll make up a spare room. Do you have Internet access?"

"Uh-huh."

"We've got a Web site. I think Owen put the directions on there. If you drive, it'll be about three or four hours from Portland to Hollis. If you take the bus, give a call and let us know what time you'll be in. I can pick you up in Amherst." Who was Owen? Was it possible that I had a nephew? Maybe she left because she was pregnant.

"Okay," I said.

Another pause. "So we'll expect you tomorrow."

"Um," I began. This was happening. This was really happening. "Yes."

"Great," she said. "I didn't think I would ever get to meet you."

Ever? "Yes," I repeated.

"Okay."

"Okay." I wasn't sure how to end the conversation.

"Do you need anything else?" she asked.

"No," I said. "That's it."

"Okay," she said. "Bye, Dara."

"Bye."

I closed my phone and stared at it in my hand. It was warm. My ear was burning hot.

I was going to stay with my sister.

I was going to meet my sister.

Now all I had to do was tell my parents.

Chapter Nine

I poured myself some cereal, took it to the den, and turned on the TV. But I was too keyed up to focus on anything, so I went upstairs to take a bath. I hadn't done that in forever. My parents had one of those big tubs with jets in their bathroom. They even had a remote-controlled sound system installed in the ceiling so my dad could listen to music while he showered and shaved. I wasn't supposed to use their bathroom, but they weren't home, and I was feeling bold. I filled the tub with the hottest water possible and tuned in the oldies station on the radio, before gingerly sinking down. The jets whirled the water so I couldn't see my body.

I hummed along with "Chain of Fools," tapping my feet on the edge of the tub. Then I let my head sink all the way under, eyes closed. My hair brushed over my shoulders and cheeks.

I loved being in the water. I always had. Even after I came to hate being seen in a bathing suit, I still went to the beach with my friends. While they sat on blankets and read their books and guilty-pleasure magazines, I'd spend the day in the ocean. "How can you stand it?" Melissa would call out to me. "It's so cold!"

Once I had called back, "My blubber keeps me warm." She shook her head and gave me a big thumbs-down. Melissa hates it when I make fun of myself.

I so wanted to call her and tell her about my phone conversation with Rachel, but she was in class. Where I should be. I couldn't believe this was happening.

I stayed in the bath for almost an hour, lost in thought, until the water had grown lukewarm and my skin was beyond pruned. I turned off the jets and opened the drain so the water could spiral down. As the water level sank lower, I could feel gravity taking over again, tugging down on my boobs and arms, making my skin fold farther over itself. I hoisted myself out of the tub and dried off quickly, then padded down the hallway to my bedroom, singing "Bobby McGee" loud enough to fill up the empty house.

It was still too early to call Melissa, so I went to my bookshelf and pulled out one of my favorites. Then I put on a Janis Joplin CD and climbed under the covers to read, but fell asleep during the third chapter of *To Kill A Mockingbird*.

I was still asleep when Mom got home, which is not the way I had planned for things to play out. She stood in the doorway and called my name until I opened my eyes. "Have you done *anything* all day?"

Damnit. I sat up and brushed my hair out of my face. "Is Dad home?" I asked.

"Not yet."

"I'll come down when he gets home."

Mom stood there for a moment, regarding me as if there were a thousand issues she wanted to point out but couldn't decide where to start. "I'll be down in a bit," I said emphatically. She sighed and yanked the door shut. I jumped out of bed and walked to my closet. I had to look pulled together. I had to show them that I was still responsible, straight-A Dara. I cringed, remembering how badly the whole artiste act had backfired. In my all-black outfit and heavy eye makeup, I must have looked like a real wackjob in Mrs. Arendt's office . . . even before I started crying.

I chose a pale green corduroy skirt and matched it with a preppy white polo I'd bought in tenth grade. It had grown tight in the arms and also hugged the bulge above the skirt's snug waistband. Morale flagging, I stripped off the shirt and changed into a pink one with thicker fabric, but it honestly wasn't much better.

I sighed. I didn't feel like squeezing into a different skirt, so I let it go. I just had to do the best with what I had. In the bathroom, I pulled my long, thick hair up into a ponytail. My hair is definitely one of my best features, but I knew I looked more mature with it pulled back. Next, I applied some light foundation and mascara; I have pretty decent skin so it didn't take much to make me look polished. Aside from the

61

bulge thing, I looked okay. My hairdresser was always telling me I looked like Natalie Portman (she was kind enough not to add the "if you lost half your body weight" part), and just then I could almost see it. As I was redoing my ponytail, I heard Dad come in downstairs; he and Mom were speaking in muffled voices and I couldn't hear what they said.

I took one last look at myself in the mirror, then went down to face them.

They were in the living room, sitting next to each other on the sofa. I sat down in the wingback chair opposite them, and smoothed out my skirt. "I wanted to apologize to you for my project. It was never my intention to hurt you. I can see now why you were upset, although I want you to know that in my mind, it was not a statement about either of you." I looked from one to the other. They seemed suspicious. Which was funny considering what I was about to say. "I spoke to Rachel this morning." I kept my voice calm and even, though I was not calm at all. My palms were damp and my heart wouldn't slow down. "She would like me to visit her."

Dad looked at Mom, but Mom stared straight at me. I had expected them to say something at this point.

"I'd like to take my car. If that's not okay with you, I'll take a bus."

Mom cleared her throat. "This is absolutely out of the question." She made a move to stand up.

"I'm going no matter what you think. You can't keep me from meeting my sister."

Mom sank back in her seat and exchanged a look with Dad. Finally she said, "You don't understand the history here."

"If I don't understand, it's because you haven't told me." I held on to the arms of the chair. I couldn't lose my temper. If nothing else, I had to remain calm.

"Your sister was wild," Mom said. "She slept around. She drank. She trashed the house whenever we were gone. And then she ran away, and when she ran out of money, she came back here and stole from us to run away again. Dara, she was a nasty person. She did everything she could to hurt us."

My heart sank. If they were right, then I was making a big mistake. How did I know they were telling the truth, though? That Mom wasn't exaggerating? "You think I wanted to hurt you, and I didn't. How do I know you're not wrong about her too?"

"She wasn't like you," Dad said.

Mom continued. "Before she left she—"

Dad stopped her. "She's probably still the same unstable, angry woman, Dara. It's not a good idea for you to go there."

"We're just looking out for you," Mom agreed.

Bullshit. They were lying. Rachel was nice. I could sense that as soon as I heard her voice. They just didn't want me to meet her. And if they cared so much about me, they would have listened to me yesterday, instead of pulling me out of school because they were ashamed. Now everyone thought I was a psycho. "I'm old enough to take care of myself. I want to meet her."

"Out of the question," Mom repeated.

That was going to be their answer no matter what I said, so why argue? "I'm leaving tomorrow," I said, and went upstairs.

Chapter Ten

I stayed up in my room all night. First I packed, and then I got online and found out how much the bus to Rachel's would cost: seventy-seven dollars. I could definitely cover that, plus a cab to the bus station. In the morning, though, Dad was waiting for me downstairs. "The car needs an oil change in another thousand miles," he said. His voice was flat. Unreadable.

"Okay," I said.

"Do you know where you're going?"

I nodded. I had directions from the Web site.

"How long do you intend to stay?"

"I don't know. I guess that's up to Rachel."

He handed me an unsealed envelope. I peeked inside and

saw some cash and a credit card. "For emergencies," he said. "Be careful."

"Thank you," I said. I meant it, but I wished he would give me something more, that he'd tell me things would be okay. As it was, I just turned and left. I pulled out of my street and drove through Portland, toward I-295, then merged onto I-95, heading for New Hampshire. The car was cool inside, so I turned off the air-conditioning. It was a wonder it still worked. My car, Bert, was seventeen years old: my age exactly. The seats were soft and pliable with age, and gave me a snug little squeeze, like sitting in someone's lap. Every time my dad saw Bert, he would knock on the hood and say, "Volvos. Boxy but reliable."

He had always cared about my safety. Even as he grew disinterested in my day-to-day life, he still did things like check the tread on my tires, and he made sure I never went on a trip without proper supplies.

Maybe my parents were right about Rachel being unstable. If she was, though, I could always just go home. Then at least I would know. I would have tried.

My directions sent me across the state of Massachusetts on Route 2, a two-lane road at times. The road was lined with tall pine trees that gave way to farms as I traveled farther west. I didn't stop for food or even go to the bathroom or anything. I just wanted to get there.

Rachel really didn't seem crazy. She'd sounded kind. She had welcomed me right away, and seemed to honestly mean it. Mom was the crazy one, and Dad always took her side. If Rachel had really stolen money and all those other things, then they had probably driven her to it.

65

As I got off Route 2 the roads got narrower and more gravelly. Finally I saw the sign at the end of a long dirt driveway: JEZEBEL GOAT FARM. My heart beat faster and my stomach spiraled. This was it. This was where my sister lived.

There were fenced-in fields on both sides of the driveway. On the right side were goats, about twenty of them. On the left side was an empty lawn. The driveway curved, and then I saw a big gray farmhouse—not painted gray, but never painted—with red shutters. Next to it was a barn with its doors wide open. As I pulled up toward it, I could see what looked like vats and a big metal table, and I really didn't want to know what they did to the goats there.

There were more goats beyond the barn. They looked up when I closed my car door, then went back to chewing their cud or whatever it is that goats chew, unimpressed. The smell was overwhelming: manure, hay. I looked down at my outfit: pleated skirt, T-shirt, and flip-flops. I had thought the outfit was sensible that morning, but now I realized I was not appropriately dressed for a farm. Rachel was going to think I was clueless. I forced myself to take deep breaths and squeezed my hand into a fist, digging my fingernails into my palm.

Just then, a woman emerged from behind one of the vats. She was about my height, but skinny, and her hair had some strands of gray mixed in. She looked more like my dad than my mom. She had his thin lips and strong chin. But we shared our mom's brown eyes, narrow nose, and pale eyebrows. She smiled tentatively. "Dara? I'm Rachel," she said.

"Hello," I replied.

We both just stared at each other for a few seconds. I tried to read her face, but I couldn't tell what she was thinking, whether she was pleased or disappointed. I guess I had hoped she would throw her arms open and say, "Welcome!" but it's not like I would have done that.

"Let me show you around," she said. It sounded welcoming, but more in a professional than a personal way.

I stepped out from behind my car and into the sour-smelling barn. She didn't look the way I had imagined. She wore old sneakers and her hair was pulled back into two long braids, more like a hippie than a rebel. She wore a T-shirt with a faded Jezebel Goat Farm logo, and jeans that were about ten years out of style, like maybe she had stopped shopping in her twenties. All the questions I wanted to ask her seemed too personal to bring up.

"We make goat cheese," she said. "We sell it at farmers' markets."

"That's awesome," I said, too enthusiastically.

She gave me a little smile and then pointed to the fields. "Our goats live out in the pastures. We grow a special grass out there and supplement that with a mix of grains. We milk the goats once a day. Then we bring the milk in here to pasteurize it. It takes twenty-four hours to curdle." The more she talked, the more I felt like I had stumbled into a job orientation.

We moved farther into the barn. "This is where we'll be doing the flipping. Basically, that's very gently putting the curd into sacks. These are hand-sewn in Montana." She paused, then looked up at me. "Sorry. We get school groups here sometimes, and bus tours from down South. I just went into my spiel."

"It's okay."

She wiped her palms on her jeans, and I noticed that her hands were shaking. "This is a little bit awkward," she said.

"A little," I concurred.

"You know, when you were born, Uncle Barrett sent me a picture of you. I thought you were the most beautiful baby."

I blushed. "Thanks. He, um, he was actually the one who helped me find you. He said the farm had a Bible name, so I was Googling all these biblical women together with Rachel Cohen until I found Jezebel."

Rachel smiled, but she seemed bewildered. "Mom and Dad could have told you that," she said.

My heart froze.

Rachel looked down toward the cement floor. "How are they doing, anyway?"

"Mom and Dad?" I felt trapped. "They're okay. You know, they work a lot."

"It's amazing that they let you come."

"Yeah, well . . ." I began. I didn't know how to respond. One look at her face, though, and I realized she had already gotten the point. Mom and Dad didn't want to have anything to do with her. "So, it's really nice here," I said. "How long have you been here?"

"Ten years," she said. "No wait, oh my gosh. It's closer to fifteen years now. Time just goes, you know? I mean, look at you, how old are you?"

"Seventeen," I told her.

"Seventeen," she repeated. "You weren't even born yet when I left."

"How did you find this place?" I asked, steering back into safe territory.

She leaned back against one of the bins. "Word of mouth, I guess. That's the way it's always been." I noticed a small tattoo of a bright red heart on the inside of her wrist.

"It's really pretty," I enthused.

"It is," she agreed. She studied me for a moment, and then said, "Oh my goodness, I'm the worst host. You just drove all this way, and here I am just rambling on. Why don't I show you where you'll be staying? You can unpack and get settled in." She ran her hand over her crisply parted hair. She still wore it the same way she had in the kindergarten picture. "When I get to a new place, that's what I like to do first."

"Me too," I agreed, although I felt paranoid that she was dismissing me.

"Good," she said. "Let's go."

We went to my car and I opened the trunk. We each took a suitcase, and I followed her to the side door of the farmhouse. She took off her sneakers and left them just inside the door, so I slid off my flip-flops. Her socks were worn at the heels. My toenails were painted magenta. "Nice pedi," she said.

"Thanks." I wasn't entirely sure it had been a compliment.

"Up this way," she said, leading me up a narrow staircase off the mudroom. Old photographs hung on the grassy-green-painted walls, but we went by too quickly for me to look at them. Rachel was fast, even with the suitcase. I struggled to keep up with her and was winded by the time we reached the top of the stairs. "You'll be in the twilight room."

She pushed open a door and we stepped into a bedroom almost twice the size of my room in Maine. On the opposite wall were two recessed windows, each with a seat big enough for one person. The silver-framed bed was pushed against the wall and covered with a quilt made to look like the night sky: squares of blue and purple with white stars sewn on them. The walls were light blue at the bottom and blended to a deep purple blue at the top. Twilight.

She put my suitcase down next to a bureau. "Do you need anything? A glass of water?"

"No, thanks," I said, even though I was thirsty. I didn't want to be any more of a burden.

"Okay, well I'll be downstairs. I'm going to get started on dinner. So you take your time, and if you need anything, let me know."

"Thanks," I said.

She stood there for a moment, looking at me, and I wondered if she was waiting for me to say more, but then she turned and left. She shut the door behind her, and I sighed and lay back on the bed, mentally replaying our conversation. I couldn't tell how I'd come off to her.

It hadn't occurred to me that Rachel might not know that I knew almost nothing about her life, or that she might be hoping for some kind of acknowledgment from Mom and Dad. I had been stupid not to think this whole thing through. Instead I just showed up hoping we'd instantly hit it off like best friends.

I got up and flopped both suitcases onto the bed. As I began to unpack, I realized I'd brought very few clothes that

I was willing to get dirty. I wore a lot of skirts with pretty details and nice fabric. I didn't own many work-type clothes, just a few pairs of jeans and some T-shirts.

I opened the closet and found shoe boxes stacked two feet deep. So someone in the house had a shoe fetish. This made me smile. I lifted the top of one to get a peek, but instead of slides or heels, I found sheets of typed paper.

```
slow summer. Not too many passers-through. The
girls are getting restless I can tell. Ought
to have some sort of party, I think, but the
goats have been hard and I don't know where
I'll find the money for anything nice.
```

The words filled the page, single-spaced and reaching for the edges. I flipped open the other boxes and they, too, were filled with type-covered paper. There didn't seem to be a beginning or end, just words, and words, and words.

```
rain for three and a half days. When the
rain slowed down, we called it stopped because
it made us feel a little better. Sarah went
into town to try to get more
buckets. She took Bette with her and I got this
feeling like they might not come back.
I always got that feeling when Bette went out.
Like she might disappear as quickly as she
appeared. But that time they did come back.
```

They had buckets and trash barrels and we set
them up under all the leaks. Sarah got the
girls to all sit around it and sing songs like
it was a campfire. We didn't have any power,
just flashlights and candles. Folks in town
would think their fears had been confirmed.
Witches! They don't say that so much
anymore. They've gotten used to us it seems.

Something creaked behind me, like a foot on a floorboard, and I turned toward the door, my heart pounding with guilt. I had just been invited into the house; I didn't want to get caught snooping through Rachel's things. Quickly, I put the pages back in the box, put the top back on, and closed the closet door.

There was no room in the closet to hang up the four summer dresses I had brought. This didn't seem like much of a dress-wearing kind of a place anyway, so I left them in the suitcase.

Unpacking took about twenty minutes, and though I wanted to stay and read some more of the pages, I knew I should go downstairs to find Rachel. Plus I really needed to pee. Fortunately, it wasn't hard to find the bathroom, as it was the only open door in the hallway. And it was golden! A gilt-framed mirror hung above a gold sink. Even the toilet had been spray-painted gold; the paint was wearing off the front of the reservoir. There was a small framed card on top that said "the throne," which I thought was a nice touch.

On my way down, I looked at the photographs. They were

of the farm, though I couldn't place the date, maybe the forties. Jezebel had been a lot livelier then. In one photograph, a group of women, about twenty in all, sat in and on a truck. Their bodies crushed together so they could all fit. One stood on top of the cab, another hung out the window. I could almost hear them giggling as they jostled for room. In another, the women square-danced, their hair and skirts swinging out behind them. In a third, a woman sat on the ground surrounded by goats. They were shoving their snouts into her long, dark, untamed hair. This woman was in all the photographs. In the picture with the goats, her eyes shone dark as marbles, and wild.

I could have stared at these pictures for hours, but Rachel had probably heard me on the stairs, and I didn't want her to think I was stalling. I followed the smell of onions and garlic into the kitchen, where Rachel stood at the counter, chopping an eggplant. Her knife moved quickly, and the rounds of eggplant fell into a neat pile.

"Hi," I said.

She looked over her shoulder. "Welcome to the kitchen," she said, gesturing with her arms like a game-show model. It was a bright room, lit with afternoon sun through one large window over the sink. The floor was black-and-white check, and there was a red valance across the top of the window. I couldn't tell if the appliances were new with retro styling, or simply old. Either way it was cool.

"I'm making aubergine and polenta terrine. We're vegetarians here. Well, technically, we're pescetarians, since we sometimes have fish."

"Cool," I said. "I don't think I'll miss meat too much. I like fish, though. Salmon, anyway. And tuna." I was rambling. I needed something to do. "Can I help at all?"

"Sure. That'd be nice." She didn't elaborate.

"So . . . what can I do?"

"Oh! Um . . ." Rachel looked at the arrangement of ingredients in front of her, nodding at each one as if ticking it off a list. "Cheese," she said. "Want to grate some cheese?"

"Sure."

"There's some in the fridge."

I opened the door and stopped, overwhelmed. Never had I seen a refrigerator so overstuffed. Green leaves pushed out of the crisper drawer. Tupperware were stacked three high on each shelf. There was milk in a glass bottle, soy milk, cream, orange juice, and iced tea in a plastic pitcher. "So, where's the cheese?"

Rachel laughed and wiped her hands on her jeans. She looked so much like Dad right then, it was unnerving. She squatted in front of the refrigerator and started to pull out containers from the middle shelf. "Just like home, right?"

I nodded. I couldn't tell if she was being sarcastic. The refrigerator at home was almost airy. I couldn't imagine Rachel in our kitchen.

"I always say I need to get some sort of an organizational system. I mean, this is ridiculous, right? I even bought the kitchens issue of *Real Simple*—you know that magazine? Anyway, I thought for sure there'd be some sort of inspiration in there." She pulled out a block of cheese. "No, that's

Gruyère. But, as you can see, I'm no better off than before." She giggled nervously, and stretched her arm into the back of the shelf and came out with another block of cheese. "Voilà!" she said. She took a grater from a low cabinet next to the fridge and held it up to me. "Have at it."

I held the grater and the mozzarella but wasn't sure what to do next. Did she want me to do it into a bowl or just on the counter? I scanned the kitchen, looking for anything. "Um, should I just grate this . . ."

"Grab one of the cutting boards by the sink," she said.

"Oh, right, of course. I mean, duh, right?" I said. I put the cheese down to grab the board, and then got myself set up. As I grated, I concentrated on what I was doing as though my kitchen prep skills would reveal something about me to Rachel. My worth as a person, as a sister. I was lucky she hadn't asked me to do something tricky, like julienne carrots, because I had no idea how to cook.

"So," she said, "things aren't going well at school?"

I cringed. "It's complicated," I said.

Rachel stopped chopping eggplant. "I'm sorry. You don't have to talk about it."

I hadn't meant to push her away. "No, it's okay. My English project was misinterpreted, and it was a big debacle. Mom and Dad freaked out. Now they say I have to have therapy before I can go back to school." It came out in a rush.

"Really? What was it about?" she asked.

I wasn't sure how to frame it. "Um . . . so we had to do these multimedia autobiography projects, and my class wanted to hear about how I was Little Miss Maine when I was little." I glanced at her, expecting a surprised expression, but she just nodded for me to go on. "So I did that, but I also used it to talk about, how, like . . . how thinness is the beauty ideal, and how even when people are basically anorexic, that's better than being overweight."

"That sounds really cool. Why did they freak out?"

"Well . . . to make my point about how people react to weight, I used some dialogue from an old pageant DVD; it was Mom talking. Like she said I was getting round and so—"

"She said that? On tape?"

"Well, I don't think she knew she was being taped. Anyway, the point wasn't her. I just used those words to demonstrate society's fear of fatness."

"But she did say it," Rachel insisted.

"Yeah, sure. But that was the only thing that was actually bad. The rest of it was stuff I took out of context, because it was good audio. But everyone thought I was accusing her of being a horrible mother."

"She probably was," she replied.

"No, that wasn't the point. I mean, I wasn't trying to get at her at all. I was trying to make more of a statement about our culture in general."

Rachel raised her eyebrows, then turned around and started chopping again. I was afraid I'd pissed her off, like I'd taken their side or something.

After a moment she said, "I got in trouble in high school too." She laughed. "I mean, obviously. But once in particular, I told my U.S. History teacher that our textbook was culturally biased." She paused. "I may have called him a bigot."

"What happened?"

"Detention, probably. Too bad they didn't ask me to write an essay explaining why I was wrong—I would have written a kick-ass defense of my position." She started chopping the eggplant slices into quarters. "Which school are you at?"

"Portland Academy," I answered.

"Of course," she said. I wasn't sure what that meant. "I did the Lower School, but said no thanks for the Upper School. I thought it was elitist." She shook her head. "It's easier to disdain something when you have a choice."

"It is kind of elitist," I said. My friends and I were always joking about how the community was tolerant and welcomed diversity as long as you could afford the twenty thousand a year tuition.

"Sure, but it's a good school. I was foolish to give it up. You should just do the therapy so you can go back." She dumped the eggplant into a bowl and tossed it with some salt. "You know, there's a great therapist here in town, Dr. Eddington. If you'd like, I can set up an appointment for you."

I didn't answer. I'd been hoping the whole therapy thing would just go away somehow. I felt kind of insulted, actually.

"Even if you don't really need therapy, she can help you. It's always good just to talk to a neutral third party, and she's really good. Really sharp." She took an onion from a bag near the windowsill.

"Have you met with her?"

"On and off," she said. She sliced the onion in half and then glanced out the window. "Oh good. Owen's home."

Chapter Eleven

I took a moment to admire the male form. The male form in general, yes, but Owen in particular, as he walked through the door and into the kitchen. He looked about my age and was tall and slight. He wore a pale green button-down shirt with the sleeves rolled up. Biracial—Asian-Caucasian—with smooth and unblemished skin. His movements were so graceful, they seemed effortless; even when he blinked his eyes, his lashes seemed to drift down to caress his skin, then float up again. I hoped like hell he wasn't my nephew.

I couldn't help but stare. His face was constructed like a work of art: high cheekbones, bee-stung lips, wide eyes. I thought that kind of attractiveness only existed in magazines and on television, with the help of makeup and good lighting. I hadn't realized that actual living people got so close to the beauty ideal.

His presence thrilled me. I think my body might have actually shook a little bit. This was definitely not something I had anticipated: arriving at my sister's house, then having the most gorgeous guy I had ever seen walk through the door. I didn't want to let myself get too excited about Owen—he was truly beautiful, and therefore out of my league—but he looked at me the way boys normally looked at Melissa: interested, curious. Usually that gaze went right past me and landed on someone else; yet here he was, looking at me like he wanted more.

I followed the muscle line of his calves, a perfect indentation. He lifted his arm and ran his hand through his spiky black hair. Dennis Epstein wanted to look like a rock star. Owen actually did.

"This is Owen," Rachel said. "This is Dara, my sister."

Owen reached out his hand. "Hey. Nice to meet you." His hand was warm, smooth. He gripped mine tightly, then let go, but his smile lingered. A flirtatious smile? Who was I kidding? Why would this gorgeous guy be flirting with me? But that look, that look—I knew it, though I had rarely been the recipient before.

"Owen's parents kicked him out because he's gay. He's staying with us until he goes to Williams in the fall."

Of course.

Owen looked past Rachel at the neat array of chopped vegetables on the counter. "Eggplant parm?"

"I'm trying something new. Aubergine and polenta terrine." She seemed really happy that Owen was home. Relieved, even.

"Aubergine," Owen mocked. "Just call it eggplant." He picked up an apple, rubbed it on his shirt, and took a bite. "Sounds good, though."

People that beautiful should not be able to move, speak, breathe. They shouldn't need to eat. They should hold still so we can admire them. Being near him made me dizzy. He stepped by me to go to the refrigerator, and brushed against my arm.

"How was school?" Rachel asked him.

"Pretty good. We're not going to have a history final, just a paper, which is awesome. I'm going to do it on the Stonewall Riots."

"Good for you," Rachel said. "I bet that'll be a first."

"Well, Mrs. Winslow is pretty open-minded, but yeah, I doubt any other student has done it."

"What are the Stonewall Riots?" I spoke without meaning to.

Owen said, "Well, there was this bar in New York, the Stonewall Inn. A gay bar. And the police raided it. They herded everybody out. Then they tried to take away the staff and three drag queens."

"It helped to ignite the gay rights movement," Rachel added. "It's one of those things they don't normally teach you about in high school, but should."

I nodded. We had learned all about the civil rights movement, the sit-ins and the protests, but even at progressive PA, nothing about the gay rights movement. "What were they arrested for?" I asked.

Owen turned to Rachel. "Where did you say she was from?"

I blushed. It wasn't my fault; Rachel had just pointed out that it was one of those things that weren't taught in high schools. He was good enough to answer my question at least. "They said it was an alcohol violation, but gay bars were getting raided all the time in the sixties, even in New York. One night, the gay men fought back."

Owen took the iced tea from the refrigerator and poured himself a glass. He lifted himself up onto the counter.

"Actually," Rachel said, "the gay men were all hamming it up and making a big show of it, but then the police actually put some drag queens in a paddy wagon. That's when people started to realize it was serious. It was a lesbian who really got things going when she resisted arrest."

Rachel hadn't said it in a condescending way, but it still made me feel better to know that Owen didn't know everything about everything.

I finished grating the block of mozzarella. "Enough cheese?"

"Perfect," Rachel said.

Owen hopped down from the counter and put his glass in the sink. "I'm gonna go feed."

"Hey, why don't you take Dara with you?" Rachel turned to me. "Would you like that? It'll be good for you to learn."

I wasn't sure if I would like it or not, but I said, "Okay."

I followed Owen to the door and slipped on my flip-flops. "You should probably wear different shoes," he told me.

I looked down at my feet, embarrassed. "I'm okay."

"Suit yourself."

As we crossed the sandy driveway to the barn, I watched Owen's back and the way his muscles moved under his T-shirt. He handed me a five-gallon bucket and we each took a scoop of pellets from a bin. A cloud of dust rose up, and when I tried to lift my bucket, it felt like it was glued down. Owen shook his head. "Carry what you can," he said. I dumped out half. He grabbed a second bucket for himself and filled it halfway. "I usually do it myself anyway. Follow me." He walked out the back door of the barn, and I struggled to keep up with him, the pail of feed smashing against my leg with every step. My flip-flops slapped an uneven rhythm. I had to breathe through my mouth like an oaf, and I was afraid he could hear me. I tried to take slow, quiet breaths, but that just made me feel light-headed.

Finally, we came to a fence, and Owen put down one of his buckets to unlatch the gate. Soft dirt slipped between my feet and the flip-flops as I followed him inside the pasture. Immediately, the goats began to crowd us, bleating in anticipation. We reached a trough, and Owen said, "Dump it."

After that, the goats left us alone, and Owen stepped back to the wooden fence. "I usually watch them," he said, "to make sure they all get to eat. Sometimes the big ones push the little ones out of the way."

"That's sweet of you." I cringed as soon as I said it.

He looked at me and arched his eyebrows. I could tell he was trying to determine whether I was mocking him. "Yeah, well, hungry goats bray all night, and trust me, they're loud."

Owen propped himself up on the top rung of the fence.

"So what are you running away from?" he asked.

"Excuse me?" Had Rachel told him I was a runaway?

"Everyone at Jezebel is running from something. I wondered what your story was."

My story. Where to start? I climbed up on the fence a few feet away from him and quickly wiped the sweat off my forehead with the back of my wrist. "I got into a little trouble at school," I said.

"Trouble? What kind of trouble would a nice girl like you get into?"

"Who says I'm a nice girl?" I asked, annoyed. Okay, so everyone back home would say I was, but Owen had no reason to assume that.

"Fair enough," he said. "All right, so you got into trouble at school. For what?"

"It wasn't exactly trouble—"

"I figured." He smirked. It was a sexy smirk, though.

"We had to do this autobiography project, and so I made a movie. And my dense teacher and parents totally didn't get it, and so I had to leave school for a little bit."

"They kicked you out over a film? That's awesome! What was it like?"

"It was a video collage," I explained.

"Cool. Very Eisenstein," Owen said. "What was it about?"

I was hoping he wouldn't ask that. After going through this with Rachel, I didn't really feel like getting into it again. But he seemed genuinely interested, so I told him the story.

"Well, yeah," he said when I was finished. His face was kind, not mocking. "It was an autobiography project, and you showed your mom calling you fat. Of course they were pissed."

One of the goats meandered to the fence and started rubbing her back on the slats next to my leg. I watched her absently, processing what Owen had said. I still disagreed. What my mother had said was representative of a larger social problem that affected my life. She needed to get over herself if she thought it was all about her.

"Anyway, none of that explains why you came here," he told me.

"I wanted to meet Rachel."

"Meet Rachel? You've never met her before?"

I looked down at my dirty feet in their ruined flip-flops. "Yeah, well . . ."

"I think your family is even more screwed up than mine." It seemed harsh, but what could I say? I didn't know his family; maybe we *were* more messed up.

"How did you end up here?" I asked.

He looked out over the field. "My parents kicked me out."

"Yeah, but how did you know you could come stay here?"

Owen picked at a splinter on the fence. "Well, that part was easy. Rachel's always been around. In elementary school she'd come in and talk about goats, and we'd take field trips to the farm. It's a small town, you know. You see people around. I guess it was in maybe ninth grade that I went to the farmers' market one summer, and she was there. I noticed she had one of those pink triangle pins on her T-shirt. I asked her all these questions about the farm, and I think she thought I was really interested in cheese, because she offered me a job.

So I started working here on weekends. When my parents kicked me out last year, it seemed like the right place to go. Like I said, it's where people who are running away end up."

"Wait, Rachel's gay?" I asked.

He shook his head. "Sister, you've got a lot to catch up on, don't you?" He didn't mean to be cruel, but it still felt like he was mocking me. "Listen, that's what I mean about this place. For decades it's been a place where lesbians whose families wouldn't accept them could come. Lately I guess they've just been expanding the criteria for admission." He raised an eyebrow at me. "Unless you have something you want to tell me."

"No, I'm straight," I said, way too quickly. He just laughed.

The goats finished with their feed and started wandering away from the trough. Owen checked his watch. "Dinnertime."

Chapter Twelve

Owen and I washed our hands in the kitchen sink, and then I followed him into the dining room. Rachel was setting out plates, and an ancient, wizened woman was already seated at the head of the table. "Belinda, this is my sister, Dara," Rachel said.

"Nice to meet you," I said, smiling. Belinda responded with a very slight nod. Her bright white hair was pulled into a large bun at the back of her head, and her eyes seemed buried in her face.

As soon as I sat down, a large man burst through the doorway.

"And this is Sascha," Rachel said, patting his shoulder on her way back out to the kitchen.

"Hello," he boomed. He sat across from Owen and me. He was a giant man: tall, broad-shouldered, and he had a thick black beard. He made me think of a lumberjack—he even wore a flannel shirt.

Rachel returned with the aubergine and polenta terrine and set it on the table next to Belinda. I'd never had a terrine before, but this one was layers of gold polenta and purple eggplant, with fresh chopped tomatoes on top. It smelled delicious, and my mouth began to water. Belinda served herself and nudged the dish toward Sascha.

"Dara was Little Miss Maine," Rachel announced.

"Congratulations," Sascha said. "What's that like?"

I felt myself growing red. "Well, it was a long time ago." Why had Rachel told them that?

"Did you have a tiara?" Owen asked.

"Well, sure."

"Sweet," he said. "I want to win something where I get a scepter."

I decided to turn the conversation to someone else. "Sascha—that's a Russian name, right?"

Sascha nodded. "My mother only read Russian literature. Tolstoy. Dostoevsky. She drank vodka straight and cursed about Stalin."

"I see," I said with an encouraging nod. Once, before a dance in middle school, my mom had coached me on body language: "Nod when you're listening. Validate what they are saying." She had been talking about boys, but it seemed applicable here.

"So she was from Russia?" I asked.

"Jersey."

"Oh. Cool."

Sascha scooped a giant dollop of casserole onto his plate and passed the dish to Owen.

"Now Rachel's going to tell her green stick story," Owen said.

Rachel's mouth was open, ready to speak. She blushed, then grinned. "How did you know that?"

"I heard you tell Didi at the farmers' market last week, and you guys had been talking about borscht. Borscht! You were just like, 'Hey, did you know . . .'"

"Oh, stop." Rachel laughed. "I'm not that bad."

"What's your green stick story?" I asked.

"Ha!" Rachel said to Owen. "Dara is intrigued by my trivia."

"Don't encourage her," Owen said to me, still holding the dish. I hadn't had anything to eat since breakfast and was ravenous. I wished he would pass it to me, but instead he turned back to Rachel. "You must be dazzling at cocktail parties. Too bad this is Hollis."

"Will had a cocktail party just last month," Rachel said.

"Okay, just because Will served cocktails doesn't make it a cocktail party," Owen countered. "I bet you were all there in your jeans. Didi probably wore combat boots. And half of you probably just drank beer anyway."

"Well, I didn't. Callie and I were drinking champagne cocktails."

"That's because Callie is from New York," Owen responded, as if that made perfect sense. Who was Callie? This conversation was making me simultaneously jealous and bored. I looked at the terrine, hoping that Owen would feel my gaze and pass it.

"Since you asked, here's my Tolstoy story," Rachel said finally. She cleared her throat. "Tolstoy had an older brother. And this older brother told him that he, the brother, had written the secret to making all men happy on a green stick, and hid it somewhere. Tolstoy searched his whole life for it."

It took me a second to realize that she was finished. "Did he find it?" I asked.

"'All happy families resemble one another, but each unhappy family is unhappy in its own way,'" Sascha recited. "So I'm guessing no."

Owen finally handed the dish to me, and I served myself a moderate-sized spoonful of Rachel's aubergine and polenta terrine. Everyone else had begun eating, so I picked up my fork and took a bite. It was the best food I had ever put in my mouth. The eggplant melted into the cornmeal and mozzarella, their milder flavors balanced out by sun-dried tomatoes and an herb I couldn't place. "This is amazing."

"You think?" she asked. "I don't know. I think it would be better with our cheese."

"Everything's better with our cheese," Owen chirped.

"No, really, this is like the most amazing thing I have ever eaten. Why aren't there good words to describe the way things taste? I can't even describe it."

"You don't have to kiss her ass," Owen said. Belinda slapped the table. "Sorry."

"I'm not. This is insane how good this is." I sounded stupid, but I couldn't help myself.

"She's your sister. She's going to feed you. Sorry, Rachel, it's not your best work."

"Well, thank you, Dara," Rachel said. "But Owen's right, I've cooked better. Still, you'll never know unless you try something new, right?"

I couldn't believe they couldn't taste how wonderful the meal was. I looked to Sascha. He shrugged. "Food's good here. You'll see."

Belinda rapped the table, and Sascha handed her the basket of rolls. This was the way she communicated throughout dinner. She'd hit the table and Sascha would hand her something. Either he always knew what she wanted, or she decided it would suffice. I snuck glances at her, knowing it was rude to stare. Plus, if I looked at her, she might rap at me, and I would have no clue what to do. She chewed her food deliberately, overchewed it, and never swallowed except by washing the food down with a sip from her glass of milk.

Rachel poured herself a glass of wine and handed the bottle to Sascha. Belinda leaned forward as if to speak—a request, a condemnation—and I perked up in anticipation. She said nothing.

When we were all finished eating, Owen got up and started clearing dishes. I jumped up to help, thankful for a chance to be useful. I carried the dishes into the kitchen while he washed them in the deep porcelain sink, and when the table was clear, I started drying. He talked the whole time. "So this is life on Jezebel Goat Farm. Goats, food, cleaning up. It's peaceful, which is good if you like that sort of thing. Everyone pitches in."

As far as I could tell, all Belinda did was sit and hit the table, but I wasn't ready to ask about her. "What does Sascha do?"

"Transportation. He brings the cheese to market, buys the feed and other supplies, and moves goats around when they need it." I pictured Sascha lifting goats and throwing them through the air, one field to another. "I feed, which I guess is what you'll do too. Unskilled laborers. Feed and water the goats and sometimes help Rachel with the cheese, the less delicate parts. She doesn't like to let me help with the cheese."

"It's because you aren't careful," Rachel said. I hadn't heard her come in. "You've ruined whole batches."

"Once."

"Twice."

"That second time was Milo's fault."

They quipped like brother and sister. But she was my sister, not his. I wondered if Rachel and I would ever be like that. "Hurry up," Rachel said. "Belinda wants her pie." She took a stack of dessert plates down from a cabinet and went back into the dining room.

"Is every night like this? A big family dinner and everything?" I asked Owen.

"It's not because of you, if that's what you mean. Well, maybe the pie is. It's crazy, right? In my family, the only time we ate together was by accident." I nodded in total agreement. He went on, "It's nice, though. Plus the food is fantastic. I have to do extra sit-ups." He lifted his shirt and slapped his lean stomach with his wet hand.

"Wow," I said, my voice flat.

"What?" he asked.

"Nothing. I just figured that's what you wanted me to say. 'Wow. Nice abs.'"

He grinned. "Okay, maybe. But I wanted you to say it like, 'Wow, nice frickin' abs!'"

"Take what you get." I laughed, and he smiled back at me.

"All right. Let's go. I hope it's lemon meringue. She makes it from real lemons. I didn't even know you could do that."

The pie was pecan, but Owen and I both sighed over it all the same. "Now this is good cooking," he said.

I let the butter-sugar filling dissolve over my tongue. "Mmm-hmm," I agreed. I don't think my mom had ever made a pie, or my dad either, for that matter. The only time we sat around and ate like this was on holidays. Mom would be all nervous and stressed, and my grandmother would drill me on my times tables. When I got them all right, she'd say, "Well, at least you've got your mind." Bubby was even more blunt than my mother.

I wondered if Bubby had tested Rachel too. No matter how hard I tried, I could not insert Rachel into our family setting. On holidays in Rachel's house, everyone would be calm, happy, and well-fed—not stressed out and eager for it all to be over. I wondered how she'd found this place. This life.

After dessert, Owen and I washed those dishes too. By the time we finished, it was a little after 8:00. "All right, I'm going up to do my homework. See you at five thirty tomorrow?"

"Morning?" I asked.

"Yes, morning."

"But it's Saturday."

"Goats don't know what day of the week it is," he said. "We've got to feed and milk."

I tried to come to terms with the idea of getting up at 5:30 in the morning. I couldn't remember the last time I'd done that.

"I can do it myself," he said. "I just thought—"

"No, I'll do it," I said. He had thought that I was part of the farm now, and I was. At least I wanted to be.

The phone rang and my body tensed. It was my parents. I knew it. We could hear Rachel pick up in the other room. "Yes, she got here all right."

When Owen heard that it wasn't for him, he said, "Good night."

I nodded but didn't say anything because I was listening to Rachel's half of the conversation. I walked toward the living room. "I'm good," she was saying. She wrapped and unwrapped the phone cord around the fingers of her free hand, and chewed on her lower lip. She saw me in the doorway and looked up. "She's fine." I shook my head to let her know I didn't want to talk to them. "Okay," she said. "Yes, well, she doesn't actually want to talk to you right now." There was a long pause. "Maybe." Another pause. "I'll let her know." She looked down at her lap. "Good-bye."

When she hung up the phone, she stared at it in the cradle for a moment before looking up at me. "That was Dad. He wanted to make sure you got here okay."

So Mom had chickened out. Had she not wanted to talk to me, or to Rachel?

"Okay," I said.

Rachel exhaled and rubbed her forehead. Opposite her, Belinda sat in an armchair knitting a blanket that looked large enough to fit a full-size bed. Rachel picked up the book she had placed beside her on the couch. "No television," she said. "We might be the last spot in America without cable, and the reception was never very good."

"That's fine," I said. I looked around the room. There was an overcrowded bookshelf, and I browsed the spines. For some reason I had expected old romances and cheap paperbacks, but instead I saw some highbrow literary works: Spenser's *Faerie Queene*, a book of Keats, *Mrs. Dalloway* and *Orlando* by Virgina Woolf. I thought about pulling out *Orlando*, but I was overwhelmed with sleepiness. "I might go up to bed. It's been a long day."

"Sure, Dara," Rachel said. "Good night."

"Good night." I turned to Belinda. "Good night, Belinda." She lifted her head and nodded at me, which I figured was the best I could hope for.

Chapter Thirteen

I brushed my teeth and washed my face in the gold sink, then gave my skin a close inspection in the gilt-framed mirror. I had one small pimple next to my nose, but other than that I looked good. Considering the events of the past few days, one pimple was manageable.

At least they had called. They weren't so mad that they didn't even care whether I was okay or not.

I had planned to e-mail Melissa, but of course there was no e-mail at Jezebel. So I pulled out one of my school notebooks and ripped out a piece of paper to write her an honest-to-goodness letter.

Dear Melissa,
      We're going to have to write

since I am sans Internet. Send me postcards from Belgium, okay?

It's going pretty well here. There's a family dinner every night. How crazy is that? Tonight we had this amazing eggplant dish. Then there was pie for dessert. Homemade pie, crust and all. I better watch out or I may get fat living here.

I reread what I had written and added a smiley face so she would know the last part was a joke.

I think it's going to be okay. My sister seems pretty cool. I can't tell how she feels about me.

I twisted my pen with my fingers trying to think of what else to write.

The other folks who live here are interesting. There's Sascha (guy), who drives things. He's the strong somewhat silent type. The truly silent one is Belinda. She does not speak at all. She's got to be close to ninety. And then there's Owen. He's one of those people who we wish went to Pla-smart, funny, etc. Sadly, gay.

As if his sexuality was the only thing keeping us from a hot summer romance.

I bet Melissa would be fascinated by Jezebel, especially the papers in the shoe boxes and the fact that Belinda didn't speak. But the thought of going into any more detail exhausted me. So I signed the letter with X's and O's, and stuck it into an envelope. I would have to ask Rachel for a stamp.

I crawled under the nighttime-patterned quilt and looked up at the ceiling. The bed was soft and creaked slightly when I moved, more comforting than annoying. Yet tired as I was, I still couldn't sleep. I heard Rachel come upstairs, and could hear Owen walking around in his room. Then after a while, the house was silent.

I slipped from my bed and went to the closet, lifted a box from the top of the pile, and brought it to the window seat. Outside the sky was dusted with stars. The moon was high and lit up the fields of Jezebel Goat Farm. It granted me just enough light to start reading the pages and pages of type.

```
used to be. We'd hear the train rumble by the
farm and the girls would run to the truck.
They'd pile into the back and drive out to
```

the station and meet the traders on the platform. Bill Whitson still wouldn't sell to us, but the guys that moved the stuff would. I couldn't keep any of the girls behind since they'd say I was being unfair and picking favorites. The traders brought extra sets of coveralls in small sizes for them. For some of them, this was enough, but others still wanted something pretty. So there were dresses and barrettes and face powder compacts. I never knew what would interest them next. Willy Whitson took over the store and realized he could make some money off of us. He drove out to Jezebel to make nice with us. He even brought me a jar of honey and some fancy tea bags. He said he was sorry we'd never done business. He looked very nervous sitting in the parlor, perched on the front of the chair like a domesticated bird. Girls peeked at him from around the door frame. I opened up an account and the girls started to get their pretty things at Whitson's Store instead of off the train. And I didn't have to lose so many afternoons of work to the run into town, so I'd say it worked out all right in the end. Still, I think some of those girls got wistful when they heard that train whistle. But the train came less and less as the years went by, and

then it stopped stopping in Hollis, just
passed through.

I could picture the women spilling out from the house,
laughing and fighting over who got to ride in the truck. It
seemed like they'd made a new kind of family. A sisterhood.
I wondered where they all ended up.

The farm operation got bigger. We started
selling cheese in other towns. Whitson's got
bought out by Agway, and they stopped selling
pretty things. Bette was in charge at that
point. I don't think she so much minded the
loss of pretty things. She could make her
own. And she liked the men at the Agway. She
could cut a deal with them. We never paid the
full prices for feed or other supplies so
long as she was the one doing the shopping.
She'd cajole them and tease them and even
flirt with them and they just could not say
no. I never saw it myself. I had stopped
going into town. But Rachel told me it was a
sight to see. She always tried to get me to
go with them just so I could see it for
myself. But I could imagine it. Bette gave
that show to everyone when she wanted
something. Maybe I was trying to keep
it a little more special. Just a little
something that was only for Jezebel.

100

Because if I saw her out in the world, being
our girl for everyone else, I would lose

When I read Rachel's name, I perked up. She was here in
the story—part of the sisterhood. But why had she needed to
leave *our* family? My parents were judgmental and mean at
times, but they weren't bigots, and I didn't think they would
shut Rachel out of their lives for being gay. They said she
stole from them and ran after making it clear that she had no
desire to live at home. So how had she ended up at Jezebel?
Had she lied to the other girls? I half wanted to pull all of the
boxes out of the closet right then and search through them,
read all night. But the other half of me, the stronger half, was
finally ready to sleep.

Chapter Fourteen

At 5:15, Shania Twain sang me awake. I reached out and swatted at the clock radio, then sat up in bed, blinking until my surroundings came into focus: blue room, gray sky, sheets tangled around my legs. I switched on the bedside lamp, kicked myself free, and slipped out of bed. I needed to figure out what to wear. It was hard for me to find clothes that fit well, so I felt protective of my wardrobe. After groggily weighing my options, I pulled on a pair of boot-cut jeans and my READING IS SEXY T-shirt, which was already sort of on the way out of favor. Socks. Sneakers.

Owen was already downstairs, alert and adorable, wearing jeans and a long-sleeved T-shirt. He handed me a mug of coffee, as if he'd just been standing there waiting for me. "Morning," he sang.

"Blah," I replied. My hair was a mess, there was still sleep in my eyes, and I knew my face probably had wrinkles on it from the pillowcase. My mouth was dry and tasted sour. I sipped the coffee.

"Not a morning person?"

"This isn't morning. This is still night."

The sun was starting to come up as we walked out toward the barn. I drank my coffee quickly. Owen could probably carry a bucket and his mug, but I knew I'd need both hands.

Owen didn't stop at the barn, though. I followed him across the field to a small low building. The grass was wet with dew, and it seeped into my sneakers. The misty air smelled fresh, like cut hay.

"This is the milking shed," he told me as he slid open the doors. Inside there was a ring of low wooden platforms, about the height of a step. On one side of every platform were two posts with two crossbars and a bucket. At the center of the ring was a large metal contraption that looked like something out of a sci-fi movie. Hoses hooked into its stainless steel frame.

Owen went to a large bin and scooped out some feed with a pail. "We need to fill each bucket," he said. I took the pail and followed his directions, dumping about a cup of feed into each of the eight buckets.

"Now we gather the goats. It's easier than it sounds."

He grabbed some leashes, which he called leads, off a set of pegs on the wall, and we headed out to the field. The goats looked as sleepy as I felt. They moved away from us as we approached, but not so quickly that we couldn't grab their collars and hook on the leads. We caught eight of them and led them back into the barn.

"So, you get it to get up on the stand," he said. "They're hungry, so they'll go for the food. And when they do, clip them in." I watched as he demonstrated. The goat didn't seem to mind having her neck clipped into place.

I took the three goats I'd caught and coaxed the first two into place easily. The third one, though, was not having it. She was pale brown and smaller than the others. When I tugged on the lead, she bleated loudly, startling me. I stepped back.

"Don't be afraid of it," Owen said.

"Come on, little goat," I cooed. "Step up on the stage. There's yummy, yummy food up there." I tugged gently, but still the goat wouldn't move. "Seriously, get up there." She chewed her cud and stomped her back hoof. "I'll give you a sugar cube."

"Sugar cubes are for horses," Owen said.

"I bet goats like them too."

He walked over to me, took the lead, and slapped the goat on her butt. She looked up at him, then moseyed on up to the stand. Owen pushed her head through the slats and snapped her in.

"Now we clean the udders."

"You're kidding, right?"

"It wouldn't be a very funny joke," he said. "Come on." He handed me a small pail and led me to a huge sink at the back of the shed. We filled the pails with warm water, then Owen squirted some soap into each, and handed me a sponge. "If you don't clean the udders, the goat could get an infection. Plus, it's not very sanitary. Would you want to eat goat cheese from dirty teats?"

This whole conversation was a little bit much before breakfast.

"Just wipe them down."

So I took one of the low stools and sat down next to my first goat. I wiped her teats with the sponge, and she didn't struggle, just kept eating her grain. Goat number two was equally cooperative. Goat number three peed. I pulled my arm back just in time to get out of the way, but the yellow stream splashed off the stand and onto me. I rocked back and toppled the stool, landing on my ass on the concrete floor. "Shit!" I yelled out. The goats all stopped chewing and tried to turn their heads to look at me.

"Oh, yeah," Owen said. "Sometimes they pee."

"Thanks," I said.

I stood up and wiped off the back of my jeans. My tailbone hurt and I could feel tears welling up in my eyes. I brushed my long bangs out of my face.

Owen took my sponge from me and wiped down the udder of the evil third goat. "The first time I did this, the goat stepped on my hand." He showed me the back of his hand where there was a small pointy scar from the tip of a hoof. "When I'm a famous director, I'm not going to tell people that I worked on a goat farm. Not because I'm embarrassed, but because I think you can get strength from having a secret. And if anyone doubts me, I'll know that they will have no idea of what I've done, and what I'm capable of." He tugged at the sleeve of his T-shirt. "Okay, now for the fun part: attaching the hose."

I wasn't sure what I was supposed to get from Owen's story, but it made me feel better. If nothing else, I knew this hadn't been easy for him either.

He pulled a hose with two nozzle-type things on the end. "So now you stick the suckers onto the teats."

"They're really called suckers?" I asked.

"No, they're called inflations, but really, they're suckers. Fun goat fact: the udder is the whole milking area, and the teats are, well, the teats. People call them udders, but animals only have one udder."

I shook my head in dismay. "And I've been making a fool of myself for all these years." Owen grinned at me.

As he shoved the suckers onto the goat's teats, I instinctively crossed my arms across my chest. I guess that's how guys feel when they see someone get hit in the crotch. "That has to hurt," I said.

"I don't think they mind. But stay to the side of them, because they do kick."

"I'd kick too."

I brought a hose over to one of the goats and gently pushed the suckers on. They fell off. I tried again. One stayed, but the other wouldn't. As I grabbed the second teat, a small amount of milk came out. I groaned.

Owen looked up. "Get used to it, sweetheart."

I pushed the teat into the sucker, harder this time. Done. On to goat number two. She squirmed a bit, but I managed to get the suckers on. Now it was time for goat number three.

My nemesis: the little brown goat. I decided to name her Fitz. I held the hose tightly in one hand and put my other hand firmly on her back. "Listen to me, Fitzy. I'm going to put this sucker on you, and you're going to like it."

"Whoa," Owen said. "I didn't think you were that kind of girl."

I ignored him and shoved the suckers onto Fitz's teats. "Ha!" I said, triumphant. Fitz didn't even look up.

Owen moved to the center machine. "Green means go," he said, then pushed a giant button. He had a smudge of something gray on his neck that made him look even sexier standing there next to the giant whirring machine. "The milk goes in there." Owen pointed to a large metal reservoir. "Then stuff happens to it, don't ask me what. Rachel does it, and then she makes it into cheese. She's the cheese artist. We're the workhorses. I'd go on strike, but I actually like the job."

"Strengthens character," I said.

"Exactly."

"What kind of movies are you going to make?" I asked. I expected him to say documentaries. Hard-hitting films that didn't flinch from the darker side of life (and maybe took themselves a little too seriously).

"Romantic comedies. Smart ones, of course, like in the 1940s and 50s. You know, Katherine Hepburn and Spencer Tracy, Rock Hudson and Doris Day. Only in my films, Rock Hudson wouldn't have to stay in the closet." As he went on, he grew more animated. "I want to make romantic comedies with gay characters, but not always as the lead. It's just as important to have gay characters as secondary characters, as part of the usual cast, as long as they aren't stereotypes. I want them to be movies, you know, not necessarily *gay* movies. We should be beyond that."

"That'll be difficult, don't you think?"

"What do you mean?"

"I mean, say there's two people who want to go to a movie, and one says, 'Oh, let's go see that new romantic comedy that came out.' And the other one will say something like, 'You mean the one with Kate Hudson?' And the first person will say, 'No, the gay one.'"

"Sure, that's the way it is now. But my movies won't be about being gay. They'll be about love. They'll transcend. Here's something else about my movies: they're going to have happy endings. You know, like Shakespearean comedies where at the end, all the problems are resolved and everyone ends up with a partner."

"That doesn't seem very realistic."

"Who cares? They'll be beautiful, inspiring films. Like Baz Luhrmann mixed with Howard Hawks."

I didn't know what he was talking about, and I was pretty sure he knew I didn't know what he was talking about.

Then he said, "You can be in them if you want."

Yeah, right. "Whenever you need a sassy best friend with a heart of gold," I muttered.

He frowned. "Do you think I'm that unimaginative? I was thinking more leading lady."

I smiled, embarrassed. "Okay then, it's a deal."

"Great." He reached out his hand and we shook.

The machine made a final whir. "Time for round two," Owen said.

We unhooked all the goats, cleaned the works, and gathered up the second set of goats. As the machines pumped out their milk, I examined a mysterious stain on my jeans. Pee? Milk?

Owen interrupted my thoughts. "So, what was your talent?"

"Excuse me?"

"In the pageant," he said.

"Singing and dancing." I mimed dancing with a cane.

"Interesting." He nodded, but didn't say anything else.

Chapter Fifteen

When we got back to the house, I went straight upstairs to my room. I smelled like goat pee and milk. My hair was flat and starting to get greasy. I grabbed my toiletry bag and the towels that Rachel had left for me and headed for the bathroom. Owen arrived there at the same time. We both stopped. Owen looked like he was about to make a move, so I preemptively leaned toward the door. He grinned. "You can go first," he said. "But I'm only being polite because you're still new here. Don't use all the hot water."

"Thanks," I said. I smiled at him, then slipped into the bathroom and shut and locked the door behind me. The golden bathroom was a shiny, clean oasis. I turned on the shower and stripped down with my back to the mirror; I had no desire to see how I'd looked to Owen. Being near a boy without any sort of cosmetic help was a new thing. Probably only Melissa and Claire had ever seen me first thing in the morning.

I let the hot water run over me. I took my time washing my hair, enjoying the familiar smells of my shampoo and conditioner.

I knew I should get out so that Owen could have hot water, but instead I put my back to the stream and let it pulse against my skin. It felt so good. Sharing a bathroom was not going to be easy.

When I emerged, I wrapped my hair in one towel and my body in the other, then went through my usual moisturizing ritual: face lotion with SPF 15, body butter, and special peppermint foot cream. I took the towel off my head and combed through some anti-frizz serum, then twisted my hair up again.

When I opened the door, Owen was waiting outside. "Oh," I said, and rocked back, blushing.

"Steamy, steamy," he said, barely glancing at me. He slid past me into the bathroom. "Holy product, Dara. Did you buy all of Sephora?" He held up my face lotion. "SPF 15, very smart. Can I use some of this? You have great skin."

"Thanks," I said. I pulled my towel around me as tightly as I could, but the ends barely overlapped. "All right, well this isn't the dollar show."

I couldn't decide if it was good or bad that seeing me nearly naked hadn't made him uncomfortable. Sure, he was gay, but shouldn't he have looked—or looked away?

I padded down the hallway to my room, again anxious about clothing. I didn't have many farmy outfits left, and I wasn't sure what the day held in store. I decided on a pair of moderately new cropped jeans and a red V-neck. I pulled my hair into two low ponytails. At eight o'clock, I went back downstairs and found breakfast waiting on the table. "Belinda made this for you," Sascha said. Oatmeal. I hated oatmeal. I took my bowl, though, and sat down next to Owen, across from Sascha, who had finished his breakfast already, and was reading *The Berkshire Eagle* while drinking his coffee.

"Where's Rachel?" I asked, poking at the beige glop in my bowl.

"Farmers' market," Sascha said, moving the paper to the side so I could see his face.

"We can go if you want," Owen told me. "She's there all day and likes it when I come and give her a break."

"Sure, okay."

Belinda came in from the kitchen and sat down with us. I took a big scoop of oatmeal, shoved it in my mouth, and swallowed right away so I didn't have to feel the mushy, lumpy texture on my tongue. It burned my throat as it went down. "Mmm, good," I said loudly.

"She's not deaf," Owen said.

Well, how was I supposed to know? She nodded at me and gave a small smile; I wasn't sure if it was a kind one or not. I took another mouthful of oatmeal, figuring I could get it down in six, maybe seven bites.

Sascha started reading aloud. "The Sox have been strong so far this June, and last night was no exception." Belinda settled back into the seat to listen. She hit the table whenever Sascha read about pitches, even the other team's.

Belinda's smile was one of pure satisfaction. So she liked baseball. I wondered if she was one of the girls from the old days. Maybe she had come back to avoid a nursing home; Rachel would have taken her in. If, as Owen claimed, everyone at Jezebel was running from something, I wondered what she'd been running from. Perhaps something traumatic—the same reason she'd stopped speaking.

Sascha read off the box score to her, and she traced the numbers on the table with her finger. When Sascha finished reading, Owen took my bowl from me and carried it to the kitchen. When he came back through, he kept walking. "Well, come on. Let's get going."

"Does anybody need anything?" I asked as I stood up. Belinda stared up at me, her eyes wide and bright. She was asking for something, I could tell. I just didn't know what it was. I looked to Sascha, but he didn't clarify. "Okay, well, I guess we'll see you later."

I grabbed my purse from upstairs and slipped on a clean pair of flip-flops. Owen was already waiting outside next to my car. "You're driving," he announced. "Unless you want to let me drive your car."

"I'll drive," I said. "Where to?"

The roads we took had no lines on them and never stayed straight for very long, always curving around sharp bends. We rounded one curve and came to a stop sign. "One of three in town," Owen said. "There aren't any traffic lights. Turn right. This is Main Street."

At first I thought he was kidding; there were no buildings, only trees. But soon the trees gave way to a smattering of businesses. There was a church, a diner, and the Agway I had read about the night before. "Hey," I said. "It's the Agway."

"You want to go?" he asked.

"No, it's just . . . never mind." I wasn't sure if it was okay to be reading those pages.

We passed the Hollis House of Pizza, and a tiny grocery store.

"And we're done," Owen said. "That was blink-and-you-miss-it Hollis."

"It's cute," I said. "Quaint."

"As a postcard," he remarked drily.

We drove a short distance out of town, and then Owen told me to take a right. I slowed as we came upon a flat-roofed brick high school. Cars were lined up alongside the road for a quarter mile. "Park here," he said. "They use the whole lot for the farmers' market." I slid Bert into a spot between a minivan and a pickup truck, and cut the engine. "Hollis High School, home of the Purple Pride," he said as we walked down to the parking lot.

"Really?" I asked, giggling.

"Really." He smirked. "And yet somehow it didn't make coming out any easier."

"Sorry," I said. "Was it really rough?" He just shrugged.

We found Rachel at her stand, talking to an elderly woman. Rachel waved to us, and the woman turned around. "This must be your sister," she said. I wondered if there was some kind of town newsletter. *In other news, Rachel Cohen's long-lost sister was kicked out of her prestigious high school and has come to live at Jezebel.* Or, of course, maybe my sister had told her.

"Welcome to Hollis," she said. "Keep an eye on this one." She hooked her thumb toward Owen. "He's a heartbreaker." Then she winked at him.

"Lucy used to babysit me and my brother," Owen explained.

"Little monster since the day he was born." She leaned in to me. "Dangerous when they're that cute."

I grinned. *Yeah, dangerous for all the girls who don't stand a chance.* "It's a good thing he doesn't know it."

Lucy laughed. "She's got you pegged," she said to Owen. "I could bend your ear off, but I should be on to Hank's to get my pork for supper."

"Try it with lime," Rachel told her.

"Lime? Well, you are usually right about these things." She turned to me. "Nice to meet you, Dara. Have a good stay here."

"Thanks," I replied.

After Lucy left, Owen said, "I'm going to go look for the honey lady."

We watched him stride into the crowd, and I found myself missing him a little. I could see why Rachel felt so at ease around him.

The whole town had turned out, it seemed like—there were so many people milling around. I saw an overweight woman in a sweat suit digging through a bin of potatoes. It always made me sad to see a fat woman in a sweat suit. It was like she had given up. Maybe she'd have to order her clothes online, and maybe they'd cost more, but still, she could find things that flattered her. I mean, it's not like I could get a dress to make me look like a waif, but I knew what suited my body—and what didn't. Really, the only people who look good in sweat suits are athletes—you know, people who actually sweat, and not just from walking around the farmers' market.

I guess I was making a face, because Rachel asked, "Is everything okay?"

"I'm great," I said.

"How was your morning?" she asked, tugging on one of her overall straps with calloused fingers. Her lips were chapped and looked like she'd been chewing on them.

"I milked the goats."

"I'm sorry I wasn't there to show you. I have to get here really early to set up." She gestured toward the white-and-purple tent top that was shielding us and the cheese samples from the sun.

I was learning that there was a lot of early when it came to farms.

"It's fine. Owen taught me."

"He's a good kid," she said. She reached up to straighten the Jezebel banner. "His parents are actually decent people. That's what's so confusing about it. They were fine, normal parents until he came out, and then it all fell apart."

"Do you think—" I started to ask if she thought his parents would ever get over it and take him back, but we were interrupted by a middle-aged woman in a pink, floppy, straw hat.

"Hello," Rachel greeted her. "How did the pepper-crusted go over?"

"I served it on melba toast, and the ladies couldn't get enough of it. I'm getting two logs this week."

I watched Rachel as she worked. She stood with her right hip jutting forward, like Mom did. She didn't have the fake smile of a salesman but seemed honestly pleased that her cheese had made this woman happy. She reached into one of the coolers in the back of her truck and pulled out two logs wrapped in brown paper. "We're featuring our spreadables this week. Two for five dollars."

"You know I can't say no to a deal."

"Personally, I'm a fan of the basil. Folks like the sun-dried tomato, though."

"I'll get one of each."

Rachel placed all of the cheese into a paper bag stamped with the logo, and passed them to the woman. "See you next week?"

"Of course," the woman replied.

Rachel leaned back on the tailgate of her pickup. It was an old Ford, maybe from the fifties or sixties. It was curvy and full, without the harsher lines of newer models, and had been painted a pale purple with white accents. "I like your truck," I told her.

She smiled proudly and patted the metal. "Sascha fixed her up for me. She runs on grease."

That was pretty cool. Maybe Sascha could fix Bert up to run on grease. "Did you name her?"

"The truck? No. She's just 'Truck.'"

"Mine's Bert."

"I remember when Dad bought that car. He was so

117

protective of it. We weren't even allowed to eat in it."

Now Bert was cozy, the leather smooth and worn. "Oh," I said. "He has a BMW now." *Like she cares*, I told myself.

"Figures," she replied.

"I'm not allowed to eat in it." This wasn't exactly the rule. It was more Mom's general anti-snacking policy.

She grinned conspiratorially. "Once, in high school, some friends and I took the car to Old Orchard Beach and—" She broke off her memory to wave at an elderly man in overalls who was loping toward the stand. "Hello there," she said to him. "Dara, this is Mr. Otis. He's responsible for this whole market."

I think the man blushed. "What else is a retiree supposed to do?"

"You're hardly retired," Rachel said as she handed him a twenty dollar bill. "See you next week."

"See you," he said, and tipped his hat to her.

We watched him leave, and I was hoping she would finish her story. Instead she asked, "Did you get breakfast?"

"Belinda made us oatmeal."

"She thinks oatmeal is the cure for everything. Make sure you don't catch poison ivy. You'll be bathing in it."

"Where did she come from?" I asked.

"Belinda? She owns Jezebel," Rachel said. "She's lived there her whole life."

If Belinda owned the farm, that made her the narrator of the pages. I felt stupid for not even considering the possibility; I had just asked a really dense question. "But you run the farm now?" I asked, recovering.

"Since I got back."

"From where?"

"I went out to California. Tried to make it as a chef." She seemed embarrassed.

"Really? You'd be a great chef. I would totally eat in your restaurant."

Rachel looked over her shoulder at the coolers of cheese. "Well, nothing is as easy as it sounds. It didn't work out. I never got my feet under me."

"You could still do it," I urged. "You could open a restaurant here."

For a moment she looked pleased, but then she shook her head. "No," she said. "I've got the farm now. I don't need anything else." She looked at me and then looked away. "It's home now."

"Is this where you came right away?" I asked, hoping this wouldn't be a too-sensitive subject.

"I worked in Hampton Beach for a while. And then I went to Vermont and worked in a ski lodge for a couple months, selling hats and mittens and stuff. I hung out at the ski bars." She laughed when she saw my wide eyes. "It might sound cool, Dara, but . . . well. Anyway, I met this woman, Sarah. She was older, maybe in her fifties. She ran one of the shops in town, and was just the kindest person I had ever met. She didn't care about anyone's past. She'd spent some years at Jezebel, and when she told me about it, it seemed like the perfect escape."

"From what?"

She shrugged. "When you go to a new place, you build a life for yourself. In Vermont, I built it all wrong. Bad job, bad guys, bad friends." She looked down at the dish of samples, and then, as if it had just occurred to her, asked, "Have you even tried our cheese yet?" I shook my head. She jumped up off the tailgate. "I'm going to start you out with the straight-up cheese. Unadulterated." She grabbed a cracker from the basket and spread some cheese on it for me.

It was smooth and creamy and a little tart, not over-whelming. The flavor almost seemed to grow in my mouth. I swallowed. "That is amazing."

Rachel grinned. "Isn't it? I still remember the first time I had it. It was taste-bud love. Try this one. This is our herbed log."

Fantastic. She gave me sample after sample, each one as perfect as the last. Rachel was a genius—a cheese genius. I only wished I had her metabolism so I didn't have to feel guilty as I appreciated her work.

"The spreadables were my idea," she said. "We whip the cheese with different add-ins. They're great for parties."

"You could go nationwide with this. You could be like the next, I don't even know what."

She shook her head. "Local," she said. "I don't care if no one in Louisiana or Chicago ever hears of Jezebel Goat Farm, but I want everyone in the Berkshires to demand it."

"Your own little goat-cheese empire," I said.

"Our own fiefdom," she corrected.

"Well, you've made me a loyal subject."

She moved like she was going to hug me, but instead just threw her arm around my shoulder. It was awkward, clumsy even, but it meant something. It meant she liked me. It was kind of a sad thing to be excited about, but I was.

Chapter Sixteen

When we got home from the farmers' market, Owen and I fed the goats, and then he went upstairs to do some homework while I went into the kitchen to help Rachel. She had made mini-pizzas, which were in the oven; the smell was tantalizing.

"Now for a salad," she said. "Hand me a tomato."

I passed her a large tomato that had ripened on the windowsill. I watched as she chopped it into thin wedges. Her knife moved so quickly, I felt like I was watching a cooking show.

"Where did you learn to do that?" I asked.

"I dated a chef," she replied.

"You're a really good cook," I said. "Especially, you know,

compared to the Lean Cuisine crap Mom always gets me."

"She never was much of a cook."

"No kidding," I agreed. "Once she tried to make mashed potatoes without boiling them first. She just put them in the microwave."

"It's like that Thanksgiving where she put the turkey in without fully defrosting it." She giggled tentatively, as if she wasn't sure it was okay to make fun of Mom around me.

"They ended up getting Mexican food delivered." My parents told the story every Thanksgiving but had never mentioned Rachel in it.

"Right, and Dad tried to say it was more authentic, because the Mexicans were like the American Indians."

"That doesn't make any sense." I laughed.

"*Now* it's funny, but I remember Mom was so mad. Of course I didn't make the day any better, right?" She laughed again, until she caught my confused expression. "Uncle Barrett and I were making apple pie?" she prompted. "And we shoved all the apple peels into the garbage disposal and totally jammed it, so the sink overflowed and the plumber had to come out and fix it?"

"Oh yeah," I said. But she knew I was lying.

"Uncle Barrett felt so bad for calling the guy out on Thanksgiving that he asked the guy to stay for tacos, which he did because it turned out he had just emigrated from Portugal and didn't have any family. We called it the Cohen-Almeida Family Thanksgiving. That's how we referred to Thanksgiving for years. They never . . ." She didn't finish her thought, just shook her head and went to the refrigerator to

122

retrieve a carrot. She peeled it vigorously, firing orange shavings into the sink. Back at the cutting board, she chopped it just as rapidly, the knife hitting the board with severe thuds.

"So they don't tell that part of the story?" she finally asked.

What was I supposed to say? They never talked about her. "Well, Mom usually talks about the turkey. I guess that's just the part that, you know, she can poke fun at herself for."

Rachel arched her eyebrows at me. We both knew that Mom wasn't one for poking fun at herself. "What about the year I decided I was going to celebrate Christmas, and I made Mom take me to get my picture taken on Santa's lap? I had Santa and Jesus confused and got in an argument with the mall Santa when he wouldn't admit he was Jewish."

I laughed, because of my nerves and the tension, and because it was funny.

"So you've never heard that one before?" she asked.

I was having trouble settling myself down. Finally I said, "It's just that—"

"It doesn't matter. I don't care."

"I'm glad you told me," I said.

"Sure," she replied. She dumped the carrots into the salad bowl. The oven buzzer went off. "Why don't you tell everyone that dinner is ready?"

I backed out of the kitchen and walked toward the staircase, poking my head into the parlor to let Sascha and Belinda know. Upstairs I knocked on Owen's door, then peered into his bright room. "Dinner," I said.

"Cool," he replied.

We arrived at the dining room at the same time Rachel came in, carrying plates of pizzas. She dropped one down at each person's place. "Mangia," she said with fake enthusiasm.

I felt horrible. I should have just lied to her and acted like I knew the whole story. I took a bite of my pizza, still so hot it burned the roof of my mouth. With my eyes tearing, I said, "This is really good."

"Thank you." Her voice was clipped.

Owen reached across the table for red pepper flakes, almost knocking over her water.

"You could ask me to pass them to you," she snapped.

"Sorry."

"Is this Jezebel cheese?" I asked, still hoping to ease the tension.

She didn't answer. Finally Owen said, "It's always Jezebel cheese."

I stopped trying at that point and kept my eyes on my plate for the rest of dinner. I could feel her brooding across from me, and I started to get angry. It wasn't my fault I didn't know her stories, so why was she making me feel awful? Then I snuck a glance at her face and saw that she was struggling not to cry, and I realized she had just now figured out the extent to which she had been excised from our family.

After dinner, Rachel and Belinda took their tea into the parlor, where Rachel read and Belinda knit. I thought about joining them, but the tension at dinner had been so painful, I decided I was better off leaving her alone. I stopped by to say good night before heading up to my room.

I got ready for bed but didn't go to sleep. Instead, I took two shoe boxes out of the closet and brought them to one of the window seats to read in the moonlight. I flipped through the pages until I found one with Rachel's name on it.

```
along the way sometime we just started to
become vaguely respectable. I suppose that's
what happens when you have been around for
years. Still, I imagine certain fathers and
mothers tell their girls to stay away from
the farm, for fear it might be catching. And
teenage boys still come round hoping to see
something illicit. But we were always just a
group of women. Girls stopped coming, just
like the trains. When Rachel came, there
hadn't been a new girl in almost three years.
Rachel was young and confused. Her hair fell
in two thick plaits down her back and her
eyes were rimmed with black liner. She
brought a backpack full of black clothes. I
put her up in the Ireland room with Bette,
thinking Bette would be a good role model for
her. Rachel was wild. She raced through her
chores. She scared the goats with her yelps
and curses. It was not clear that Jezebel was
the place for her. But she came to us and we
had not turned anyone away yet, not even when
```

we were full up and I had five or six girls
in each room. I told myself I wasn't going to
start turning girls away. I said, "Let's just
see how it works out. Let's see." In the
first week, I almost made her leave. It was
Sascha who found them all, Rachel and the two
boys with a box full of wine coolers down by
the river, whatever a wine cooler is. Rachel
in her underwear, the boys in the same. He
brought her home with a shirt on, clutching
her skirt and shoes, her hair still wet,
sweet alcohol stink on her breath. How she
met the boys was beyond me. Most likely the
boys were hanging around Whitson's. Celie
asked me why she was even here. "Isn't
Jezebel for women who aren't accepted at
home? What did she do? Why did she have to
leave?"

Though I wondered the same thing, I found myself getting
angry at Celie. This was the safe place that Rachel had found,
and her reasons were none of Celie's business.

I tried to explain that there was room at
Jezebel for whoever needs sanctuary, but
was that true? If I let every wayward girl
who passed through stay here, what would
have become of us? My girls were always
responsible, honest, and hardworking. They

were not welcome at home, but they were
welcome here. Rachel, though, was a puzzle.
My girls were looking for a home, and I was
never sure what Rachel sought. She was quick
to anger and to break our rules. For the
other girls, talking about families was like
talking about a broken heart. Rachel kept her
story to herself, and that made it harder for

The text cut off there, and I couldn't find the next page. It
could be anywhere in the stack of boxes. I looked out the
window at the moon, the fields, the dark sky. It was such a
peaceful place, but downstairs I knew my sister was still
angry and hurt.

Chapter Seventeen

Sunday was lonely. Owen and I fed and milked, and then he disappeared to do homework. Rachel stayed holed up in her office. I could have studied for exams, but I didn't have to take them for another couple of weeks. So I took *Wuthering Heights* off the bookshelf and went outside to read in a sunny patch of grass. It was kind of like being on vacation, lolling about in the sun. I dozed off, woke up and read, dozed off again, then woke up feeling hungry for lunch. Little spots danced in front of my eyes as I walked toward the house.

I found a leftover pizza in the fridge and took it into the dining room. A few minutes later, the phone rang, and I heard Rachel come out of her study to answer it. "Sure, I'll be there," she said, laughing. Her voice lowered after that, and all I could hear was its rise and fall, not the words.

I finished my pizza, but she was still on the phone, and I didn't want to bother her. I couldn't just leave the plate in the dining room, though, and I wasn't going to sit there all afternoon—who knew how long her conversation would go on? When I entered, she turned her back to me and started speaking in monosyllables: "Yes . . . hmm . . . oh?" Feeling like an intruder, I left my plate and started to walk out when she said, "Hold on," and put the phone to her shoulder.

"I was able to get you an appointment with Dr. Eddington for tomorrow," she told me.

It was nice that she'd thought of me, but at the same time, I wondered if she was trying to send a message.

"Eleven forty-five. Is that okay?"

"Sure."

Outside, my sunny spot had moved, so I had to find another one. I didn't even feel like reading anymore.

Why hadn't my parents told me the whole story of that Thanksgiving? Why did they have to cut out Rachel's entire childhood from our family history? They'd ruined it for me before I even had a chance.

I was mad at Rachel too. Why was she blaming me?

I curled my knees up to my chest. I could feel the tears burning my eyes as my chest constricted. I was stuck here. My sister was ignoring me and just might hate me. My parents were pissed at me. I hated crying. *Blubbering.* I tried to stop it, but I couldn't.

Chapter Eighteen

Dr. Eddington's office was in her home, a little two-story on a stretch of the main road where a crush of houses seemed to have been dropped out of the sky. I rang the bell and she called from inside, "Come on in!"

I felt weird turning the doorknob and walking into the home of someone I had never met. If I were a doctor, I don't think I would want patients to see my home. It violated something in the doctor-patient relationship.

Dr. Eddington emerged from a doorway at the other end of the house and walked toward me, smiling. She was in her forties, petite, and her head was covered with short, tight curls. Her long, tan dress swished around her ankles; she seemed like one of those earth-mother hippie types. Maybe we'd be doing art therapy, or maybe she'd try to cure me with crystals.

"Follow me," she said, and led me around the corner to her office. Tan-walled and lit by low-wattage bulbs, the room exuded calm. She indicated an armchair, then picked up a notebook and sat down on the chair across from me. "Welcome," she said.

The room was over-air-conditioned, and I shivered as I looked around. Two tapestries hung on the opposite wall, one of a unicorn, the other of a sleeping lion curled up in a forest. There was a shallow bowl of pebbles next to my chair, and also a box of tissues, in case I needed to do any crying.

"Have you ever been in therapy?"

"No," I said.

"It's normal to feel uncomfortable at first."

Well good, then, I was normal. I picked up one of the pebbles, a green one shaped like a tooth.

"Do you have any ideas about how you want your therapy to go?" she asked.

I thought about telling her that I'd be okay with the crystals, as long as it meant I didn't have to keep defending myself to thin people who assumed I had self-esteem issues. "I have no clue," I said.

She jumped up and crossed to her desk. "I forgot a pen," she explained as she returned to her seat. "So, what are your goals from therapy? That's always a good place to start."

"I don't really have a choice," I told her.

She frowned and tugged on one of the curls on the back of her head. "What do you mean?" Her face was kind, concerned.

I felt snide, but my being there wasn't her fault, and she seemed nice enough, so I decided to lay it all out for her. "The truth is, I don't think I need therapy."

"Okay," Dr. Eddington said. She wrote something down. "In my experience, parents don't just throw their kids into therapy. What happened?"

Maybe she would understand my project—I still thought I had done a good job. So I told her the whole story, starting with Katie North and ending with the scene in Mrs. Arendt's office.

Dr. Eddington didn't say anything at first. She just kept writing on her yellow legal pad, and my gaze wandered back to the decor. There were dozens of unicorn figurines reclining on the windowsills. A glass unicorn, likewise in repose, sat on her desk, which was tucked into the corner. What was with all the unicorns? It was like my therapist was secretly a nine-year-old girl. She got up and went back to her desk, where she started sifting through her papers. Finally she asked, "So you think your parents put you in therapy to save face?"

"Yeah. And I think they also wanted to make a point."

"What's that?"

"That it's not their fault that I'm screwed up and depressed."

"Do you think you're depressed?"

"No. Not really," I replied.

She tugged on one of her curls. "So why here? Why didn't you stay in Portland?"

I looked down at the green pebble in my palm. "My parents never told me about Rachel." I looked at her for a response, but she kept her face neutral. "I found out I had a sister when I was nine. I found her birth certificate."

"Wow, what was that like?"

No one had ever asked me that before. Of course, I had kept the secret of Rachel a secret. "It sucked," I replied.

"I'll bet. Were you angry?"

"Confused. My parents didn't talk about her. And I guess I had been thinking about her a lot this spring, and so then when all of this happened, I was so upset, I finally got up the nerve to call her."

"What did your parents think of that?"

I laughed.

"But you're here," she said.

"We had a fight about it. They told me all these awful things about Rachel. I don't know if they were true or not. But I told them I was coming no matter what."

"Good for you," she said. I hadn't realized psychiatrists were allowed to judge your actions.

"Thanks," I said.

"How's it going?"

"Good," I said. I unclenched my fist, which had tightened around the pebble.

"It must be a little weird to be living with a sister you've never really known."

"It's a little awkward sometimes, but it's nice." Awkward was an understatement, but I didn't want to tell her how lonely I felt, how Rachel seemed to be avoiding me. Dr. Eddington knew Rachel—I didn't want to make my sister look bad.

We talked a little bit more, mostly about life on the farm and how it was different from Portland. I couldn't see how it would help me, but at least she wasn't trying to get me to talk about my weight. We set up a schedule of times to see each other, and then she photocopied my insurance card.

I was tucking my wallet back into my bag when Dr. Eddington made a final comment. "I get where you were going with the thinness obsession in our society, but an autobiography is supposed to be about you."

I started to protest, to make the comparison to Maya Angelou and how her autobiography was as much about race in America as it was about her, but Dr. Eddington kept going. "I think your project really was about you, about how you feel about yourself and how you think other people see you."

Great, so we get through the whole session, and then she tells me she thinks I'm bullshitting her. Just like everyone else, she assumed I must want to be thinner—must hate myself for how I looked, and blame everyone around me.

"Think about it," she said. "I'll see you next week."

Outside, I slammed my car door. I had almost resigned myself to therapy, but with that last comment, she had lost me.

Chapter Nineteen

When I got back to the farm, Rachel was in the barn, her hands encased in plastic gloves. She waved when she saw me pull up. I shouldn't have come straight home. I should have driven around for a while; the last thing I wanted to do right now was talk to her about therapy. I was beginning to wish I had done my project on something—anything—else.

"So," Rachel said, bracing herself, "you look unhappy. How did it go?" She sat down on one of the swings that hung from the oak tree in the front yard.

I remained standing. "She kept, like, losing her pen and stuff."

"She can be a little unconventional," Rachel said.

Unconventional. That was one word for calling your

patient a liar. Why had Rachel sent me to this woman in the first place?

"She is good, though," Rachel continued. "She gets more than you think she does."

Everyone thought they got me. They saw me and thought, *Fat girl. Must want to be thin. Must hate herself.* "It sucked," I said.

Rachel looked beyond me for a second, and I realized I was just making things worse between us. "Do you want to make cheese?" she asked abruptly.

"Now?"

"It's completely soothing. I always feel better after I do it." She hopped up from the swing. "Come on. If you're still stressed out after a little bit, you can stop."

"Okay," I said.

"Go change into clothes you can get dirty, and then meet me in the barn."

She trotted off toward the barn, and I went up to my room. As I changed into a T-shirt and dirty jeans, I wondered if Rachel really thought making cheese would soothe me, or if she was just tired of my whining and needed help.

In the barn I found Rachel dumping a huge metal bowl of milk curd into a vat. "Phase one," she said. "Flipping the curd into the bags. It separates the curds and whey." She explained how much to put into each bag, and I watched her fill one and then hang it over a slanted metal counter. "We collect the whey and give it back to the goats." That sounded a little gross to me, but I didn't say so. I just started working. My hands grew prunelike in the still-damp curds.

"What's phase two?" I asked.

"We salt and season the cheese and then put it into molds or roll it into logs. Some gets aged. Some goes right out. And actually I went to a tasting and had some blue goat cheese, and I'm trying to make that. It was really spectacular—so smooth."

It was clear when she talked that she wasn't just some hobbyist. She knew her business, and she was good at it. "How do you make blue cheese?" I asked.

"It's like making sourdough bread. You need a little bit of blue cheese to start. And then you introduce that into the curds. It's called an inoculum. You have to aerate it, so the mold can grow. It's pretty interesting to watch."

We worked in silence for a long time, and it *was* satisfying and soothing, as Rachel had promised. I filled nearly a dozen bags.

"I'm sorry I've been so pissy lately," she said suddenly. "Sometimes it's easier than dealing with things."

"Oh, that's okay. Don't worry about it," I said.

"I saw you crying," she told me.

I cringed. "Yeah, well, it's just been a long couple of weeks." I corrected myself. "Days."

"I didn't mean to get so angry. I wasn't really even upset with *you*. I guess I just thought I was still . . ." Her voice trailed off. "It's not your fault. I used to get angry like that a lot. You should have seen me when I first came here. The littlest thing would set me off. Someone would ask me to sweep out the stalls, and I'd act like they'd asked me to lick shit off their boots. Sorry, that was crass." She hung a cheese bag up on a hook. "Anyway, after some time here, I guess I just saw how things worked, the pattern of it, the way everyone chipped in—I don't know, I guess it calmed me down."

"That's cool," I said, because I didn't know how else to respond. I thought about how unstable Mom and Dad said she was. It seemed like maybe she *had* been. She'd obviously changed a lot since then, but still, I felt uncomfortable, and I think she felt it too—it was like a thin wall between us.

Rachel picked up a hose and started spraying down the tub. "Thanks." She smiled. "This was nice." Then she hefted the box and disappeared deeper into the barn.

Chapter Twenty

As I left the barn I nearly walked into Owen, who was holding a small digital video camera in front of his face. "Say something," he said. "Be natural."

I put my hand up, blocking the lens. "What are you doing?"

"I'm going to help you with this autobiography project."

I dropped my hand, but looked at the ground. "You don't need to do that." I had planned to procrastinate on the project for as long as possible.

"No shit, but maybe I want to."

"Why?" I asked. He put the camera down and indicated for me to follow him, so I kept walking.

"Maybe I like making movies. And maybe I actually want

to help you out. I promise you'll get an A. So now I want you to stand in front of the barn and say, 'Hi, I'm Dara, and this is my autobiography.'"

I looked behind me at the bright red barn. "But this isn't my regular life. We'd have to go to Portland to do it right— to do it accurately."

"I'm the director here. You know what Alfred Hitchcock thought of actors? They were like cattle, the same as props, no artistic direction of their own."

"Thanks." I wiped my legs where the cheese had splattered on them.

"I don't believe that. I'm just letting you know how bad it could be. You look fine. Natural. So just say it."

"I do not look fine. I'm covered in goat milk." I hadn't generally avoided cameras, because I didn't want to be the big girl hiding from photos, but I wasn't exactly comfortable in front of them.

"You don't have goat milk all over you. You look great."

I was learning that sometimes it was easier to appease Owen than to fight him. I probably wasn't going to use his footage, but it wouldn't hurt to let him have his fun. So I squared my body in front of the barn. The sun was behind him, and I had to squint. "Hi. I'm Dara, and this is my autobiography."

"Now in front of the tree."

He pointed to the large oak whose branches reached out over the sandy driveway. I crossed over. "Hi. I'm Dara, and this is my autobiography."

Owen looked around. "In front of the house."

"This is going to make for a gripping documentary," I said.

Owen pointed at himself and said, "Director."

"Why do we have to do it so many times?"

"Good movies are made in the editing room. We need to make sure we have lots of options."

As we walked back toward the house, I said, "You know, this is my *auto*biography project, right? It doesn't really make sense to have someone else do it."

"It's a lame assignment and you shouldn't have to redo it, so it's okay if I help you." He put the camera back in front of his face. Every time he lifted his arm, his bicep muscles popped. "Just go in front of the house. We'll do that, and then out in the field with nothing around you."

The whole thing was silly, so I sucked in my cheeks and tried to say the line with a French accent. "Bonjour! I am Dara, and zis eez my autobiography." I started to giggle.

"In the field," Owen said.

I perched myself on the top rung of the fence and clumsily swiveled to the other side, somehow not minding that Owen had filmed it. When I turned around, I did my best impression of a country jig. "Hi y'all," I said. "I'm Dara, and this here is my autobiography."

I thought Owen would be annoyed with me, but he smiled. "Do you speak Spanish?" he asked.

I shook my head and called out, "Hola!"

"Lean against the fence seductively," he said.

It was an old split-rail fence, ragged and splintering, but I did as he said, draping my arm along the top rung. With my back to him, I looked over my shoulder and said the line in my deepest, sexiest voice.

We did a couple more, then sat down on the picnic table. He turned the viewer so I could watch the clips with him. I leaned away. It had been fun to goof around in front of the camera, but now I was reluctant to see myself. "You look great," Owen said. "Seriously, look." He thrust the viewer in front of my face. The early shots were boring, but the later ones were goofy in an endearing sort of way. It was a little bit cringy—I looked even wider on camera—but some people just look good when they're performing, regardless of their weight, and I think I'm one of those people. I looked charismatic and confident. Almost sexy.

I turned back to Owen and smiled. "All right, Mr. Director, you're hired."

"You don't hire me. You're the talent."

"I'm the talent and the producer," I said. "I'm like Tom Cruise." We shook on it. His hands were so smooth, like he didn't spend his days feeding and milking goats. Mine had already grown dry and calloused. Like I needed one more reason to envy Owen. "So what's the plan?"

"No plan yet. This is gonzo filmmaking."

"I'm not Hunter S. Thompson," I said, hoping I could throw a reference over his head, that of the *Rolling Stone* reporter who had led a wild, drug-filled life.

"Clearly," he replied. The corners of his almond-shaped eyes crinkled as he smiled, and I wondered what it was like to be so beautiful.

"I like plans."

"Producers usually do." He drummed his fingers on the picnic table. "Okay, have you seen *The Breakfast Club*?"

142

"Sure," I said. The movie was one of my favorites, even though the plot was kind of a stretch—all these kids from different cliques have Saturday detention and realize that they all can like and respect each other. Then they all pair up at the end, except for the poor dweeby guy. But of course they were all fairly good-looking and thin to begin with, so there wasn't that much radical mind-opening going on.

"So they're supposed to write an essay about who they think they are, which is kind of like your autobiography project, but instead they just write the one letter. 'We accept the fact that we have to be here on a Saturday, et cetera.' And it ends with them saying that they aren't just the stereotypes, that we're all unique."

"Yeah, yeah, yeah."

"We could have footage of you with something like that as the voiceover. 'I accept the fact that I have to do this project over.'"

"I don't accept that fact."

"You're doing it, aren't you?" He continued drumming his fingers and added a foot tap. The guy never held still. "Okay, how about a *Casablanca* thing?"

"I don't know what you're talking about," I said. "Movies are your thing. Not mine."

"So what *is* your thing?"

I started to tell him that it was English: books, words, poetry. But that seemed boring compared to Owen's aspirations. I scratched my neck where sweat had gathered and dried. "Music," I said.

His face lit up. "We are *so* doing a music video. Not like a choreographed dance-along video, but one of those great videos that tells a story that may or may not have anything to do with the song."

"Like a Michael Jackson video?"

"Exactly. But without the budget."

I took my hair out of its ponytail, shook it out, and pulled it right back up. The music video idea had promise. After watching myself on his camera, I could sort of see how he might edit it. But we didn't have a cast or, for that matter, a song. "Maybe," I said.

"I'll keep thinking about it. Don't worry. It's going to rock." His confidence was almost catching.

I realized it was getting late. "We should feed those goats," I said.

Owen dropped his camera off inside, and we headed out to the fields. I watched his loping stride as we walked. It was going to be hard not to get a crush on him. He was gorgeous and still he had a way of making me feel comfortable and confident, without being patronizing. I was going to miss him when I left.

Chapter Twenty-one

For dinner that night Rachel made broiled snapper with a garlic port wine reduction. It was incredible.

It's fair to say that my relationship with food was complicated. I loved good food and considered bad food a waste of time and calories. The relationship was also antagonistic: food was, after all, what had made me so fat. Living at Jezebel was adding complications. It was only my fourth night, but, gluttonous as it sounds, dinner felt kind of like the highlight of the day. It was the social part of it that I really loved. I wished food was both unnecessary and incorporeal so that it would be a purely social and pleasurable experience, like going to a concert. Instead, enjoying it had a price; for people like Owen, it was low, but for me, it was high. It wasn't fair.

Rachel placed the tray down on the table and served each of us, starting with Belinda, then settled into her seat. "How was Northampton, Sascha?"

He buttered an ear of corn as he spoke. "Hansen's upped their order. I put the paperwork on your desk."

Rachel passed me a bowl of green beans. "Good. Thank you. How's Sylvie?" she asked. A grin spread across Owen's face. Belinda frowned at him.

Sascha kept his eyes on the ear of corn he was buttering. "Fine, I guess." His cheeks were turning pink—or at least pinkish. Owen looked at me and raised his eyebrows.

"Who's Sylvie?" I asked.

"Sylvie Hansen owns Hansen's Gourmet Market," Rachel answered. "They're a big buyer for us."

"But only since Sascha came back from visiting his mother and Rachel stopped making the deliveries," Owen interjected.

"It's true," Rachel agreed. "I couldn't get any traction with them."

"It's coincidental," Sascha argued.

"Rachel could sell cheese to vegans," Owen said. "And you aren't exactly Mr. Sales Pitch."

"I don't need to have a sales pitch. People want to buy the cheese, so Sylvie sells it to them. Simple as that." Sascha's voice was gruff.

Owen snorted. "Whatever, Casanova, you should just embrace it."

Belinda rapped the table. For the first time, I understood her.

"We're just jealous," Rachel said.

"There's nothing to be jealous of," Sascha snapped before taking a huge bite of his fish. He looked like he was under siege.

They meant well, but it also seemed like they were amused, like the idea of him dating was inherently funny. "Do you even like her?" I asked casually. "Because it's not that unlikely that she likes you, and you don't want to give her the wrong idea."

Sascha's shoulders relaxed. "She invited me for coffee today."

Owen started to comment, but I kicked him under the table. Rachel clasped her hands. "Oh, Sascha! Next thing you know you're not going to be coming home to us."

Sascha looked angry again, so I pointed at his ear of corn. "You eat the cob down to a square," I said. "Some people make it round. If you make it square, you're more left-brained. If you make it round, you're more right-brained." Everyone, even Belinda, looked down at their plates to check out their corncobs.

"Really?" Rachel asked.

Melissa had told me this one summer when she saw my round corncob. "Supposedly."

"Wait, which side is the creative one?" Owen asked, holding up his round cob.

"The right," Rachel answered.

"Good," he said.

Across the table Sascha subtly shrugged at me and shook his head. I smiled and shrugged back.

"You must have the magic touch," Rachel told me as I was scraping the dishes. "He's never confessed that much about her."

I blushed. "He doesn't want to be teased. I understand that."

Rachel paused, just a beat, but I noticed. "You're a good kid," she said. Then she went back out to the dining room, calling, "Tea, anyone?"

Owen came into the kitchen, rolled up his sleeves, and turned on the water. "Four more days of school. Then finals. And then I am done. Done."

He lowered a stack of plates into the sink just as the phone started ringing. We both froze.

"Can you please get it?" I asked.

He shook his head, then wiped his hands on his pants and reached for the receiver. "Hello? Oh, hey." He leaned back against the counter, smiling. "Yeah sure." For a guy who had just been so eager to get out of school, he seemed perfectly happy to talk to whoever was on the phone. He acted like school was so awful, like the people there sucked, but I knew he had to be incredibly popular. He was perfect-looking. As he talked, he twisted the cord between his fingers. Maybe it was some guy he was dating. "Yeah, I'll bring it tomorrow."

I tried not to listen to his conversation as I folded and refolded a dish towel. When he hung up, I asked, "Friend from school?"

"My brother," he said.

I perked up. "Older or younger?"

"Younger."

"So he's still at home?"

"Uh-huh." Owen turned back to the dishes.

"You seem to be on good terms."

"Yep."

"He should come over sometime."

"He does—when he has a good alibi for my parents. He's got no balls when it comes to them." He was trying to sound lighthearted, but his tone had an edge to it.

"They don't want him to see you?"

"I don't want to talk about them," Owen said quickly, and I immediately felt chastened. His shoulders had tensed, and he looked straight down into the sink.

"Sorry," I murmured. I was. It was a stupid question. I wanted to tell him it would all work out somehow, but I wasn't sure it would. So I took the casserole pan he passed to me, and dried it off in silence.

Chapter Twenty-two

The good thing about therapy was that it had taken up some of my time. Tuesday, I was again left alone with nothing to do. Rachel and Sascha were both missing in action, and Belinda was Belinda. To top it off, it was raining. After chasing the goats down to milk them, I had no interest in going back outside.

I walked around the first floor of the house, sitting down at the piano in the parlor and running my fingers over the keys, though I didn't know how to play. I wished Rachel had left me a note. Even if it were a list of chores, that would be something. She'd been friendlier yesterday, but I got the feeling it took some effort, that she still wasn't sure she wanted me around.

I poked around the bottom floor of the house, but the rooms held no secrets. On the second floor, I pushed open the door of an unused bedroom. Two brass beds were placed side by side, each made with a calico quilt. Though dusty, it looked like someone had left the room behind—and might come back at any minute. I closed the door and went to my own bedroom. I took one of the boxes from the closet, sat on the bed, and started reading.

love. Impossible, but that's what they're calling it. Bette says it's not that she's changed, it's that love is different than we thought it was. I've never been one to follow the rhetoric, but my understanding is the fight was to convince people that this is not a choice, that it's just the way we are. And here go Bette and Rachel, flying in the face of that. Acting like all that matters is that they love each other. Celie is livid. She threatened to walk away from Jezebel. She said, "I had to leave my home for this. I had to leave everything, just to feel safe." Bette and Rachel just go on smiling doe-eyed at each other. Curling their bodies into one another, as they had been from the beginning, but now it's clear what's really been going on. But if we are angry at them, aren't we as bad as the families they left behind? Why should they have to fight for their love?

That's what Jezebel was meant to be: a place where women didn't have to fight anymore. So really, they are just fulfilling the promise of the place. This is what I wanted, isn't it? A place for women to come, to have a new family, to maybe even fall in love. It's happened before. Liza and Helen were the first. They stayed at Jezebel together until Liza got sick. Helen went into the home with her, as a dear friend, still unable to call it what it was. So if I'm angry, is it because Bette has changed her mind about who she is, or because she has chosen Rachel? I remember Rachel running around, her wildness, but then I remind myself it's mostly gone now, and she's one of the best workers on the farm. Still, if Bette was sure she was straight, then how did these two

So they had fallen in love, Bette and Rachel. It must have been weird, sharing a bedroom, then having their friendship secretly change into something else, wondering what others would think. Is that how Rachel found out she was gay? Or had she always known? And after all that, what happened to Bette?

That afternoon Owen didn't show up to feed the goats, so I had to do it myself, one bucket at a time.

Owen never really mentioned anyone from school,

except his teachers, and never said anything about any extracurriculars—so where was he? The least he could have done was tell me he wasn't going to be here, so I didn't wait around for him. Beautiful people, though, didn't always think of common courtesy; Owen didn't need my approval to feel good about himself.

I was sweating as I walked back to the barn for the second bucket. It occurred to me that he might not talk about school because it actually did suck for him. His school probably wasn't like PA, where it was cool *not* to be straight.

Thinking of PA made me feel like an exile. I wondered what people were saying about me. Probably nothing at this point. It was finals week back home, so everyone would be thinking about summer. Melissa and I had this finals week ritual of going out for banana pancakes before our first exam, and for frozen yogurt after our last one. She'd probably go with Jeremy instead.

I scooped up the second bucket of feed and trudged back to the pasture. Since no one was around, I started to sing "The Lonely Goatherd" from *The Sound of Music*. It was the only song I knew about goats. But I couldn't really yodel, so I segued into Eric Carmen's power ballad "All By Myself." I totally rocked that song. After I hit one of the long, aching high notes, I heard clapping behind me, and all the blood in my body raced straight to my face.

"You can actually sing," Owen said. He stood on the other side of the gate, still in his school clothes: a tight black T-shirt and khaki pants. His messenger bag was slung across his chest.

"Where have you been?" I demanded.

"Sorry. I had a study session for physics. The exam is going to suck."

I climbed up on the fence, and we watched the goats for a minute.

"I'm serious," he said. "You're really good."

"Thanks." I could still feel my cheeks burning.

"Do you still perform?"

Still? The only performing I had ever done was in the pageants. "Not really. Unless singing in the car counts."

He didn't answer. He was staring at the goats, deep in thought.

"What?" I asked.

"I might have an idea for your project."

"I thought we were doing a music video."

He brushed that idea away with his hand. "This idea is much better. I just need to look into a few things first."

"Don't you want to run it by me?"

"No." He checked his watch. "It's almost dinnertime. Thanks for taking care of this. Next time I'll let you know if I'm not going to be here."

"Sure," I replied. "I did okay by myself, though." I wanted that fact noted: Dara Cohen had fed the goats by herself. She can actually pull her not-insubstantial weight around here.

Owen picked up the empty bucket. "Young lady, may I escort you to dinner?" he asked.

"You may," I replied. We walked back to the farmhouse arm in arm.

154

Chapter Twenty-three

"Crap, I'm late," Rachel said as she burst into the kitchen, where Owen and I were washing dishes the next evening. She wore dark jeans and a deep purple V-neck shirt that actually showed some cleavage. Instead of her usual work boots, she wore beat-up cowboy boots. Her hair was down, for once, and fell in loose curls over her shoulders. "Where are you going?" I asked.

"Brennan's," she said. "Wednesday night is Trad Night. Traditional Irish music."

"She likes Irish music," Owen said. He mimed tossing back a mug of beer.

Rachel rolled her eyes and hurried out of the kitchen. A moment later I heard her truck start outside.

"She could have asked us," I said, feeling dismissed. Not to mention stir-crazy. It seemed like weeks since I'd gone out.

"I don't think you would like it very much," he said.

"Why not? I like all kinds of music."

"She doesn't exactly go for the music, if you know what I mean."

I raised my eyebrows. In fact, I had no idea what he meant.

"It's Ladies Night."

But I *was* a lady. Then I realized he meant it was a night for ladies who were interested in ladies. "Oh," I said.

"Yeah," he replied, and turned back to the sink. "Anyway, even if she wanted us to come, and we wanted to go, we can't. It's at a bar. Massachusetts has these draconian alcohol laws."

"Sure, whatever. It would just be fun to go out at some point." I tried to cover my anxiety about Rachel. I didn't want to seem needy.

A moment later, the phone rang. Owen was elbow-deep in the soapy water, but when he looked at me, I shook my head. I was sure it was my mother. "Fine," he sighed. He took a dish towel and dried off his hands before he grabbed the phone. "Hello?" He raised his eyebrows at me. "Owen," he said. "I live here." He nodded while he listened. "No, Dara's not available right now." He paused. "Um, she's in the shower. Do you want to leave a message?" He picked up a pen and leaned over a notepad on the counter. "Okay," he said without writing anything down. "Bye."

He hung up the phone. "It was your mother," he confirmed.

"Why did you lie to her?"

"I couldn't tell her that you didn't want to talk to her. Trust me, you'll thank me later. You don't need to add to the shit between you."

"Did she leave a message?" I asked.

Owen looked at the soapy sink full of dishes. "She wanted me to remind you to work on your college essays." He paused. "She said you were going to have to find a way to explain what happened."

I laughed. Cackled is more like. Owen gave me a weird look.

"She's such a witch!" I exclaimed. "I wonder why she even bothered to call."

"To find out how you were doing."

I started drying a casserole dish. "But did she *ask* how I was doing?"

"Not exactly. No. Did you want her to?"

"What kind of question is that?" I snapped. "Yeah. I kind of wanted her to ask about me. If your mom called, wouldn't you want her to wonder about how you were doing?"

"*If* she actually called, yes."

We finished working in silence, and then I went upstairs. I sat on the edge of my bed and looked at the small bookshelf. Most of the books were children's books, and I wondered why they were at Jezebel. I scanned the labels on the spines until I found one that I knew would comfort me: *Little House on the Prairie*. Now *there* was a family. They all worked side by side, fighting the harsh environment together. The sisters did their schoolwork at the kitchen table, while Ma cooked supper. Ma was tough but not hard-hearted. Laura was always able to pour her heart out to her, tell her all her problems. Pa, too. He listened and gave back sage advice.

I settled into bed and opened the book, and slipped into that other world, all the while trying to ignore the fact that it had been Mom who had read me this book in the first place.

Chapter Twenty-four

My friends and I had always studied for exams together in each other's living rooms. That weekend, after days of completely ignoring my books, I studied with Owen. We lay across the bed in his room—the Wheat Field room—and flipped through our textbooks and notes. Owen slapped his history textbook shut and pulled a tattered copy of *The Great Gatsby* out of his satchel. "Snooze time," he said.

"What, *The Great Gatsby*? I'd think you'd love that book."

"Just because it has some supposed homoerotic scene in it—which I never could find, by the way—doesn't mean I'm automatically going to love it."

I rolled my eyes, embarrassed and annoyed that he

thought that's what I meant. "It's so atmospheric and sexy," I sighed. "Plus it has the best last line ever."

He flipped to the end of the book. "Okay," he said. "That's pretty good. But it's a depressing ending."

I looked back down at my Pre-Calc; it was definitely the class I struggled with the most. Up until Pre-Calc, math had made sense. But this year, I'd needed my math-geek friends to help me get through. "What do you know about parabolic functions?" I asked Owen.

"Only everything," he replied.

Owen was a natural teacher, which surprised me, but probably shouldn't have. Teaching is a kind of performing, and he reveled in that. He traced graph after graph for me until finally I understood the complex process. On Monday when my exams arrived in a big manila envelope with the Portland Academy logo in the upper left-hand corner, I took the math one first so that it was still fresh in my mind. The instructions stressed that these exams were to be proctored with someone watching and timing me, and at no time was I to be left alone with the exams.

Belinda took the job of proctor. We cleared off the dining room table, and I laid out a set of pens and pencils. I also placed the green pebble from Dr. Eddington's office on the table, like one of Melissa's good luck charms. Belinda sat in her usual seat at the head of the table and watched me. Just watched me. In school, the teachers sat at their desks and graded papers or flipped through textbooks. Belinda's attention was unwavering.

As I worked on the problems, I heard Owen's voice in my

mind: "Don't think of it as a logarithm. Think of it as an exponent problem. You can do exponents."

Belinda rapped three times on the table when my time was up. She stood, reached over to grab the test from me, and put it in the return envelope.

The next day I did U.S. History. Then French. Physics on Thursday. I saved English for last. When Belinda placed the exam in front of me, I noticed Mr. Fitz had attached a note to the front.

Dear Dara:

I hope this note finds you well. We have missed you at PA. It was not my intention to have you removed from school. I was merely concerned about your emotional well-being. At any rate, I trust your break from school will provide adequate respite from the stresses of high school—believe me, I understand how tough it can be. Good luck on your exam.

—Mr. Fitz

P.S. I hope your new autobiography project is coming along well.

I thought about writing "Bite me" on the exam and turning it in without even doing the test. Belinda had her eye on me, though, so I started working. The first section was definitions. And then we had some grammar, which he'd said was to get us ready for the writing section of the SAT, but I think he was just a grammar geek and used the SAT excuse to make it palatable to us. I breezed through these first two sections, and then I got to the first short-answer question: What is the significance of the poetry Angelou tries to recite in the beginning scene of *I Know Why the Caged Bird Sings*?

I knew the answer. We had talked about it for three class periods. The poem sets up the issues that Angelou struggles with for the rest of the book: her appearance and the way she feels like she's always out of place. It hadn't occurred to me until that moment, though, that the same struggles were captured in my autobiography project. I wrote:

American society is filled with prejudice. Racism, sexism, ageism, homophobia. These prejudices victimize us all, but the lasting effect is most severe on the targets of the prejudice. Maya Angelou's family called her ugly. Society saw her as just another black girl, another way to be unattractive at the time. She never feels like she belongs. The poem she struggles to recite highlights these issues and sets them up as the touchstones for the book. It's important to note that within the confines of a set task (reciting the poem), she wasn't quite able to make her point come across. The assignment gave her limited means by which to express herself. Moreover, though it seems that reciting a poem—like, say, creating a work of art—should leave room for artistic expression, Angelou's teacher clearly had one interpretation in mind. One could argue that it was the narrow expectations of the teacher, and not Angelou's reading, that caused the problem.

My attack was veiled, but I knew Mr. Fitz would get it: he was the teacher with the narrow preconceptions—*she's fat so she must be unhappy*—and I was the artist getting my vision squashed.

When my time was up, Belinda took my exam, but instead of sliding it into the envelope, she sat down with it. She hadn't read my other exams, but she read each page of this one. Here and there she'd nod or shake her head, and when she finished, she took my pen and scrawled something across the bottom of the page.

"Belinda! What are you doing? That's my exam."

She snapped her head up and looked at me with her dark eyes. A smile spread across her lips, and then she winked at me. I was too shocked to say anything. She slipped the exam into the envelope. On the way out of the room, she put her hand on my shoulder.

I told Owen about it while we walked out to the field, carrying our buckets of feed. "What do you think she wrote on it?" I asked.

"'Dara really is crazy. Please save me.'"

"Very funny."

"She probably wanted to see what kinds of questions he asked. She loves literature. She was an English lit major at Smith."

"Really?" I asked.

"Yeah. I interviewed her for my Oral History project last year."

"Wait, she talked to you?"

Owen emptied his bucket into the trough. The goats butted past me and shoved their heads in.

"Well, she wrote her answers. I told the school they had to let me do it that way, because it would be a violation of the Americans with Disabilities Act if they didn't."

A goat pushed his snout into my bucket and pulled it from my hand. Owen lunged and stabilized the pail before picking it up and pouring in the rest of the feed. "Sharpen up there, Cohen. I don't want to be doing this all day."

"What else did you talk about?"

"With Belinda? Well, mostly the farm and its history."

We went to the fence and climbed up to watch the goats. "What is the history?" I knew some from the pages, but not all of it.

"You've seen the pictures on the stairs, right? Jezebel was an escape for gay women starting around 1940. The farm was here before that. In Belinda's family. But then her parents died, and she was all that was left. So she opened her doors to lesbians who'd been kicked out by their families."

"Did she say why she stopped talking?"

He shook his head. "I don't know why, but I got the sense that it was the one thing I couldn't ask."

In Owen's mind, it was probably something dramatic. But maybe she just got tired of talking. Or maybe she had some kind of aphasia, making speech harder and harder, and she was embarrassed at the struggle it caused her. We'd learned about aphasia in science class, and I couldn't imagine anything more terrifying.

When we got back inside, I looked at the pictures on the wall. The woman was strong, fiery. Everything about her face was expressive—her eyes, her mouth. Even without words, Belinda still managed to get her point across.

Chapter Twenty-five

Owen graduated the Saturday after we finished our exams. I was excited to go to this graduation, not only for Owen, but also because it felt like I hadn't seen another kid my age in eons, though I'd only been at the farm about two weeks.

I spent a little more time in the bathroom than I'd intended, trying to do the au naturel, flushed, berry-stained makeup thing. And I couldn't decide whether to pull my hair back or leave it down. I was going to wear a white eyelet skirt with a navy blue cable knit—the classic nautical look—which went better with an updo, but I looked thinner with my hair loose around my shoulders. I wanted Owen's friends to see me and think, *Who is that girl?*

Despite my protracted obsessing, I was ready before

everyone else. While I waited for them on the front porch, I read a letter I'd received from Melissa.

Salut!

My parents and I are in Paris on the way to Belgium. It's not really "on the way," but you know my mom. I think we walked up and down the Champs Elysées about seventy-two times today. On the plus side, she bought me a Fendi bag. Not that I care about Fendi, but it's a really nice bag. She said that now that I'm intercontinental, I need a more sophisticated look. Whatever. My journal and my camera fit in it. How are you holding up? Any apology from the school? I let Mr. Fitz know exactly how I felt about the whole thing. He said he was sorry, but I said he was not forgiven.

You know, this is so romantic! In the literary sense, not the lovey-dovey sense, although of course I do lovey-dovey you. We're separated by oceans and can only communicate by letters. It's like something Jane Austen wrote about. Or Emily Brontë. Are you out wandering on the heath and thinking of me?

I did think of her while I was out feeding the goats. That probably wasn't what she had in mind, though.

I can be like a governess sent off to Europe. And we are soul sisters, kindred spirits, *missing each other. It's much better than e-mail. By the way, Dennis Epstein asked about you. I ran into him downtown before I left, and he said he thought your presentation was righteous and that it totally sucked that they sent you away.*

Dennis Epstein. I could picture him standing out in the sun, still wearing his leather jacket. He seemed even more ridiculous now that I had some distance. But still, the fact that he was thinking of me made me a little fluttery.

"Ready?" Rachel asked. She was wearing a sundress in a deep red that made her brown eyes seem even darker.

"Yep." I tucked the letter into my purse.

"You look really pretty," she said. The compliment made my heart swell a little.

"Thanks. So do you."

The ceremony was held outside in the late afternoon sun. It was like all the other graduations I had ever been to: premature nostalgia in student speeches laced with promises of always sticking together, which the speakers must know are lies. I was surprised by how anonymous Owen was. It seemed like he should be one of the speakers; he'd definitely be a star at PA.

Owen found us as soon as the ceremony was over. He was grinning and his mortarboard sat askew on his head. "Well, that's over with," he said. His gown was unzipped, and underneath he wore a pale purple button-down shirt with a darker purple tie and gray dress pants. I wondered if the good people of Hollis had ever seen a man in lilac before. The color was great on him. I gave him a hug. "Congratulations, sexy," I said.

Before he could reply, Belinda squeezed his arm, and Sascha boomed, "Good work, Owen." Rachel hugged him tightly, her eyes welling up. I stepped to the side to give them some space.

Owen let go of Rachel and scanned the field. "Anyone seen Milo?" he asked. "I just saw him a few minutes ago." He rubbed his head vigorously, making his hair stand up in wild spikes. I glanced past him at the sea of families; the groups split and re-formed like amoebas while the five of us from Jezebel Goat Farm stood just outside, looking in. Belinda coughed. Sascha shifted his weight from foot to foot. Rachel crossed her arms over her chest, looking solemn as she surveyed the crowd. I knew she and Owen weren't looking for Milo.

A group of girls approached, tipsy in their heels on the grass. "Owen!" they cooed. One wrapped her arms around his neck. The other handed me a camera. "Will you take our picture?" They didn't even introduce themselves or ask my name. Still, I snapped a photo as the girls grinned and Owen struck a silly-serious glam pose. He gave them each a kiss on the cheek, and then they were gone, back into the crowd to join their families. I couldn't believe Owen's parents hadn't even come to his high school graduation. It seemed like maybe they would lay aside the gay-hating thing for a couple hours so they could see their son graduate.

"I've made reservations for dinner. My treat," Rachel announced.

"Where are we going?" I asked.

Sascha chuckled. "The choices are endless in Hollis."

On our way back to the parking lot, Rachel looped her arm through Owen's, and I took the rear, my kitten heels sinking into the soft ground. So much for turning heads.

When we got to the truck, there was a round-faced boy waiting, his shoulders slumped forward and his hands sunk deep in his pockets. He was cute, though not striking like Owen; his face was broad, with big, wide-set eyes. He had a shaggy hairstyle that seemed more by neglect than design, and he wore rumpled khaki pants with a blue chambray button-down that was too short in the arms. Clearly Owen was the fashionista of the family. Owen detached himself from Rachel and jogged toward his brother, grinning. He collared him and ruffled his hair, ignoring his brother's grimace. "I'm glad you came." Then he introduced us, "Dara, Milo. Milo, Dara."

"Hey," Milo said.

"Hey," I returned.

"I'm glad you could make it, stranger," Rachel said.

He blushed, looking more embarrassed than flattered. "Thanks. I um . . . I've got a new bike now, so maybe over the summer I can come over more."

"New bike, huh?" Owen smiled, but I could feel tension between them.

"Pile in," Rachel told us.

"Someone's going to need to sit in the bed," Sascha pointed out.

I looked down at my white skirt. Owen was also far too dressed up.

"I'll do it," Milo offered.

"That's okay," Rachel replied. "I can sit back there."

"I don't mind," Milo insisted.

Somehow, it was settled that they would both sit in the bed of the truck. I stole glances at them as we drove the short way into town. They weren't talking, but I guessed it was too noisy anyway. Milo held on to the edge of the truck, while Rachel sat on the wheel well, totally natural, her hands holding her hair out of her face. She looked beautiful.

Owen stared out his window the whole time, drumming his fingers against the armrest in an uneven rhythm. I reached for his other hand and squeezed it. He squeezed back but kept looking out at the tree-lined street.

A few minutes later, we pulled into the parking lot of the Hollis Village Inn, a large Victorian house painted pale yellow with blue trim. While I waited for Sascha to help Belinda from the cab, I watched Milo jump off the bed of the truck. He reached up a hand to help Rachel, but she didn't notice and hopped down easily. Milo quickly tucked his hand back into his pocket.

The hostess smiled when she saw Rachel. She came out from behind her little podium on the porch and embraced her, giving her a kiss on each cheek. I glanced at Owen to get a sense of whether this meant something, but he was lost in his own thoughts. The hostess, a petite woman with spiky black hair, put her hand on Rachel's back and led her to our table. Sascha and Belinda followed, arm in arm. Then someone took mine, and I turned, expecting to see Owen, but instead there was Milo. "Oh," I said.

"It seemed the thing to do," he replied. His sneaker was untied, and I really, really wanted to tell him to tie it, but I felt like it was the wrong moment. I let him walk me to the table, where he pulled out a chair for me. As I sat down, he pushed it in, but our timing was off, and he ended up smacking the chair into my knees, so I fell down with a soft *oof*. Blushing furiously, I stared at my place setting—the napkins had been folded into flowers—while the others filed into their seats.

Owen sat down to my right, and much to my relief, Milo sat down next to him. He seemed sweet, but I didn't want him passing things to me, or I'd probably end up with water spilled in my lap or the dessert on my beautiful white skirt.

The dining room was filled with families in their Sunday best; most men wore suits, or at least sports coats, and the women all wore skirts and dresses. Some of the people looked polished and fashionable, almost like my own classmates' families, while others looked uncomfortable in dress clothes.

Owen abruptly leaned toward me. "After this summer, I may never see these people again," he said. Just then, a cute girl seated a few tables over with her grandparents gave Owen a finger wave. "She's decent," he conceded.

Everyone at Hollis High seemed to like Owen, but Owen showed indifference or disdain for them all. They acted kind of phony, but they all honestly *liked* him; it annoyed me that he could take his popularity for granted like this.

While a busboy filled our water glasses, a tall man wearing tiny spectacles came to take our order. I hurriedly scanned the menu, unable to decide; I ended up ordering the same thing Rachel did: the tuna special—"rare, like sushi."

We could hear piano music from the next room, and I really wanted to see who was playing. They were really good. Snobby as it sounds, I was surprised that someone so talented lived in Hollis. He or she finished a Beethoven sonata, then launched into *The Rite of Spring*, a piece so unusual in its use of rhythm, it had caused a riot when it was first performed. My dad liked to play it while working out on the treadmill. "Who is this composer?" Rachel asked.

"It's Chopin, isn't it?" Sascha answered.

"Shame on you." I was about to chide Sascha for not recognizing a Russian composer—his mother would be so disappointed. Before I could, Milo said, "It's Stravinsky."

"*The Rite of Spring*," I added.

Milo was mostly hidden behind Owen, but I could see him smile.

"Well, isn't this a sophisticated table," Rachel said. She grinned at me, impressed.

I was dying to see the pianist, so I excused myself to go to the restroom. When I saw her, I stopped short. She was a gorgeous young woman with long blond hair that cascaded over her shoulders as she played. She reminded me of Uma Thurman—her face long but delicate, and her skin pale and rosy. A few minutes later, a waitress came up behind me and asked, "Can I help you?"

"Oh, sorry," I said. I'd probably been gaping. "I'm just looking for the bathroom." She pointed out the way to me.

Our food had arrived by the time I got back. Owen had ordered a steak—something he never got at Jezebel. Milo had just gotten a bowl of soup and a side salad.

My tuna was good, but after getting used to Rachel's cooking, I doubted I would ever again be thrilled with a restaurant meal.

Rachel tapped her water glass with a spoon, then held up her glass of white wine. "Owen, do you have anything profound to share with us?" She beamed at him with love and pride, and I felt an annoying pang of jealousy. I tried to push it away and just be happy for him.

Owen straightened and picked up his ice water. "Actually, I'd like to make a toast to Jezebel Goat Farm. If it weren't for you all, and that includes you, Milo, I wouldn't have made it."

I thought he was being a tad melodramatic, but then, I guess I didn't really know how bad it had been.

"To Jezebel," Rachel said, and we all clinked our glasses.

Milo tapped his fingers along with the pianist's next selection. This one was some kind of jazz piece that I couldn't place. "Who's this?" I asked him.

"Cole Porter," he replied.

I recognized it as soon as he said it: Cole Porter was a favorite of Dad's for his funny, romantic lyrics. The pianist was playing "Just One of Those Things," but slower and bluesier. "I've never heard it played this way," I remarked.

Milo nodded. "It's good, though. It actually sounds like a breakup song now."

He didn't look at me as he said it, and I could only glimpse his profile around Owen. He had long eyelashes—longer than Owen's—and from this angle his cheekbones were more pronounced.

"You think it's a breakup song?" I asked, trying to remember the lyrics. "I always thought it was about a fling. It could have been something more, but it wasn't."

"I thought it was a kiss-off, a really cruel way to dump someone—like it never even mattered."

"I knew you two would get along," Rachel chimed in. Which, of course, is the fastest way to kill something. Milo and I both shut up.

When we had all finished our dinner, our plates were cleared away. A moment later, our waiter placed a large cake in the center of the table. *Congratulations Owen* had been carefully spelled out in pale green frosting across the top. Rachel clapped her hands together. "I might have dropped this off earlier today," she confessed.

"A Rachel cake?" Owen asked. "This is fantastic. Thank you."

"It's nothing," she said.

She cut me a large piece of moist, yellow cake—probably more than I could eat. At home, I would have gotten a look letting me know that I should stop after three bites. It didn't even occur to Rachel to give me less than everyone else. Cake was happiness and she wanted me to be happy. "Thank you, Rachel," I said, hoping she'd see how much I meant it.

"No problem," she replied. "It's what I do."

* * *

That night, Owen went out to "make the rounds." I guess I shouldn't have expected him to ask me along for his classmates' graduation parties, but still, sitting in the parlor listening to the click of Belinda's knitting needles, I couldn't help feeling a little bit like I had during middle school dances. I was all right when the music was fast, and we danced in a circle of girls. But when the slow songs came on, and my friends all started scanning the room for their crushes, I suddenly felt panicked. I'd always pretend I desperately needed to reapply my lip gloss or mascara. I probably spent about forty percent of those evenings in the bathroom. Why had I even bothered to go?

Rachel had also gone out. She left right after dinner, but didn't say where, and I didn't ask. She was still in her red dress, so she just threw on a black cardigan and went out the door. After an hour or so of reading downstairs, I went up to my room. It was Saturday night and I was in bed by 8:30. Pathetic. I was exhausted, though—the 5:30 a.m. thing was catching up with me—and I fell asleep almost immediately.

I was awakened a few hours later by a crash and giggling downstairs—Rachel's and some other woman's. I sat up and listened like a total snoop. I even thought of creeping down the stairs to take a peek. Had Rachel brought someone home to spend the night? I heard them coming up the stairs whispering, and at that point I wasn't sure I wanted to hear what they were saying to each other. I lay back and tried to sleep, which proved difficult because Rachel's room was directly above mine.

Chapter Twenty-six

In the morning, Rachel's visitor was gone, and Rachel made no mention of her previous night's activities. None of us was talking much; it was the first day of summer, and as if on cue, the temperature had spiked. Even feeding the goats at 5:30 a.m. had been torturous. Owen and I were drenched with sweat by the time we were done. The one plus side was that it was even too hot for oatmeal; a family-sized box of cornflakes had mysteriously appeared in the middle of the dining room table.

After breakfast, I went out to join Rachel in the barn. I got to work readying the cheese sacks while she checked the curdled milk. She had a special order for a wedding—a bride in New York City wanted fresh goat cheese for the cocktail hour of her reception, complete with a quaint story about a farm in western Massachusetts. Sascha was ready to drive it down to the city early the next week, so it would arrive at the caterer mere hours before it was served. We had to get all the wedding cheese done on top of our regular orders, so we worked quickly.

I wanted to ask about her evening visitor, but couldn't think of a way to bring it up without sounding like a nosy parent. ("So, I heard you come in last night . . .") Rachel was humming, totally off-key, and maybe making up songs, because I couldn't recognize any of it. Finally I asked, "Did you have fun last night?"

She considered the question and then smiled and said, "Yeah."

I'd been hoping for a little more detail. I bet that Owen wouldn't be afraid to ask—and that she would tell him.

"So . . . was that your girlfriend?"

Rachel laughed. "Oh my God. Were we loud? I'm so sorry."

"No, you weren't that loud." I was already pink from the heat, but she could still tell I was blushing like crazy.

She giggled and gave me a teasing nudge. "Dara!" she said. "Sorry you had to hear that with your poor, virgin ears. Don't worry, it was just an isolated incident."

"Really? It seemed like you really . . . got along." This made Rachel laugh even harder. Now my face was probably maroon. "Not like it's any of my business."

"Hey, we all live in the same house, right? I'll try to keep it down next time."

I stirred the cheese curds with a metal paddle, staring at

them instead of her. I felt like an ass. I just wanted to chat, you know, about crushes and other sister stuff.

After several minutes of awkward silence, Owen rescued me. He stuck his head into the barn. "Swimming," he said, "is necessary."

I looked at Rachel. "Go ahead," she said. "We're about done here. I can finish up."

I pulled off my plastic gloves and burst outside. "Be right back," I called to Owen as I ran into the house. Upstairs, I shimmied into my one-piece black suit and put on a T-shirt and a pair of cotton shorts over it. I threw a denim skirt, some underwear, and a T-shirt into a bag and ran back downstairs. Owen was already in the front passenger seat, and Milo was in the backseat. When I saw him there, I hesitated. I didn't want him to see me in my swimming attire. The sun beat down, and Owen said, "Come on," so I got in the car.

When we got to the river, I dove straight into the water while they were still busy taking off their shoes and shirts. The water was cool and pulled the heat from my skin. My hair tickled my neck, and my T-shirt and shorts clung to my body in a way that I had grown used to—I always swam in my clothes. I rose to the surface.

"Clothes off, then swim, Dara," Owen called. He stood at the riverbank, feet hips-width apart, looking a bit like a Greek statue. "What the hell goes on up in Maine? They don't teach you the basics."

"I like to swim in my clothes," I told him, wishing he would shut up.

"You like to? Nobody likes to swim in their clothes." Milo

dove in, but Owen stayed on the shore, teasing me. "That's why they make bathing suits, so you don't have to swim in your clothes."

"I have a bathing suit on," I called back.

"A bathing suit *and* clothes? Dara, you make no sense."

"Let it be," Milo said.

Somehow this made it worse. He realized why I was wearing my clothes, and why Owen's teasing was actually mean.

Owen shook his head at Milo. "Whatever," he said before diving in to join us. Then we were three little heads bobbing in the river, our bodies obscured by the cool, dark water. My toes rubbed pleasantly against the smooth stones on the bottom of the riverbed.

"Where does this river go?" I asked.

"Into the Connecticut, I guess," Owen said.

He swam toward me. With the water on his skin and eyelashes he looked impossibly beautiful. It triggered a strange pain inside me, something I couldn't quite articulate. Envy and something else. I shook my head.

"What?" he asked.

"Nothing."

Milo swam up to us, and we moved farther toward the center of the river. The boys could reach the bottom, but I had to tread water and swim against the current to stay with them. My body felt light, though, and strong. I slipped under and felt my hair swirl all around me. When I came up, I had strayed several yards away from them. I didn't mind drifting, not because I wanted to be alone, but because it felt so good to be cool and weightless for a while.

Chapter Twenty-seven

That night after dinner, I went out to the back porch to write a letter to Melissa. My mind wandered, though. I'd been at Jezebel almost three weeks. My parents hadn't called in over a week—a bad sign—but at the same time, I was feeling less and less upset about it. Things with Rachel were about the same: not exactly BFFs, but friendly, and she hadn't said anything about my returning to Portland.

Owen poked his head out the back door. "What are you doing?"

"Writing a letter."

"I need to show you something," he said. "Let's go. You can drive."

I was about to ask where, but decided it didn't matter. I

left the letter paper on the glider, and followed him to the car.

After a fifteen minute drive to the outskirts of town, he pointed to the side of the road. "Here," he said. I pulled off to the shoulder. We were on the edge of a large, empty expanse of land, dotted with sheds. But what stood out was an old Ferris wheel that rose up in the center of the lot, taller than anything else for miles.

"What are we doing here?" I asked.

He was already walking toward the field. "You'll see."

I followed him to a tall fence, and we walked beside it in silence. Owen trailed his fingers along the chain link as he went. He walked quickly and occasionally broke into something like a skipping run, turning back to grin over his shoulder at me. Finally we turned a corner and came to a large sign painted on a piece of plywood—HOLLIS TOWN FAIR. AUGUST 4–14.

"What?"

Owen's eyes glowed in the fading sun. He was tapping his foot on the sandy ground, watching me impatiently. "Read it," he said at last.

I stepped closer, reading out loud. "'Fireworks, demolition derby, truck pulls, horse pulls, agricultural displays, family fun and games including keg toss, performance by the Yankee Ramblers, baked goods, antique fire engine.'" I couldn't imagine what any of these had to do with me. Then I read the last line. MISS HOLLIS, AUGUST 14.

"I don't think so," I told him.

"What?" He actually looked surprised.

"No way."

He stopped tapping. "Well, you're already entered." Then he started up again.

I sighed to show Owen how uninterested I was. Then I sighed again to make sure he got the message. "I'm not strutting around in a bathing suit at the county fair, thank you very much."

He pointed at me like he had caught me in a lie. "There's no bathing suit competition. There's a talent portion, an evening dress competition, and that section where they ask you silly questions and you answer, 'World Peace.'"

"No."

"I'm your escort for the evening-dress part. I get to wear a tux. We're going to look fabulous."

"No."

"It's for your project. We're going to film the pageant, and then we'll make up a little thing with footage from your first pageant. You'll do a voiceover: 'I'm still beautiful, no matter what people think.'" I wanted to laugh, but Owen kept going. "Actually, I thought you could sing that Christina Aguilera song for your talent. You're a wicked awesome singer—you're going to blow everyone away."

"I'm not taking on Christina Aguilera," I said. The girl weighed maybe ninety pounds, but her vocal range was enormous.

Owen laced his fingers through the fence and smiled at me. "So you'll do it?"

"I didn't say that." He had such a smug little smile, like I didn't even have a choice, like he had already made up my mind for me. But he didn't realize how demeaning this could be. Most of the girls I'd seen here had fake tans and tacky chunky highlights in their hair and acted like they had never set foot outside of Hollis and didn't care to. I should be able to beat them. No, I should be able to crush them, based on singing ability alone. But what if I didn't? What if my weight meant I couldn't even win some dinky little town pageant? I didn't think I could handle that.

"You're already signed up," Owen said again. "Come on, let's go on the Ferris wheel." He pivoted and walked back along the fence.

I chased after him. "The fair's not open yet."

I followed Owen toward an old man in overalls who was bent over the control box of the Ferris wheel. "Hey, Mr. Otis," Owen called.

The man looked up, and I recognized him from the farmers' market. "Owen!" he said. "How's the news?"

"Good. Getting ready for the Fourth?"

"Yep," Mr. Otis said. He looked past Owen at me. "Rachel's sister, right?" I nodded. "Is this your girl?"

"Yep," Owen said. "She's my girl."

I blushed.

"I've got to run a test. Want to be my dummies?"

In fact I did not want to be the test rider on the world's oldest Ferris wheel, but Owen was faster. "I was hoping you'd offer," he said.

I shot him a look.

"Coward," he replied, and the way he said it, I could tell he wasn't just talking about the ride.

I opened my mouth to protest, but then he reached back

and grabbed my hand. I thought, *Screw it, what's the worst that could happen?* and followed Owen into one of the small cars.

As the ride started to move, I tried not to think about how many laws and insurance regulations we were violating. When we got to the summit, it stopped. Was it broken? I peeked down at Mr. Otis, who was examining his wrench, unconcerned.

"Look out there," Owen said, pointing to a distant cluster of lights. "That's Jezebel."

"Really?" I asked. I didn't quite believe he knew which lights were ours.

"Uh-huh. Make a wish."

"Why?" I asked.

"Because the top of a Ferris wheel is as good as any other place to make a wish."

The wish I made surprised me. It came out of nowhere, just popped into my head and was made.

I wish to win this pageant.

Chapter Twenty-eight

Owen needed all of thirty seconds to get everyone at Jezebel involved in the pageant, even Belinda. "Dara's entering Miss Hollis," he announced at dinner the next night.

I took a bowl of green beans with mushroom Madeira sauce from his extended hand. "Owen entered me in the Miss Hollis pageant," I corrected him, making sure they could see how nonplussed I felt about the whole thing. I passed the green beans to Belinda. Her eyebrow was cocked, and she looked skeptical.

"Her talent is singing, so we need to pick a song," Owen continued.

"Yeah?" Rachel asked. "I didn't know you were a singer!

If I could sing, I'd do Patsy Cline. Definitely 'Walkin' After Midnight.'"

Owen frowned. "We're going to use this for her autobiography project. It needs to be more upbeat. We're going to show that she was beautiful when she was young, and she is beautiful now." I started to interrupt him to say that I wasn't so sure about this thesis. He continued before I could say anything. "She won't sing Christina Aguilera, even though it's perfect." He sang the refrain in a low gravelly voice, like Lou Reed. It was horrifying—even Rachel grimaced. "My second choice is 'I Will Survive,'" he went on, unfazed.

"Cliché," I said.

"Classic," he responded. "Plus you could have a fabulous costume with a feathered headpiece."

"That's the gayest thing you've ever said."

Belinda rapped the table and shot me a disapproving look. I felt stung. Though silent, Belinda's disapproval cut through me.

"Respect," Sascha said.

"She does respect me," Owen said. "It's just a word."

"I meant the song," Sascha said.

We all paused for a moment. It was a fantastic song, and I did love to sing it. Still, Aretha Franklin—taking on one of her songs was worse than taking on Christina Aguilera. "I don't know," I said. "It's hard to do a song so associated with one person."

For the first time, I missed Dad: he'd be full of good suggestions.

"We're overlooking show tunes," Owen said.

I was about to say, "Actually, *that* may be the gayest thing you've ever said," but one look at Belinda stopped me. I wrinkled my nose.

"Well, you're not coming up with any ideas," Owen said. "You need to have the whole vision. The dancing, the lights. That's why 'I Will Survive' would be so great. Imagine a dark stage. A single spotlight on you. You lift your head with its glorious headpiece. You're totally still as you sing the first few lines. And then the fast part starts, and you grab the microphone off the stand and strut out to the front of the stage. The lights come up, the disco ball drops down. It's perfect."

Across the table, Rachel was desperately trying not to laugh. I had to lean forward and shield my eyes with my hand so I couldn't see her, or we'd both crack up. "It will come to us," I said. "Right now I'm a little more concerned about costuming. I mean, if I'm going to do this, I don't want to look like a dork." I had to look good. If I had any chance of winning this and not going down in a blaze of embarrassment, I had to make the most of what I had. I couldn't wear one of those awful dresses with petticoats and puffed sleeves that would made me look like a pastel marshmallow. "Where am I going to find an evening gown around here?"

"All right, Miss Big City, we do have stores," Owen said.

Belinda tapped her fingers on the table softly and looked upward.

Rachel bit on her thumb, thinking. "Belinda's right. We have trunks of old dresses upstairs. Something there might work. I can help you put something together."

Musty old farm dresses were not going to win a pageant for me. I couldn't say that to Rachel or Belinda, though.

"What else?" Sascha asked. "What else do you need?" I was surprised that he would take an interest. He cleared his throat. "I have that run to New York City coming up soon."

"I'll make a list," Owen said. "Or I could go with you." He looked to Rachel hopefully.

"Sure, that makes sense," she said. "Dara?"

Normally, I would have loved to go to New York. Mom used to bring me down once a year. We stayed with her college roommate on the Upper East Side, had lunch in the Oak Room with Uncle Barrett, and then went, just the two of us, to the Metropolitan Museum of Art. When I was very young, I held her hand as she led me from room to room, stopping the longest to look at Degas's dancers. Now, though, I didn't want Rachel to think I would bolt at my first opportunity. Maybe we could do something together, just us. "I'll stay here."

"Suit yourself," Owen said. "But that means surrendering yourself to my whims."

I was pretty sure I'd already done that just by agreeing to do the pageant.

In fact, by conceding, I had more or less signed myself up for abject humiliation: I had six weeks to learn a song, get costumes, and rehearse. All this in an attempt to convince people who didn't even know me that, fat as I was, I was better suited to the title of Miss Hollis than the girls who had lived here all of their lives.

Chapter Twenty-nine

After dinner, Rachel and I went up into the attic. The air was hot and dry, and dust motes hung in the light of two naked bulbs. Together we pulled three antique trunks from under the eaves to an empty spot on the floor. I saw stacks of shoe boxes and wondered if they, too, were filled with stories about the farm.

Dresses had been neatly folded, wrapped in now-yellowing tissue paper, and stacked in the trunks. "Probably not the best way to store them," Rachel said, holding up a stained petticoated skirt—exactly the type of thing I feared we would find up here.

Next out was a 1950s-style Donna Reed homemaker dress, red with white polka dots and a wide white sash, followed by a Chanel-esque wool sheath in faded black. These dresses were beautiful and could sell for a ton of money at used clothing stores. Maybe there would be something in here after all. Rachel lifted up a red slinky dress with large crystals around the choker neck. "How's this?"

"Maybe for my right thigh," I replied.

"You know, I read a biography piece on Marilyn Monroe. Everyone talks about how she was so big compared to today's actresses, but really they've just changed the sizing. She wasn't emaciated, but she was smaller than the average woman."

"That's not making me feel much better."

Rachel flipped open a second trunk and dug out a long flowing skirt with a brightly colored pattern. It looked like something the hippie girls would wear in Monument Square. She laughed. "This was Celie's, and I cannot tell you how much I wanted it. I thought it made her look so free and gorgeous, but it's kind of frumpy, isn't it?"

"Definitely."

I removed a long black trench coat. Rachel turned crimson and put her hand over her mouth. "God, how embarrassing. Why did I even keep that?"

"It's cool," I offered unconvincingly.

Rachel laughed, still embarrassed. "It's appalling."

She turned back to the trunk and unwrapped a midnight blue silk gown, floor-length, with a deep V-neck and an elaborate crisscrossing pattern of straps along the back.

It was perfect.

"Wow," I said.

"Try it on."

The beauty of the dress made me panic a little bit. I'd let myself want it—the pageant, the dress. If it didn't fit, I was going to feel so stupid. "I don't know."

"Come on, just try it."

I stood up and wiped the dust off my knees. My heart sped up as I pulled off my T-shirt and stepped out of my jeans. I felt Rachel's eyes on my round stomach. She saw the way it pushed over the edge of my panties. She saw the folds of fat on my back, squeezed and pinched by my bra. I avoided her eyes as I took the dress from her and slipped it over my head. The straps caught on my fingers and arms, but I shimmied and managed to pull it down. I let out a sigh of relief. It fit! Rachel stood to arrange the complicated tangle of straps, her fingers cold on my back.

"Just think," I ventured. "In some alternate universe this could be you getting me ready for the prom."

She stood behind me, not saying anything. Finally she laughed. "Oh, you wouldn't have wanted me to do that. I was a fashion disaster. My freshman year my boyfriend was a senior. He didn't want to go to prom, but I begged and begged him to take me. You know, I tried to be all badass, but really I wanted the girly stuff—the prom, the boyfriend who wrote me sweet notes. Mom took me shopping for a dress, and we must have gone to a dozen stores. You know I was kind of surprised, because she was really into it, like she wanted to make sure that I got a dress I loved. And I did—embarrassingly enough."

"What was it like?"

"Pink." She laughed. "Pink, pink, and more pink. It had an empire waist, sweetheart neck, lace sleeves, and the skirt—I don't even know if there's a name for it. It kind of came out here." She made cupping motions around her hips. "Kind of like a smaller version of something Marie Antoinette would wear." She shook her head. "My boyfriend came to pick me up in the rattiest suit you've ever seen, smelling like an ashtray. I thought Mom was going to keel over. She had the camera all out and ready to go, but then she didn't even take pictures."

I thought of my prom back in May. None of us had dates, except Melissa and Jeremy, and we went in a big group. I wore a black A-line dress. We found Dad in the den and conscripted him to take our picture. Mom caught us on the way out the door and pulled me aside. "Didn't you get the Spanx I put on your bed?" I was wearing them, but I said, "No, I didn't see them, sorry." My skin burned and I couldn't look at my friends.

"It was stupid how mad I got—I mean, it basically ruined the prom," Rachel said. "He brought a flask, and as soon as we got outside, I polished it off. Mom probably saw me through the window. We went to the dance for a minute, but I was so trashed." She glanced at me. "I wouldn't have been the best influence on you."

Something in the way she was confiding in me made me bold. I'd been careful not to bring up home since that awful Saturday, but now it seemed like it might be okay. "Rachel, why did you leave home? I mean, why at that moment?"

Rachel let go of my straps. "I was just done. Done with

high school. Done with Maine. I was ready to get out."

That didn't explain anything.

"Okay, let's see how this looks on you," Rachel said, forcing us back into the present. She took a step back and looked me up and down, and I wondered what she saw, what she was thinking about me. Her face didn't reveal much. "Gorgeous. The color is perfect for you. I'll need to let it out in some places, take it in in others. Now let me see you strut like a supermodel."

I turned and walked toward the far end of the attic, feeling the silk swirl around my legs. My walk turned to a slinky strut. After a few steps, I paused, posed, then turned and walked back. Rachel was smiling. "Wonderful. I can see how you won those pageants. You've got that something. It's like that light some people have—you just want to be near them, to watch them."

"Thanks," I said. It was one of the nicest things anyone had ever told me.

"Let's get out of this hot box and go downstairs, so I can measure you."

I followed Rachel down to her bedroom on the third floor. She'd never shown me her room before, and what I saw surprised me. Her four-poster bed was neatly made with a patchwork quilt, and flanked by identical nightstands. A bud vase on one held a single iris in full bloom. The only other furniture was a rocking chair draped with a multicolored afghan, and an oak bureau. But the floor was covered with stacks of magazines. Hundreds of them, maybe thousands. *The New Yorker, Harper's, Gourmet, Cook's Illustrated,*

Biography, Goat Biz, Cheese Digest, Vegetarian Times. I hadn't realized some of these magazines existed.

"So you're going to need to take it off," she said. She opened the drawer of the right bedside table and took out a faded orange tape measure.

I struggled again with the straps, and flinched when I felt her hands on my back, undoing the zipper and lifting the dress over my head. "Thanks," I said, instinctively crossing my arms over my stomach.

"You need to put your arms out," she said. I reluctantly obeyed. She stretched out the tape measure and wrapped it around me, just below my breasts. "Don't tell me," I blurted. I knew what the ideal measurements were. I didn't want to know how far off I was. Her cold fingers brushed my skin as she reached for her pencil. She wrote the number on a small scrap of paper and then moved on to my breasts, then my waist. "Hold this on your hip bone," she said.

I took the end of the tape and pressed it on my hip. I yearned to put my clothes back on. I was actually fidgeting with anxiety. "Hold still," Rachel said.

"Sorry. Whose dress was this?" I asked, trying to ease the tension.

"I'm not sure," Rachel said. "Someone before my time. Now up on your shoulder where the top of the strap will be."

"Why would people have evening dresses here?"

"I think when girls left home, they just packed up their favorite things. These dresses probably meant something to them, even if they never wore them here." She lifted the end of the tape measure a little higher on my shoulder. "We

195

should really be doing this in the shoes you're going to wear. Heels?"

"Sure. Of course."

She stood up and went to the closet. She rummaged around for a minute, then emerged with a pair of black heels with tiny ankle straps—a bad style for me, but they would work for now.

I slipped them on, and she measured from my shoulder to the floor, then wrapped the tape measure around her hand. "We're all set."

"Thanks," I said. A weird happy-sad emotion swept over me, and I started to tear up.

"Hey," Rachel said. She put her hand on my bare shoulder. "Hey, what's wrong?"

I shook my head. "Nothing. I'm just happy." Happy she was helping me. Happy she believed in me.

She smiled. "Good." She paused. "Me too."

In bed that night, the feeling stayed with me. Happiness mixed with loneliness and guilt. It was like the more time I spent at Jezebel with Rachel, the farther I drifted from home. I was afraid I was closing a door.

Chapter Thirty

Dr. Eddington had a new unicorn figurine. It was made of clear glass with gold eyes and horn, and she left it on the table by the chair, next to the pebbles. I picked it up when I sat down and flipped it over—crystal. So not only was it an ugly unicorn, it was an expensive, ugly unicorn.

She sat down across from me and rearranged her skirt.

"How are things? Settling in okay?"

"Sure," I said.

"Have you talked to your parents at all?"

"No."

She didn't say anything.

"My dad called on my first day. Rachel talked to him. I guess it was just to make sure I got there okay. And my mom called a few weeks ago. I didn't want to talk to her, so Owen did. She just wanted to remind me about my college essays."

"Let's talk about your mother," she said.

"This is very Freudian."

She grinned a little sheepishly. "I'm asking more to get a sense of what your life is like. How would you describe her?"

"That's a loaded question," I warned. I ran my fingers through the pebble bowl.

"Start with the good."

"She's very professional. Polished. Organized. She has high standards." I snickered at that last one. "On the other hand, she's a control freak."

"She tries to control you?"

"Me, my dad, everyone, and everything. Like, take the whole college thing. I wanted to visit a school with my friends, but I wasn't allowed to go. She likes to take me herself. But she totally monopolizes the tour guides and embarrasses me, so that I'd rather crawl under a rock than go to college." As I spoke, my words came faster and angrier. "And the thing is, it's not just that she wants me to get into a good college so she can brag to her friends. It's also like she can't stand the idea of me making a choice on my own, of pursuing something she can't appreciate. So it's not like *I'm* applying to college, it's like *we're* applying to college. She tells everyone I'm going to major in English, but I don't know if I want to do that. I like it, but there's so much out there. Maybe I want to be—I don't know—maybe I want to perform show tunes on a cruise ship. I just haven't had a chance to try it yet.

"The worst thing is, she's right. I can't just not have a direction. Colleges expect you to have some sort of a hook—something you're good at and have demonstrated an interest in. All of my friends have theirs. Owen's going to make films. Melissa wants to work for an NGO. Jeremy wants to be an engineer. I'm the only one with no clue. How do they know this already? How are they so sure?" I looked to Dr. Eddington for an answer.

"Maybe they aren't so sure. Maybe they're just playing the game, too."

I shook my head. I wished that were the case, but I knew it wasn't. "What about you? Did you always know you were going to be a therapist?"

"It wasn't a straight line, but, yes, the interest was there for a while. My father tried to discourage me. He told me that my patients would never get better. So for a while I thought I would be a medical doctor. In college I told everyone I was going to be a heart surgeon. But it didn't work out."

"What happened?"

"I just wasn't very good at it. You don't want someone who's shaky with her scalpel working on your heart. So I changed my specialty to psychiatry."

"Proving my point," I said.

"What point?"

"That most people know generally where they're going. I mean, most people can at least picture themselves doing *something*."

"Most people," she said, "are afraid to wander off the path."

It seemed like something that should be on one of those hokey posters in a dentist's office, the phrase written in script below a picture of a straight path through an autumn forest. Rachel insisted that Dr. Eddington knew what she was doing, but I was becoming less and less impressed with therapy at each session.

Chapter Thirty-one

The Fourth of July started like any other day at Jezebel: milking, feeding, racing Owen for the shower. But when we came down for breakfast, Rachel was rushing around the kitchen with her braids pinned to her head like the Swiss Miss girl's. "Hurry up," she said. "We're going to be late."

"Late for what?"

"Oh, yeah." Owen gave me a devilish grin. "I forgot to tell you."

"What?" I looked from Owen to Rachel, who hadn't stopped scurrying.

"It's almost time for the parade," she said. "Your costume's up in my room. You're going to be Martha."

"Martha?" I asked.

"Washington," she replied. "Owen is George."

"Little-known fact that George Washington was a brown boy," Owen said.

"You just forgot to mention that we had to dress up and be in a parade?"

"She wouldn't let me," he replied.

Rachel paused and smiled at me. "It's the type of thing where if you think about it too long, you might not want to do it. But really it's a lot of fun. I promise."

Belinda was sitting at the end of the table holding her teacup and looking as devilish as Owen. "Who are you?" I asked.

"I'm Betsy Ross," Rachel answered, thinking I was talking to her. "Sascha is Paul Revere. Come on, let's go."

I put my cereal bowl down in the kitchen and went up to Rachel's room. Sure enough, lying across the bed was a blue dress with big wavy sleeves and a full skirt, complete with crinoline. It appeared to be the right size. She had used my measurements for the pageant dress—that was sly. And she'd made it in days; apparently she didn't need much sleep. I wanted to be excited, for Rachel's sake, but I was pretty sure the whole experience would be mortifying. On the plus side, no one really knew who I was.

I stepped into the dress, which, thankfully, had a side zipper, and looked down at myself. The dress cinched in at the waist, which was good, because at least it showed I had curves. In the Revolutionary era, I probably would have been considered a catch. Full figures were okay back then, and people cared more about faces and gracefulness. The dress sleeves fluttered when I moved my arms, and I had to lift up the skirt as I walked downstairs. Owen had changed into a pair of knickers with a bright blue military jacket and knee-high boots. "My lady," he said.

"Mr. President," I replied. This might be okay. Maybe we'd just sit in the truck and smile and wave at kids, and then it would be over. "So is this parade a big deal?"

"Only in the sense that the whole town is there."

Perfect.

Rachel tore down the stairs in her Betsy Ross outfit: a cotton dress with an apron and a cute bonnet. She was totally into it. She had a flag as a prop and a handful of what looked like sheep's fur. "Wigs!" she cried.

Oh, God, no.

She tossed me a white beehive, and I pulled it on. Owen snickered as I struggled to get all of my hair tucked into it. I ignored him and persevered.

"You're crooked." She reached over and tugged on one of my fake ringlets.

Then Sascha clumped down the stairs, looking more like Paul Bunyan than Paul Revere in his white button-down shirt, vest, and tricorner hat.

"Perfect!" Rachel said.

"Where's your horse?" Owen asked.

"My horse is a truck," Sascha replied.

Owen and I followed Rachel outside to Sascha's pickup. "Belinda isn't coming?" I wondered out loud.

"No, she's not into the Fourth. Too much noise," Rachel answered.

Owen, Rachel, and I climbed into the bed of the truck, and

Sascha drove to the high school. "Here's how it works," Rachel explained on the way. "The parade goes right through downtown." She passed each of us a canvas bag. I peeked inside and saw about four pounds of hard candy. "Just smile and toss it. Make sure you get it back to people who are farther away." To Owen she added, "Don't peg it at them."

"What?" Owen protested.

"Last year he almost took the high school principal's eye out with a butterscotch," Rachel told me.

"It wasn't on purpose. But if it had been, it would be justifiable, given he's a homophobic tool."

Rachel seemed about to comment, but she changed her mind and refocused on the parade. "The most important thing is to smile."

I wished my parents could see her, this giddy costumed woman who loved what she was doing and where she was. If they hadn't tried to control her, I bet everything would have turned out okay.

Sascha pulled the truck in line behind three antique automobiles, and a fire engine filed in behind us. It seemed like the order had been determined ahead of time, because everyone knew where to go. Leading off the parade was the high school marching band, which consisted of about twenty-five kids wearing uniforms that made them look like tin soldiers.

The parade began its slow lurch toward town. People lined both sides of Main Street, waving flags and clapping along with the band. I had never seen anything quite so Americana. Older people sat in folding lawn chairs. Small children ran around the legs of the adults; sawhorses kept them from running out in front of the vehicles.

"Throw!" Rachel yelled, laughing. So we threw. We tossed the candy in high arcs out to the crowd. Kids scrambled for them like they were gold coins. It was a hot day, and my wig itched horribly. But Rachel's glee made it fun.

In less than half an hour, we'd come to the end of the parade route. Once we were out of the downtown area, the parade vehicles all pulled over, and a woman with bleached blond hair appeared from out of nowhere, pouring glasses of lemonade.

In the field behind us, a member of the marching band drifted away from his comrades and began strolling toward us. It was Milo, holding a trumpet. When he realized I'd seen him, he took off his funny little marching band hat. Likewise, I pulled off my wig. "God, I'm so hot," I said.

"For Martha Washington, sure."

I rolled my eyes. It was a totally cheesy line, and I had asked for it. But did it still count as a compliment? It seemed backhanded: not empirically hot, just hot compared to our nation's first first lady.

"Hey, Milo," Owen said. "You coming to the fireworks tonight?"

"I don't know. Mom and Dad want to go with the Pembertons. You know, the weird neighbors?"

"I remember the neighbors," Owen told him, annoyed.

"Yeah, well, anyway, their daughter kind of freaks me out, so I don't know."

"Honestly, I don't care if you go with them, I was just asking," Owen replied.

"I don't know if I'm going to go with them. She's actually really annoying. She keeps bugging me to join her youth group, like *hinting*, you know?"

"Then why are you even torn about it?" Owen asked. "Whatever, maybe I'll see you there." He turned and walked toward the truck.

Milo glanced at me, then back at his brother. He'd come off sounding lame, but I could understand how he felt. "So, yeah, I should get back to the band. We're going to get pizza. And milk shakes."

"Cool," I said. "Bye." I watched him go, and then I went to join Owen.

The fairgrounds were already covered with families by the time we arrived for the fireworks. Rachel and I spread out a plaid wool blanket on the ground and began unpacking our picnic. It was just the two of us—Sascha had decided to go see the fireworks in Northampton, and Owen had hitched a ride with him. Still, Rachel had made a huge feast for the two of us: red bliss potato salad (with potatoes from her garden), lobster rolls, melon balls, and iced tea.

The sun slipped completely below the horizon while we ate, and the fireworks were going to start soon. "I have a surprise for you," she said. "Come with me." We left our blanket and everything else behind, and walked to the Ferris wheel. "Best seats in the house."

It was nice to hang out with her outside of the farm. She was so in her element in Hollis, and I felt some of that ease wearing off on me. I wondered if people could tell we were sisters. The Ferris wheel slid up a quarter rotation, then stopped while people below us boarded.

"I'm almost finished with your dress," she said.

"Thank you."

"You're going to look gorgeous."

I felt a nervous flutter when she said that. I couldn't believe I was entering a beauty pageant.

The wheel started moving again, lifting us closer to the sky, then halted. "How old were you when you did those pageants?" Rachel asked.

"Seven."

"And things were pretty good then?"

"I guess." I shifted in my seat.

"When I was seven, I fell down the stairs and knocked out my two front teeth." She wasn't looking at me but out at the landscape around us. "Well, not so much fell as decided to slide headfirst down the stairs just to see what it was like. I think that was also the year I tried to climb from my window to the tree out in the backyard."

The Ferris wheel was all filled up and began to rotate. Rachel leaned out over the edge of the car. The wind caught stray strands of hair and blew them around her face. I tried to think of something to say, anything. But maybe it was okay that we weren't talking. Maybe that meant we were comfortable together.

The Ferris wheel stopped, and almost immediately the first fireworks exploded in the sky: red, white, and blue sparks raining down. I had never been at the same height as the fireworks. One after another they exploded, then slipped away, like pebbles dropping into a pond. "Wow," I said.

"See? Best seats in the house." She pulled out a camera. "Lean in." We leaned toward each other across the center of the car, our cheeks pressed together. She took the picture with explosions behind us.

The fireworks crescendoed into a fury, one right after another, making my ears ring. The sky was as bright as daylight. And then, nothing.

"Wow," I said again as the Ferris wheel lowered us down to the ground. When we got off, Rachel was immediately snagged by Didi, the hostess from the Inn, who tucked her arm into Rachel's and pulled her aside. I waited a moment for Didi to say something to me, but she didn't. I decided I didn't like her. Even Rachel looked a little bored by her, but didn't make an attempt to disengage. I wandered away from the crowd down a small hill on the other side of the ride. Then I saw Milo sitting on the ground, head up to the sky. "Hey, Milo," I called out to him.

"Oh, hey," he said when I got closer. I stood next to him for a moment, not sure if he wanted me to join him. But standing felt awkward, so I sat down next to him on the cool grass.

"Good show," I said.

"It was better last year," he replied. He tilted his head back up toward the sky. I was beginning to wonder if maybe he didn't want me there after all, when he said, "Shooting star."

"What?"

"I saw a shooting star." He moved his arm in a wide arc, tracing the star's path with his finger. While Owen was frenetic, Milo was subdued. He was so still, he barely seemed to breathe.

"There's always something a little sad about a shooting star." Milo's face was lit up by the moon, pale and wondering.

We sat there for a while longer. I racked my brain trying to think of something to say to him, but couldn't come up with any small talk. "Rachel's probably looking for me," I told him finally.

"Right," he said.

I stood up and brushed off my butt. "So, um. Good night."

"Good night."

I walked back up the hill to find Rachel, thinking about what a strange boy he was.

Chapter Thirty-two

The next morning, Owen and Sascha left for New York long before dawn. I had expected to feed and milk on my own, but when I got to the fence, Milo was waiting there. "I'm filling in," he announced.

"Oh, thanks," I said.

He was a little sweaty from riding his bike, and his hair was twisted in all different directions from the helmet, but he didn't seem to realize how disheveled he looked. The morning was cool, and I shivered as we walked out to the paddocks. When we got to the fence, I unhooked it for Milo and let him go in first to meet the goats.

One was especially bold, and Milo reached out his hand to her, as though she were a dog. "Milo!" I blurted. But instead of chewing Milo's fingers, the goat rubbed its body along his hand. "You're like Snow White or something, taming all the wild animals."

"These goats aren't wild," he said.

"Yeah, well, neither are you," I replied, not making sense. He raised his eyebrows. "Whatever you say."

Ugh.

We gathered the goats and led them to the milking barn. Milo was quick about it, better than Owen even. The goats held still for him, while for me, they twisted and nipped. Once all the goats were connected, we just stood there and waited for the machine to finish.

The silence was getting awkward, worse than the night before, so I asked, "How much younger are you? Than Owen, I mean."

"Three years." His hair had settled down, and he looked less goofy and more cute.

"You're a freshman?" I asked, surprised. I'd thought he was older.

"Well, technically a sophomore," he replied.

"Oh, right." That made me a senior; it hadn't really occurred to me. "So do you like Hollis High School?" I asked.

He shrugged. "It's fine. We have a decent orchestra."

"Trumpet, right?" I said.

"Piano in the orchestra. Trumpet in the marching band."

"Cool." And that was all I could think to say.

The milker pumped on. I felt strangely tense standing there while the machine yanked on the goats' teats, but Milo didn't seem to mind. Still, it made me uncomfortable not to have a conversation going, so I blurted out the first thing I thought of. "What was it like when they kicked Owen out?"

"They didn't really kick him out," he said. "The way they were acting, it was like they couldn't even look at him, they were so disappointed. So he left." He pressed the tips of his fingers together, index then middle then ring then pinky, over and over again. "Do you miss home?" he asked. It wasn't really a non sequitur, but it was a surprising shift.

"Uh, yeah. Parts. I miss my friends."

He turned to face me. "Not your parents?" He watched me intently as he waited for my answer.

"No." I felt many things toward my parents, but when it came right down to it, I didn't really miss them.

When the milking was done, we brought the goats back into the paddock. "Do you want to stay for breakfast?" I asked.

"Sure," he replied.

He waited downstairs while I showered. I can't imagine what he did. Just sat there, probably. When I got down to the dining room, Belinda placed bowls of oatmeal in front of us, and watched us as we ate. None of us said anything.

After we finished, I picked up our bowls and took them into the kitchen. "Want to go for a swim?" he asked as I washed up.

"Well, I—" I began. I was supposed to go to therapy, but a swim sounded so much better. "Actually, that sounds nice." I should have felt guilty, but instead I felt light.

Upstairs, I tugged on my bathing suit, and then shorts and

T-shirt. I forced myself to take a quick glance in the mirror. It was a mistake. I hated my thighs and there was nothing I could do to cover them. It's not like I could go swimming in jeans or a skirt. I ran back downstairs and outside, where Milo stood waiting next to my car.

We went to the same spot on the river, and as I got out of the car, I realized with a jolt that I had forgotten to bring an extra set of clothes. If I went swimming in what I had on, my wet clothes would be clinging to me the whole way home. I watched Milo pull off his shirt and dive clumsily into the water. He wasn't perfect either—his skin was doughy, and he had a few pimples on his back. I pulled off my T-shirt and shorts, and dove in.

Upstream, the river curved deeper into the forest. Our spot was its own little clearing, dappled with sunshine. This could be the place where Rachel had been caught with the boys. Here I was, years later, swimming with a boy when I should have been somewhere else.

"Listen," Milo said. We were both quiet, and when I strained I could hear very faint shrieks and laughter coming from down the river. "Most of the Hollis kids swim at the trestle," he said.

"Wanna go?" I asked. I skimmed my hands over the surface of the water and watched the ripples spread outward.

"I'd rather not deal with them." Milo stared at his reflection as it wavered in the ripples. I didn't want to go either, so I didn't press for details.

He abruptly clapped his hand on the water, making a splash. "Ever play Floater?"

"What's that?"

"It's a game that me and Owen made up."

"Well then, obviously, I haven't."

He shrugged. "You close your eyes, take a deep breath, and float on your stomach. Dead man's float. And you go as long as you can until you have to breathe. Whoever goes the farthest wins."

This seemed dangerous to me. "Aren't there rocks and stuff in the way?"

"That's the game." He paused. "Want to play?"

"Do we go at the same time?"

"Uh-huh."

"So how do I know that you didn't pop your head up before me and then put it back down again?"

"I don't cheat," he said.

It sounded like a pretty stupid game, but I was feeling too lazy to argue. "Let's go, then."

"All right. On three."

What Milo hadn't considered was the advantage my fat gave me. While his legs cut through the surface at an angle, I floated up on top like a bathtub toy.

My face in the water, my arms hanging down, the river caressed me. I lost my sense of direction. Had I spun? I was having trouble telling if I was headfirst or feetfirst. A rock brushed against my side, startling me, but I kept my face in the water. I began to feel drowsy. It was like after spending the day in the ocean, you can still feel the waves as you lie in bed at night.

The peacefulness passed. My lungs tightened and my

limbs went weak. *It's only a game.* I lifted my head.

Blinking to clear my eyes, I looked to see where I was. I could just make out our stuff on the shore, maybe a hundred yards away. Then Milo floated past me, looking like a dead body. I reached out and let my fingers trail along his back, but he didn't respond.

It seemed impossible that he could hold his breath for so long. Maybe he had hit his head. He drifted farther away from me, and my lungs tightened again, the panic palpable. "Milo," I called. "Milo, you win!"

I swam after him, struggling to keep him in view. Swimming was suddenly difficult with my breath coming so fast. He was too still. "Milo!" What would I do when I caught him? I didn't know mouth-to-mouth. I probably couldn't even get him to the shore. I'd hold him and we'd float down the river until someone found us.

I reached out and grabbed his shoulder. He jerked his head up, angry.

"You can't touch the other person."

"You won," I breathed out. Looking back up the river, I couldn't see our clothes anymore.

"You're not supposed to touch the other person."

"I was just . . ." I began, but couldn't finish because I was so out of breath—and pissed. "Fine. Now what do we do?"

"Get out and walk back."

"Floater is a dumb game."

I swam to the shore and climbed out. The pebbles and sticks dug into the bottom of my feet, but when I tried to tip-toe around them, I jiggled. I should have left my shirt and shorts on. Milo caught up to me, and I let him pass. I didn't need him staring at my cellulite.

We walked in silence to our clothes. I pulled mine on over my wet bathing suit and walked toward my car. "Are you mad?" Milo asked. I took off my flip-flop and swiped at a pebble on my heel. He walked up beside me, still shirtless and dripping like a drowned gopher. "Don't be mad."

My body was tense with anger. "You looked like you were dead."

"I'm not, though. See?" He touched both hands to his chest.

"What's the point of that game? It just seems like your weird way of freaking me out."

Milo looked bewildered. "You were scared?"

"Of course I was scared. This dead body comes floating by, and I touch you, and you don't even look up. I thought you had hit your head on a rock or something."

"You were seriously worried about me?" The idea seemed to both please and perplex him.

"What the hell is wrong with you?"

"Huh?" he said.

"Huh," I said back to him, and started walking again. He trotted behind me on his bare feet.

When we got to the car, Milo hesitated. "Got a towel? For the seat?" he asked.

"No." I twisted my hair to wring the water out before I got into the car. "Just get in. Where do you live?"

"Can you take me back to Jezebel? I rode my bike."

I nodded and started driving. The dirt road curved like a

snake in the dappled sunlight, skirted town, and passed Dr. Eddington's house. I pictured her sitting in her armchair, still waiting for me to show up, pulling on one of her curls.

"I live down there," Milo said, pointing to a fake-rustic wooden sign that said OCTOBER GROVE, one of those developments full of identical beige houses crammed onto tiny, treeless lots.

I slowed at the entrance. "I thought you wanted me to take you back to Jezebel."

"I do. I was just saying."

I shook my head and put my foot back on the accelerator.

"Don't be mad. I swear, I wasn't trying to scare you."

"Whatever."

I ignored him for the rest of the drive. As soon as we got to the farm, Milo jumped out and walked to his bike, and I popped the trunk to grab an extra pair of flip-flops. Then Milo pedaled right up to me and stopped. "I'm sorry," he said. Without warning, he leaned over and kissed me. His lips were warm and soft. He held them there, just for a second. Didn't try anything, just pressed his lips to mine; my stomach fluttered. He pulled back and started pedaling.

"What the hell was that for?" I called after him, stunned.

He shrugged and coasted down the driveway.

Chapter Thirty-three

In the shower I examined myself. I could tell I had lost some weight and gotten some muscle, especially in my arms—my biceps didn't sag as much. My stomach also seemed a little smaller, although it might have been my imagination. Stomach fat is just about impossible to burn off. My thighs were the worst. It was hard to believe there'd been a time when I could see between them. When I was ten they were still sticks. Now they were like whales. If I could get liposuction, I'd definitely change my thighs before anything else.

I must have looked awful when he kissed me. I wasn't wearing any makeup, my hair was matted, and my bathing suit had soaked through my clothes, leaving large wet blotches on my boobs and belly. What had he seen in me? What made him want to kiss me? And why had I liked it so much?

It had been four years since I'd been kissed. That had been at a party in eighth grade, when we still played spin the bottle. Trevor Dodds, on the cusp of being a high school lacrosse star, had put both of his hands on my shoulders and barely touched his lips to mine. I knew he'd only done it out of politeness. While the bottle spun, I could see him willing it to land on anyone else, like a contestant on *Wheel of Fortune* tries to make the wheel avoid BANKRUPT.

Before that had been in seventh grade, not too long before the doctor's visit. My boyfriend, Tim, and I were in a closet at a birthday party, mashing our tongues into each other's mouths, while he felt my exceptionally well-developed breasts through my sweater. We stopped when the other kids flung open the door, giggling and whistling. I wiped his saliva from the corner of my lips, absolutely humiliated.

Milo's had been a chaste little kiss. He had probably never kissed anyone, and just wanted to try it, and thought I'd be too flattered to push him away. I didn't want to keep thinking about it. Milo probably wasn't.

Back in my bedroom I pulled out my drawer of shirts and stared at it. I knew I wouldn't see him for the rest of the day, but still I wanted to put on something nice. So if I did see him, I'd look composed. Maybe a little intimidating. I put on an eyelet peasant shirt that Melissa once told me was sexy, but when I looked in the mirror, I just thought I looked trashy, like a buxom barmaid. I was being stupid. Finally I just grabbed my softest T-shirt, one I only wore for sleeping—and pulled it on over a pair of yoga pants.

I tried to read for a while, but my attention span was shot, so I went into the parlor to look at the record collection. Maybe I'd find some inspiration for the pageant. The records were mostly country. They had Johnny Cash, who I adored but knew he wasn't quite right for a beauty pageant. And Patsy Cline—I *had* always liked "I Fall to Pieces," but Owen had already vetoed her. I flipped past a few classical records, then stopped when I found Dolly Parton's *Just Because I'm a Woman*. I loved this album.

The speakers made a loud pop when I started the record. I dropped the needle down. There was crackling and static, and then Dolly began to sing. On the album cover she was beautiful; she wore her hair piled up on top of her head in a crazy beehive, and she had a soft, lovely smile. Most people think of her as all big hair and boobs, if they think of her at all. But she is actually an amazing songwriter.

Rachel came in and sat on the armchair next to the stereo. Underneath her tan, her cheeks were pink and glowing, and just then she looked like a younger version of our mom. It startled me. "What are you up to?" she asked.

"Trying to find a song for the pageant." I knew what was coming next.

"Dr. Eddington called," she said.

A thousand little lies flitted through my mind. I said, "I went swimming with Milo."

She toyed with one of her braids. "I know you aren't self-destructive, or whatever it is Mom and Dad think," she said. "And frankly I'd be pissed too if they forced me to go to therapy. But even though you may not need it, it's what you have to do so you can go back to your school. So you might as well go. None of this is Dr. Eddington's fault; why blow her off?"

"I'm running out of things to talk about." It was true. After my long rant about Mom and colleges, now all we talked about was what I might like to do. Whenever I told her new thoughts I'd had, she just nodded and said things like, "And how do you think your mom would react to that?" It was kind of disappointing, actually.

"Tell her about the pageant." Rachel grinned at me. "She'll eat that up."

I rolled my eyes. "She won't get it. She'll think it means way more than it does."

"She's not that bad," Rachel said, starting to sound defensive.

"Sorry," I replied.

She glanced down at the stack of records I'd pulled out of the cabinet. "I'll cover for you this time, if you go the rest of the summer. And bring her some cheese next time, as an apology. She likes the sun-dried tomato."

"Okay."

"Since you're here, you want to help with dinner? It's an experiment, since it's just us chickens tonight."

"Sure." I smiled. I liked cooking with Rachel—it was like being a magician's assistant, watching the way she transformed raw food, a lot of it still coated with soil, into delicious meals. I reached to stop the record.

"Leave it," she said. "Belinda loves Dolly."

Chapter Thirty-four

I had forgotten Rachel had plans that night. Someone's birthday. I didn't feel so bad about it, though. It wasn't fair to ask her to sacrifice her social life just because I wanted more attention. For a second I thought about calling Milo. But then I got real: even if I had his number, there was no way. Instead I went upstairs to read the shoe box memoir. When I found a page with Rachel's name on it, I grabbed the next fifty or so and took them to the window seat, so I could watch for Owen and Sascha, who were due back from New York any minute.

```
        organized the whole thing. Rachel turned the
        barn into a haunted house. She got the guys
```

from Heritage Farm to bring a couple of ponies for rides. Celie drew posters and put them up all around town. I expected Rachel to dress like a witch or a devil, but she came floating down the stairs as a fairy, with layers of tulle, gossamer wings, and a wand she'd made with a dowel and old ribbons. "I am going to grant all of the children's wishes." And she did. I heard laughter coming from the barn all night. Bette led me through so I could see what was happening. Celie popped out of a stall, mouth painted to look like it was dripping blood. Sascha rose up from a table: a woodsman with an ax in his back. "Excuse me," he'd say. "Could you scratch my back? I've got an itch." At the very end, Rachel stood on top of an apple box, which was concealed by her long skirt. She appeared magnificently tall to the children. She tapped each child on the head and bent low to whisper something in his or her ear. The children ran out of the barn, laughing, chasing each other around the yard. Parents stood around drinking apple cider. That was the first year. She did it every year until she and Bette moved away. We thought of doing it without her, but none of us had the heart, or the drive. Children came to the door, and we gave them candy. Celie said, "I'm sorry, dears, no haunted house this year." Celie left a few months after. She'd never warmed up to Rachel, but even Celie could recognize the hole she left. We said it was Bette's absence, but we all knew it was both of them being gone that made the place so empty. So for a while it was just me and Sascha and a string of farmhands whose names I could never

The story didn't continue on the next page, but I read anyway.

guess word must have gotten around that Jezebel was a place for girls whose families didn't want them. I opened the door to call the girls in for supper, and she just was there, in a little plastic bathtub. Not crying, but smiling up at me. I ought to have given her to one of the girls, or to one of the women who had moved on. I was fifty-three years old. What was I thinking taking in a baby? But the way she looked at me, I had no choice. I picked her up out of that bathtub and held her to my chest, smelled her sweet baby smell, and she was mine. I knew she was mine. We called her Bette because the girls thought it was a glamorous name, like the old movie actress's. I knew there wasn't much room for glamour in Hollis, let alone on Jezebel Goat Farm, but I agreed after I saw the way she cooed when Sally called her that. It's like she picked her own name. Looking back, it's not surprising. She picked her own way throughout life, reinventing herself as she raced forward. Didn't care what she left behind. Was that the way she always was, or did it come from being at Jezebel? None of us knew too much about raising babies. Some of the girls had had younger siblings, but still we were all so tentative with her. As if it were possible that people were right about us, that just being near us could taint a child. She slept in a cradle in my room. It was my old bassinet, actually, dug up and brought down from the attic. I wrapped her in oversized blankets and put her down to sleep that first night. When I turned the lights off, she began to cry. I held her, and she stopped. But when I put her down again, she started crying once more. I carried her into my bed, and there she slept for the next few months. Such a lovely, perfect

I heard a truck rattle up the driveway before the headlights bathed my room in golden light. I quickly gathered the pages and put them back into the box. I couldn't wait to see what Owen had brought back from the city.

I skipped down the stairs in my socks, and ran out to the porch to meet them. It wasn't Sascha and Owen, though, but Rachel, home from the party. Her cheeks were glowing. She had let her hair loose from its usual braids, and it flowed around her head almost like Belinda's in the old pictures.

"Come swing with me," she said, slurring her words in a singsongy way. She was definitely tipsy.

I pulled off my socks and followed her barefoot across the front yard to the old oak tree with the swings. She immediately pushed off and started pumping her legs. I let my toes hang down and swayed back and forth.

The night had grown cooler, but the air was still heavy with the fragrance of honeysuckle. Rachel let her feet drag to slow her momentum. "You really are lucky to be able to sing," she said. "I wish I could sing, but I couldn't carry a tune in a bucket." She giggled. "Like Mom. She used to try to sing to me, and I'd hold my ears."

I couldn't remember Mom ever singing to me. Maybe Rachel had turned her off of it. "I've never heard—"

"Dara, I'm in love with the most beautiful woman," she declared. She swung herself higher and higher. "But, Dara, I don't wanna get my heart broken again." She stopped her swing abruptly and looked a little ill for a moment. Then she coughed. "I was in love with Belinda's daughter. Did you know that? We went to California together."

"Really?"

"Yep," she sighed. "We broke Belinda's heart when we left." She tilted her head back and looked up at the tree. "They're so pretty, all the leaves, and it's like the tree, you know, this tree is so old and so wise, you know what I mean?"

"I think so," I replied.

"I don't know if I can go through that again. I thought that was *it*, you know? Like, who cares about everyone else in the world because we had each other. Everything made sense." She sighed up at the leaves. "But then she left me, and I lost it. I stopped going to work. . . . Just stayed in bed and drank." *Oh, Rachel.* "She threw me away like she threw Belinda away. She was so *selfish*. I hated her so much, Dara. I just . . . can't handle being thrown away again."

I didn't know what to say. It was strange and kind of hard hearing this story from Rachel. Her memories were so messy and raw compared to Belinda's. And I didn't know enough about her current love life—whether she'd chosen a better woman this time.

"Sorry, I'm freaking you out," she said abruptly. "Just swing with me!" She started pumping again, and I did too. We rose higher and higher until the leaves shimmied, and the lights of the stars blurred. My arms and legs began to burn as I lost myself in the thrill, the joy of swinging. Rachel started singing "Dancing in the Dark," way off-key, and I joined in. We sang at the top of our lungs until we were laughing, howling into the night.

By the time Sascha's headlights shone down the driveway, I was helping my very nauseated sister walk back inside. She stumbled and caught the banister. "Are you gonna be okay?" I called up after her.

"Not tomorrow!" she answered, strangely cheerful.

"Um. Well, good night, then," I said.

She muttered something unintelligible and disappeared around the corner. I turned to go meet Owen, and nearly bumped into him as he rushed into the house loaded with bags. "Come on," he said as he headed for the stairs. "I have so much to show you. New York is awesome. I should have applied to Columbia, or NYU, or Barnard."

"Barnard is a girls' school," I replied.

"Yeah, but look where I live. It would be nothing new."

"Now that's a compelling argument."

In his room Owen ushered me to a chair, then sat down on the bed, letting the bags fall to the floor. "I got you stuff." I hoped there wouldn't be too many feathers involved. He peeked into one of the bags, then removed a long black vintage wrap dress. "For the singing," he said. "Or the talking. Black is sexy and slimming."

Thanks, Owen, I thought. The dress was beautiful, though. He'd chosen well.

"It goes great with these," he went on, fishing through a different bag. "Here." He held out a pair of dangly faux sapphire earrings. "Fabulous fakes. There's a necklace to match, but it might be overkill." He dropped the earrings back in the bag without showing me the necklace. "The next thing is the best. Are you ready?"

"Sure," I replied.

He rustled tissue paper in the bag for suspense. "Ready?" he asked again.

"*Yes*, just show me!"

He slowly lifted out a black leather jacket, then slipped it on. "For me."

"Fierce."

"Too much?"

I shook my head. "No, it's good. Sexy, really." He shrugged off the jacket. "Wanna go out on the roof?"

"Uh, sure."

I let him crawl out first. He stepped up on the sill, then scrunched himself in half and ducked out. I couldn't do it that way. Instead I put my knees on his desk and lifted myself out with my hands until I was far enough to swing my legs through. My back brushed along the window sash, but I fit through okay. Owen graciously pretended not to have seen my awkward passage.

"Anything exciting happen here?" he asked.

"Rachel's in love," I told him.

"Yeah, right," he scoffed. "She's the biggest player in town."

He thought he knew her so well, but she had secrets she kept, even from him. I had a secret too—Milo's kiss. I thought about telling him, but that would only make him think I was interested in Milo. "Have you ever kissed a boy?" I asked.

"Nah, slim pickings in Hollis." He scratched at one of the shingles. "High school romances never last anyway, so why bother?" He was probably right, but it seemed too cynical for him.

"Have you ever been interested in anyone here?"

"Sure." He paused. "But just crushes. They last, like, a minute."

I rested my head on his shoulder. "Thanks for getting me the stuff in New York. Why do you care so much about this pageant?"

"First off, I like you. Second, it's what I do. I mean, I feel like I need to fight against things like this. Prejudice against you is like prejudice against me. Maybe worse."

I tensed. "How do you figure?"

"People make fun of me, but they know they shouldn't. They know it's not cool. But people get made fun of all the time for their weight. I mean, the things they do to not-even-that-fat people in movies, the stereotypes, you could never get away with that sort of thing with gay people, or black people, or whatever. At least not to that extent."

He was so frank, I was caught a little off guard by what he said. No one had ever spoken to me so matter-of-factly about weight stereotypes before, expecting me to be personally indignant about them. But he was right, they were terrible. I'd seen so many movies in which the fat characters were waylaid with humiliating physical mishaps; their bodies and pain used as comic relief, like they were only half-legitimate people. Whenever I watched these movies with my friends, they would laugh at every fat joke without thinking, and I'd sit there trying not to take it personally. Owen was the first one who seemed to understand how it felt.

"You are smart, and funny, and genuine. Just because you're not skinny doesn't mean you aren't beautiful."

"But in a pageant—"

"You *are* beautiful. Skin, eyes, hair—it's all perfect. It's just this one element that doesn't fit into society's idea of

230

beauty, so some people think you're totally out just because of that."

It hurt to hear it so bluntly, but I believed he thought I was beautiful, and that gave me a lump in my throat.

"It's too bad you're gay," I said.

"It's too bad you're a girl."

The rough shingles pressed into my hand. A mosquito buzzed near my head. But I didn't move. I didn't dare disturb that one perfect moment.

Chapter Thirty-five

As July pressed on I settled into a routine. Owen and I milked and fed in the morning, and fed in the afternoon. In between I either helped Rachel with the cheese, or hung out with Owen—reading, swimming, trying to think of a good song for my pageant performance. My parents didn't call, but I didn't care. What bothered me more (and it bugged me that it bugged me), was that Milo wasn't around. He just kissed me and disappeared.

In August the Hollis Town Fair began. Owen decided we needed face time there, so the town could get to know me. "This is a campaign," he'd announced the night before the fair opened. "You're the outsider. The dark horse. We need to press hands and kiss babies." He presented the idea to Rachel as we washed dishes. "It's a win-win situation if we run the stand."

Rachel bit her lip. I'd seen her sell the cheese. She was basically a genius. "Maybe we can trade days."

"Rachel, really, you're much more valuable to the business here. The farmers' market is one thing, but that's just a few hours a week. The fair is all day, every day, and we have more orders than we did last year."

Rachel flipped a dishrag onto her shoulder. "All right. You can leave after the morning feeding. But you're going to have to wear the polos."

"Rachel—" Owen started.

"I don't care if they're uncool. Pop the collar. You have to wear it. It's branding. Customers need to see a logo at least three times per visit if they're going to remember the company."

Owen grinned. "That was in your *Small Business Monthly* newsletter. Verbatim." Rachel threw the dishrag at him. He dodged, and it fell to the floor. "Nice throw, quarterback."

She grinned back at him. "Watch it, buster."

The next morning, we left right after chores—no time for showers. Owen waited until we got there to change into his polo. He peeled off his black T-shirt and basked for a moment in the morning sun; then, slowly, he looped first one arm and then the other into the sleeves and pulled the shirt over his head. As Rachel suggested, he popped the collar, and smoothed out his recently self-inflicted faux hawk.

This accomplished, Mr. *GQ* and I lifted the rolling coolers from the truck and dragged them to the booth, two apiece.

While I spread cheese onto wheat crackers, Owen opened a large umbrella that slid into a hole in one of the corners of the booth. "My beauty queen is not getting a sunburn," he said.

The gates opened at 8:30, and the first group of fairgoers was the walking moms. In brightly colored tracksuits, they pushed their strollers around the fairgrounds, chatting and drinking coffee from travel mugs.

"Ladies!" Owen called to a trio as they passed the stand. "Care for a snack break?" His repertoire of smiles was impressive; the one he gave the women was wide and flirtatious.

The women shrugged at each other, none making a commitment one way or the other. "Well, we . . ." one began.

"Did you know that goat cheese has one-third the fat of cheese made from cows' milk? One-third!" Owen marveled. I wasn't sure if this was true or not, but it sounded good. The women moved closer to the stand. Owen stepped out from behind the counter, carrying a tray of samples. "Also, it's part of the Mediterranean diet, which experts agree not only helps you lose weight, but also aids in longevity."

They weren't offended by his comments; they didn't assume he was telling them they needed to lose weight. The women reached for the tray and took a cracker each, then daintily brushed the crumbs from their lips and sighed at how good it was.

"The cheese is made daily on Jezebel Goat Farm, right here in Hollis. Dara and I feed and milk the goats— all-natural feed, of course, and Dara actually helped make the cheese herself. Amazing, right? She's Rachel's sister, in town for the summer."

The women nodded excitedly. "I love what Rachel has done to help bring local foods to the area," a blond woman said. She reached out and took a second cracker. "All the processed foods we eat are *killing* our kids." She automatically glanced at me.

Owen didn't seem to notice. "Dara's really getting to love this town. As a matter of fact, she's going to compete in the Miss Hollis pageant."

The women turned to me. The blond had her lips in a small, round O.

"Fun."

"Lovely."

"Good luck."

They thanked Owen for the cheese and started walking their circuit again. Owen returned to the stand. "Okay, you're going to need to be more proactive."

I picked at a splinter in the plywood counter. "I don't see why it matters. It's not like people vote."

"Public support. You want the audience clapping like crazy every time you come onstage."

I could still see the women power walking in their tracksuits. They bounded along like ex-cheerleaders. "I don't think those women are going to be clapping for me."

"Not with that attitude."

I arranged more crackers on the serving plate.

We were tucked away in the Local Artisans Alley: a sandy strip on the edge of the fairgrounds where everyone from the

235

farmers' market decamped for the two weeks of the fair. Our neighbors sold pies, beef jerky, apple cider, quilts, felted art, and scarves out of brightly painted booths and trucks.

A man in brown Carhartt overalls approached the stand. "Where's the john?" he barked.

"Next aisle over," I answered proactively.

"Have some cheese," Owen offered, extending the platter. The farmer paused for a second, then walked toward us and snatched a cracker. His cuticles were dark with mud.

"Thanks," he said.

"Listen, since you're here—"

"I don't need to hear your cheese talk."

"Actually, it's about Dara," he said. The farmer looked at me, curious. "She's going to be in Miss Hollis—"

"The beauty pageant?" he asked. As if there might be some other Miss Hollis.

"Yeah, and we're hoping to drum up as much support as possible. So, if you go, and we really hope you do, could you make sure to cheer extra loud for her?"

"Why should I cheer for her over the other girls?"

This, to me, seemed a legitimate question, and I looked to Owen to see how he would answer it. Owen rolled his eyes. I realized I was supposed to make my platform speech, but I had no idea what to say. So Owen took over. "Because she's like you. Know what she did this morning? She got up and fed twenty head of goats, and then she milked them."

"I've got pigs."

"Well, how many of the other contestants do you think know anything about livestock at all?"

236

"Where'd you say the john was?" he asked.

"One aisle over." I pointed the way out to him.

"Thanks," he said. He looked at me for a moment longer, shook his head, and then was on his way.

"Well, at least you said something that time," Owen said.

As the morning wore on, the trickle of walking moms gave way to a horde of hungry visitors. We handed out tray after tray of samples. Mostly through Owen's excellent salesmanship, we sold more than half of our cheese before 12:30.

We were discussing who should go to lunch first when a group of preppy girls cast their shadows over the stand. "Hey, Owen," one of them said. She was a tall, slim girl with dark hair that fell to the middle of her back. She was intimidatingly beautiful. Narrow features and deep-blue eyes, and a perfect tan with just a few adorable freckles on her nose and shoulders.

"Hi," Owen replied coolly.

"Sucky way to spend a summer," she went on, ignoring me.

"I kind of like it, actually," he said. "This is my friend, Dara. Dara, this is Maddie, Charlotte, and Jenna."

I figured the slim girl was Maddie. I wasn't sure which of the other two was which, but I got the impression that it didn't matter—they were interchangeable. "Nice to meet you," I said.

Maddie appraised me for half a second, then decided she could stand to talk to me. "You're new in town," she stated.

"I'm just here for the summer." I smiled politely, then looked away for a second, pretending something more interesting had caught my eye. "I'm staying with my sister,

Rachel. She runs Jezebel. Owen lives there too. We live together."

Maddie gave Owen a too-sympathetic look—terribly overacted—and said, "I'm so sorry about what happened with your parents, Owen."

I didn't believe her for a second. I sidestepped a little bit closer to him. We all stood there without saying anything. Owen had to fill the silence. "You and Dara actually have something in common."

I couldn't imagine what I had in common with this skinny, catty girl.

"She's going to be in the Miss Hollis pageant too."

I should have known.

Maddie's eyes lit up like a crocodile's before it snatches its prey. "That's so cool. I was the first runner-up last year. It was so much fun."

She had to get it in there that she was first runner-up. But she hadn't won. "Yeah, well, I used to do pageants when I was little, so I thought it might be cool to try one again." I tried to sound bored with it all, like I didn't really care.

"You weren't just in a pageant." Owen did my bragging for me. "She won Little Miss Maine."

Maddie's confidence faltered for a second, but then she smiled. "It's great to have a different . . ." she paused. "You know, a new face." She threw her hair one last time. "We're on our way to the tarot card lady. You ought to get your fortune read, Owen."

"I'd rather not know," Owen said.

She wiggled her fingers at us as she strolled away with

her posse. Then the three girls leaned toward each other and giggled.

"So," Owen said, "if you want to go get lunch first, that's okay by me."

"Who was she?" I asked, still watching their backs.

"What? Maddie? Total bitch."

I knew there was more. "Why does she get to you?"

Owen shoved his hands into his pockets. "Ancient history."

It sounded like they'd had a breakup or something, but that didn't make sense. "Wait, did you date her?"

"Sort of."

"How do you sort of date someone?"

"It was tenth grade. She broke up with me to go out with some other guy. It wasn't anything."

The girls had disappeared into the crowd. "She's really pretty," I commented.

"Yeah, sure, in a superficial, manipulative, cruel sort of a way."

"What's her talent?" I asked.

"Singing. But she's not as good as you."

"Wonderful," I whispered. I'd be up onstage with Maddie, looking gargantuan next to her, while the whole town sat in the audience thinking I was delusional. "This is going to be humiliating."

"What are you talking about? Don't worry about Maddie. Seriously, she's a real bitch. Everyone thinks so."

"It's not just her. It's everybody. The way they look at me when they hear I'm in the pageant."

I had been stupid to agree to this, pathetic to want to win. And everyone who saw me knew it. Already they made me feel fat and ugly, and I hadn't even stepped onto the stage yet. "Do you think I need to lose weight?" I asked.

"Do you want to lose weight?"

I dropped down onto a stool. It wasn't so long ago that he had told me I was beautiful, no matter my weight. "You think I should, don't you?"

"Only if you want to."

"But what do you think?"

"You know I think you're gorgeous. But, I mean, it's healthier to be thinner. And as long as you don't go crazy with it, I think it could be okay. Because it would help you out in the long run, not because it would change the way you look." He was backing out of his compliments, hastily erasing everything good that he had said. "I mean, really, it doesn't matter to me how you look. But I guess if your weight meant that you were unhealthy, that would be a problem. I don't want you to die before you're thirty, like Mama Cass."

"Isn't she the one who choked on a sandwich?"

"Whatever. The point is, that's the only reason I can see that you should lose any weight. If it's because of what other people think, well, screw them. But if it's because of what you think, then do what makes you feel good."

It had made me feel good to think I had a friend who didn't care about my weight, someone who could really relate to what it was like to have people stereotype you. Now here he was, taking it all back.

"I don't think I can do this pageant," I said.

"Okay." He didn't even put up a fight. He knew. Maddie had come and forced him to face reality: this was a beauty pageant, and I had no chance.

I stood to go, biting my lip, trying not to cry. What the hell had I been thinking? It was stupid—just a stupid town pageant, but for whatever idiotic reason, I'd wanted to win it.

"I'm going to lunch," I told him.

"Are we good?"

"Sure," I said. "We're good." But I couldn't meet his eyes.

Chapter Thirty-six

I walked dazedly into the main rush of the fair. The air reeked of frying oil, with an undercurrent of hay and manure. My options were Italian sausage, french fries, hot dogs, or pizza. Nothing sounded appetizing. All of it would make my fingers and face greasy, make me feel uglier than I already did.

The sun and the overpowering smells were giving me nausea. I needed shade so I stepped into the nearest building—one of the showcase halls—and found myself surrounded by pigs of all sizes and colors. At the far end of the row, I saw the farmer we'd talked to that morning. I slipped deeper into the building. The pigs in the next row were tiny. Cute, even. One of them rolled onto its back like a puppy.

In the row after that, I found the biggest pig I had ever seen. He had a fan blowing on him, and occasionally he turned his head from side to side. He was like a Roman emperor holding court in the corrugated steel building. Someone tapped my arm. I looked down and there was a boy, maybe four years old, smiling up at me. Then he put his finger on his nose and pushed it back so it looked like a snout. "Piggies say oink, oink."

I backed away from him and rushed out the side door. It took a second for my eyes to adjust to the light, and then I saw a glass case containing a huge butter sculpture of a woman milking a cow. The sight of all that butter turned my stomach. I could hear cows mooing. It was surreal, and I felt dizzy. I spotted a bench toward the back of the pig building. Tucked out of the way, it seemed quieter than the rest of the fair, and I sat down.

Milo came from out of nowhere. "Hot day," he said, sitting down next to me. "You feeling okay?"

I'd been missing him, but he'd appeared at the wrong moment. "I'm fine," I snapped. I shouldn't have. He wasn't the one who'd compared me to an obese singer from the sixties. "Sorry."

"You look a little upset is all."

"Yeah, well, sometimes people suck," I said.

"That's true." He turned to face me; though why he would want to get a better look at my sweaty, fat face and frizzy hair was beyond me. I scratched my leg. A fly buzzed around us and landed on the back of the bench.

"Do you know who Mama Cass is?" I was fixated on the

comparison. It might have been easier if Owen had just called me fat.

"From the Mamas and the Papas?" He sang a few lines of "California Dreamin'" and then added, "She's the one that choked on a ham sandwich."

It was that detail—she was so gluttonous that she had died eating—that hurt the most.

"I'm quitting the pageant," I said.

"Why?" He wasn't quite sure how to react. "Wanna go for a walk?"

Yes. Maybe. I didn't know, but I stood up.

We walked through the main part of the fair, past the misting tent, past the giant slide kids rode down on old potato sacks, and on toward the rides. We walked down the midway, where hucksters heckled Milo to win me a stuffed monkey or turtle.

"It's all rigged," he told me. "Like in that one, they weight the bottles. It's almost impossible to win."

"Yeah?"

He walked slowly, and I had to adjust my pace to match his. I had grown used to keeping up with Owen. "I never understood why you'd want to do a pageant, but I wanted to hear you sing," he said. "Owen told me you were really good."

I looked down at the dusty ground. "Thanks." He was being so nice, I was afraid I would cry.

"Maybe some other time?"

"Sure," I croaked.

"Cool."

Then he asked, "Want to go in the haunted house? It's only three dollars. I'll pay for you." It seemed like he might be asking me on a date, but he spoke so casually, I wasn't sure.

As soon as Milo paid, the ride conductor ushered us into a small red cart. We hitched forward through a black curtain into a cool damp chamber. Though it was meant to be completely dark, light crept in through the spaces between the boards of the building. Definitely not spooky, but at least there was air-conditioning. The first scare loomed about thirty feet from the entrance, shaped like a body, draped in black. Just as we reached it, it spun to reveal a green, sagging face made out of Styrofoam. It was missing a chunk of its chin.

I raised my eyebrows at Milo, but he looked more annoyed than amused. "Were you expecting it to actually be scary?" I asked.

"It's supposed to be a haunted house."

The cart was too small for us; we were pressed together, the skin of our arms and legs touching. I wished I were smaller, that I didn't take up so much space. God, this was awful. I thought I had moved past this disgusting feeling.

The cart made a sharp turn to the right as we began to snake deeper into the building. How much weight, I wondered, did Owen think I should lose? Thirty pounds? Forty?

We cruised past a trio of skeletons poised around a large cauldron. They were completely out of proportion: the arms were too short, the torsos way too long. One was missing a hand, and its absence didn't seem to be a deliberate part of the effect. They started swaying and stomping their feet and cranking their heads up and down.

We were jerked around so the cart went in reverse, the motion snapping my head back. I rubbed my neck.

"Are you okay?" he asked.

"Tiny whiplash," I said. But I thought maybe he was asking more in general, so I asked, "Do you know anything about Maddie?"

Milo glanced at me. "So you met Cruella?"

We spun back around just as a giant CAUTION! sign appeared. Followed by NO! and ABANDON HOPE ALL YE WHO ENTER HERE.

"I always like my carnival rides with a little bit of Dante," I said. He smiled. We didn't get an inferno, though, or the nine circles of hell. Instead we passed through a graveyard with headstones like I.M. ROTTING and JUDGE DEAD. One green light flickered, on the verge of burning out.

"Is this for real?" Milo asked.

"It's kind of funny," I said.

"This has to be the lamest ride I've ever been on."

"It's not so bad."

Milo put his hand on the bar at the front of the car. "What happened with Maddie?" he asked.

"Nothing. It doesn't matter."

Milo looked at me, and then at the track ahead. "Suit yourself. But you shouldn't quit the pageant because of anything Maddie said."

"That's not it. It's just not my thing anymore."

He tapped his fingers on the bar in front of us, as if he

246

were playing the piano. "Mama Cass was a pretty awesome singer."

I didn't get to respond because the ride abruptly shimmied and stalled. I cast a glance over at Milo, but he didn't look concerned—he actually had a small grin. And dimples, I noticed. The creepy music got louder, and there was a sizzling and snapping sound. Flashes of light came every few seconds, but we couldn't yet see what was around the corner. We made one small final turn, and there in front of us was a chair with a neon sign that said JUST PUNISHMENT floating above it. Then the snapping, cracking sound started again, and the whole chair lit up. There was a body strapped into it that shook whenever the light came on, its eyes bugging out of its head.

"Oh my God," I said. "Is that an electric chair?"

"That's the most tasteless thing I've ever seen."

The ride chugged back outside to where we had boarded, and we climbed out of the cart before it cycled around.

"I can't believe we paid three dollars for this," he said.

"Actually, you paid six dollars. I didn't pay anything."

"Sorry I made you do that."

"No, it was good," I told him.

"You don't need to lie to me."

"I'm not lying," I protested. "Really, it wasn't terrible."

"Not terrible," he repeated. "Just what I was aiming for."

Chapter Thirty-seven

Milo hung out with us for the rest of the afternoon, and I was grateful for it. I didn't really feel like talking to Owen. After Milo left, Owen and I packed up in silence. We were on the road before either of us spoke.

"Rachel should be happy with how much we sold," he said.

"Mm-hmm."

"I think we made over four hundred dollars. I can count it all when we get home."

I turned on the indicator, which made a *click click click* sound that filled the truck.

"What did you think of the fair? Did you and Milo get to walk around much?" He tapped his foot relentlessly on the floor of the cab.

"A little." I realized that I was going ten miles over the speed limit, and eased off the gas. Slightly.

"Definitely go to the Hall of Innovation—it's all these people selling things you see on infomercials."

"Hmm," I replied. And then he finally gave up. We drove the rest of the way in silence, and I disappeared into my room as soon as we got home. I wanted to take a shower, but Owen beat me to it. Rachel had already fed the goats, so there were no chores to do.

She had left a postcard from Melissa on my bed. The front showed a picture of a wheel of cheese. On the back she wrote,

Oui oui, c'est le fromage! You make it, and I eat it.
C'est magnifique!

I didn't see anything too *magnifique* about Melissa getting to eat *fromage* in Belgium. Her tone was so carefree—like she was preoccupied and happy and not really thinking about me. I tossed the postcard back on my bed. I knew that if I read any more, I would get angry at Melissa, and she hadn't done anything wrong.

At dinner Rachel was eager to hear how the day had gone.

"Fine," Owen said.

"Fine," I agreed.

She looked from one of us to the other.

"Were people interested in the cheese?" she asked, a little anxious.

"You mean did we sell a lot?" Owen replied. He took a huge bite of his burrito.

Why was he being such a jerk? "We sold a lot," I answered, cutting my own burrito into small pieces.

"Good." Rachel relaxed. "Well, I have exciting news!" She looked around the table, waiting until we all seemed sufficiently intrigued. "We've got an order from upstate New York." She paused dramatically. "The Moosewood Restaurant. Can you believe it? I've got all those cookbooks. Our cheese is going to be featured on the menu! They're calling Jezebel a 'collective of like-minded men and women.' I thought you would like that, Belinda."

Belinda smiled.

"I hope they send us some of the recipes. Maybe they'd let us put them in with the cheese, in the packaging."

Belinda leaned forward and slapped the table, her eyes bright.

"I know!" Rachel said. "We were already planning on buying a dozen more goats, but we might have to do more."

"Where are you going to put them all?" Owen asked.

"We've got eighty acres," Rachel replied.

Sascha leaned back from the table, considering. "What if we got a vacuum packager? We'd have a longer sell-by date, and I think we'd get more buyers."

"I don't know. Maybe. We have a lot to think about."

I pushed my half-full plate away from me. "I'm not feeling so well," I said. "I think I might go up to bed."

Rachel looked concerned, but no one argued with me. I pushed my chair back, and carried my plate into the kitchen.

Upstairs, I picked up the postcard again.

In Belgium, they give a three-kiss greeting, not two. We will have to remember that when we come back here—which we will do! I want to show you all around. I want to introduce you to my friends, and take you to the cafés, and parler français avec vous. It hardly seems real that you aren't here.

How much could she really miss me? She was gallivanting around with her new friends in Belgium, and I was . . . what? What was I doing here? I had been feeling good about things. Owen had trashed it in a single conversation. Of course Maddie and the walking moms hadn't helped. Or the oink-oink boy.

Being fat sucked. I had to do most of my shopping online—a lot of stores didn't stock my size. The chairs at school were always too tight, pressing my stomach up against the built-in desktops. People I had just met told me about diets that had worked wonders for their sisters, cousins, aunts. Those were the day-to-day things, and I could deal with them. Or so I had thought—but here I was almost in tears again because some skinny girl was going to get something I wanted, almost by default. Whenever I went for anything, people thought I was crazy, or sad, or acting in poor taste.

I turned off the light and slid under the sheet. I lay there for hours, watching the sky grow dark. The half-full moon cast a shaft of pale light across the bed. It was a beautiful, perfect night, but that just made me feel even sadder.

*　*　*

A moment later, it seemed, I woke up to find Owen lying next to me, his weight pulling the sheet tight against my arm. "I want to tell you about Maddie," he said.

"Owen," I mumbled.

"Here's what happened. She broke up with me and started dating Andy Temple. A senior. A gorgeous senior on the lacrosse team with amazing green eyes."

He rolled over onto his side. My eyes began to adjust to the dark, and I could see his face in the bluish tones of the twilight room. He looked haggard.

"I tried to pretend I wasn't gay for a long time. I knew I was, and I was coming to terms with it, but I didn't want anyone else to know. I don't know why I dated Maddie. She was pretty and popular, and she really liked me—that felt good." He rubbed his nose. "But I started hanging out with Andy Temple. I mean, he had always been there, but it's like all of a sudden he was *there*. I couldn't handle it. It was so intense, I couldn't believe he didn't feel the same way. It had to come from somewhere, right?"

I nodded.

"So I told Maddie. I told her how I felt about him, and how sorry I was. I thought she would understand. I mean, I didn't love her, but I liked her, and I thought we were friends."

My stomach tightened—I could see the trap he'd laid for himself.

"She went after him. There was a part of me that felt sorry for her. I didn't think she had a chance. But then one day I came into school, and she was hanging all over him. She smiled at me and then kissed him. Like, frenched him."

"I'm sorry," I whispered.

He shook his head. "It's weird, though, 'cause that moment made me decide to come out. It was like, 'Well, screw this.' I didn't make a big announcement or anything—I told a few people, and it took maybe two seconds for it to get around. It was rough at first. People would stop talking as soon as I came up. Some guys would fake-accidentally bump into me in the hallways, a little too hard. The principal had been right down the hall once when it happened, and he totally pretended not to see it. And suddenly my friends just weren't there. I'd sit with them at lunch, and we'd talk, but no one called me.

"No one threatened me or called me names—not to my face, anyway. Some kid wrote some crap on MySpace about how I didn't need to shove it in everyone's face that I was a fag; and it's not like anyone stood up for me, but it could have been a lot worse, I guess. Everyone at Hollis High likes to *think* they're all liberal and open-minded. As long as I wasn't flamboyant, and didn't stare at guys' dicks in the locker room, or actually make a play for anyone, I was fine. It was a novelty. I made people feel better about themselves—'See, I'm not biased. I like Owen, and he's gay.' But they wouldn't actually let me be me."

"I'm sorry," I said.

"Not your fault. Anyway, Maddie didn't have it so easy either. I think I really hurt her when we broke up. She didn't get it and thought she just wasn't attractive enough, or something."

I was having a hard time feeling sorry for her. He put his head down on one of my pillows. His face was inches from mine. I loved the way he smelled. I loved the warmth of his body. He shifted his body again, moving closer to me.

"She's beautiful, but that doesn't mean she'd beat you. I'm sorry if I made it seem like I thought she would beat you."

I checked the clock: 3:27 a.m. Had he been up all this time, wondering what to say to me?

"I'm sorry if I made you feel bad today."

He meant it, I could tell.

"It's just that, you asked . . ."

I *had* asked him what he thought about my weight, and he had told me. It wasn't his fault that it wasn't what I wanted to hear. It wasn't my fault either, but what was I supposed to do? Only be friends with people who denied I was overweight?

"Did you ever tell him?" I asked.

Owen took my hand in his. "No. I never told Andy Temple."

I curled my body toward his, and rested my head on his shoulder. He combed my hair with his fingers until we both fell asleep.

Chapter Thirty-eight

When my alarm clock went off in the morning, Owen was still asleep beside me. I climbed out of bed, trying not to wake him, and went into the bathroom to wash my face. When I went back to my room to get dressed, he was gone. I met him in the kitchen, and we went out to feed and milk the goats.

As we were hooking up the first round, I accidentally bumped into him and spilled soapy water onto his legs and sneakers. Normally he would have chided, "Cohen, watch it!" But that morning, he just said, "Excuse me."

"Sorry."

"No worries," he replied.

While we waited for the milker to finish, he asked, "You still want to work at the fair today?"

Networking wasn't important now that I wasn't in the pageant, but that didn't mean we had to stop, as long as Rachel was okay with it. "Sure," I told him.

"Good."

He didn't speak again until we were snapping in the second group. Out of nowhere, he said, "My brother would be so jealous if he knew I spent the night in your bed."

Immediately my face got hot. "What are you talking about?"

I gave him a quick glance, but avoided his eyes—he'd see right through me. His old, sly grin was back. "I'm not stupid, you know. I see what's going on."

"Whatever. You see what you want to see." I walked over to the nearest goat and pretended to adjust its feed bucket.

"Denial is the first stage," he remarked.

"Like I'm addicted to your brother."

"That's a sexy way to put it."

I couldn't help but smile. "Let's not fight again," I said.

"Deal." He reached out his hand, and we shook on it.

When I got out of the shower after an uneventful day at the fair, I went into the kitchen to help Rachel make dinner. "Hey," she said as I walked in. "Cut me some beets?"

"Sure. Beet salad?" She had this salad that she made with roasted beets and almonds over spinach, sprinkled with, of course, goat cheese.

"You got it," she replied. I dug the beets out of the refrigerator and brought them to the sink, where I ran them under cool water to wash off the dirt.

"Another good day?" she asked.

"Yeah, but not as busy as yesterday," I told her. The crowd had been steady but thinner.

"First day is always a big one."

I started to peel the beets, letting the skin fall into the white ceramic sink. "Rachel?"

"Yeah?" She looked up from the tuna steak on which she was spreading an herb rub.

"What do you know about Mama Cass?" Owen and I had goofed around all day at the fair, and it was like normal. But then all of a sudden I'd get this image of a big woman in a muumuu, and it would bring me back down. I could not get the comparison out of my head.

"She was the singer for the Mamas and the Papas."

I chose one of our sharpest knives, one that was probably a little too big for the job. I liked it, though, because it made a satisfying noise when it hit the cutting board.

"Yeah, I know. Anything else?"

"Her real last name was Cohen."

Perfect. Not only was I fat like her; we might also be related. As I sliced the beets, they let out a purple-red juice that soaked into the wooden board.

"Also, she didn't really choke on a sandwich." Rachel flipped the steak over. "She died of a heart attack."

"Really?" That was terrible. I could understand how a rumor like that would take hold, though. It was such a juicy cautionary tale: the fat woman dying from eating.

"Uh-huh. Here she was this great singer, and someone started this rumor about her. It's worse than the Elvis dying on the toilet one, I think."

How had the rumor started? Who would do such a cruel thing?

"I read an article about her once," Rachel went on. "She had been in a different group with one of the guys, but when she wanted to join the Mamas and the Papas, there was already a woman in the group, Michelle Phillips. They told her her voice didn't blend well with Michelle's, but probably it was really because of her weight."

Blown off because she was too fat. In the sixties. Weren't they supposed to be all free love and tolerance back then? I wrapped the sliced beets in tinfoil and threw them in the oven. Rachel had already preheated it, which was good since that was the type of thing I always forgot to do. "Forty minutes, right?"

"Right."

With my pink-tipped fingers, I set the egg timer, leaving a tiny smudge.

"Anyway," Rachel continued, "even though they wouldn't let her join, she followed them around while they toured, and the story goes that they were on some island somewhere, and she got hit in the head by a copper pipe, and that magically changed her voice, so they let her be in the group after all. I think Cass made up that story because it was easier than the truth."

"That doesn't make any sense. At least she could have made up a believable story."

"It was the sixties. There were a lot of drugs."

I got out a small cast-iron pan that had to weigh at least five pounds. I added a little bit of oil and then poured in

258

some sliced almonds. I stirred them with a wooden spoon as they toasted.

Belinda walked into the kitchen, her strides small but strong. I stepped out of her way as she came up to the stove. With knobby fingers, she turned on a burner for the kettle, then took her teacup and saucer from the cabinet.

"Dara says the fair sales are going well," Rachel reported to her. "With the Moosewood sale, this is going to be a great quarter."

I didn't know anything about the finances of the farm. Were we on the edge? Did we do all right? Rachel never talked about it, so I assumed it was okay. Farming, though, seemed like the kind of business that could turn at any moment. Even though math was not my strongest subject, I still did pretty well with it, and I wondered if the finance end of things was something I could have helped out with. But the summer was quickly coming to an end, and I'd be going back to Portland. The idea brought a vague feeling of dread.

Belinda took out an Earl Grey teabag before she acknowledged Rachel. She nodded toward me, and then she nodded upstairs.

"Well, yes, of course. Once Owen's at school, we can think about hiring a farmhand."

The kettle whistled, and Belinda turned the heat down. She poured the water over the tea, then shuffled out of the kitchen.

I hurried back to the stove, hoping the almonds hadn't burned. "How do you understand her?" I asked.

"I've known her a long time," Rachel said.

"But still."

"People are predictable, Dara. Once you get to know someone, it's easy to know what they want."

I spooned the almonds into a small dish, then dumped the oil into a bowl to make the dressing. "When did she stop talking?"

"It wasn't all at once. It's just that over time, she spoke less and less. Once the writing really took over, that's when she stopped altogether."

"Don't you worry about her?"

"Why?"

"It's not normal."

Rachel opened the oven and slid the baking tray in. "What's normal, Dara?"

She probably meant it on a deeper level, but all I had meant was "typical." "Healthy," I told her.

Rachel started to smile, but then she shook her head. "Is anyone really completely healthy?" she asked.

"That's not very comforting." I opened the cabinet to find the vinegar.

"Really?" she asked. "I feel much better knowing I'm not the only one who has no clue."

No clue. Just like me—no clue where I was meant to be, no clue what I was going to do at the end of the summer, let alone five years from now.

What had been Mom's hope for Rachel? Certainly not this. I wanted to ask her if Mom had controlled all their conversations in the same way, but at the same time I wasn't willing to ruin the mood. I whisked the salad dressing together and tossed it with the spinach in a large bowl. Then I got the beets out of the oven and set them on a cooling rack. "This is all set to go," I said.

"Great." Rachel gave me an appreciative smile, and I think if I had been five years younger, she would have reached out and tousled my hair. I felt an ache then. This is what I had lost. I could have had this love, this friendship all along. I had been up and down so much the past few days, and feared I might start crying again, so I excused myself. I went outside and sat on the old swing next to the picnic table, waiting for dinner, trying to make the ache go away.

Chapter Thirty-nine

"We should see the fair at night," Owen announced as we were washing the dishes. "You really haven't experienced rural life without it." He turned to Rachel. "Want to come?"

"I'm about fifteen years too old for that scene," she replied.

Owen called Milo's cell, and we arranged to pick him up at the end of his street at 8:30. Which gave me little time to change. I wasn't really sure what constituted a good fair-going outfit. I'd probably want a sweater, in case it got cold, so I picked out a cotton zip-up. Then I took out a pair of nice dark-wash jeans—ones I never wore for work—that were starting to fit a little loosely. I pulled out a couple of T-shirts, a pretty one with silkscreened birds and an old New Kids on the Block concert shirt. Milo might think that was funny. Or lame. In the end, I decided you could never go wrong with simple slimming black, and put on a V-neck T-shirt.

"Are you coming?" Owen called from downstairs.

"Be right down!" I did a quick face check, but not a full-body evaluation. I didn't have time to change if I didn't like the whole picture.

Owen fiddled with the radio until he found the hip-hop station. He turned the volume way up, and we rolled the windows down.

"I could hear you guys from a mile away," Milo said when he got in.

"What?" Owen called back. He slapped his hand against the outside of the car and bobbed his head. I looked at Milo in the rearview mirror and grinned.

We stepped through the main gates into a transformed world. Flashing neon blotted out the light from the moon and stars, and cast a multicolored glow on our skin.

The junk food stands shone with flashing lights, bright and aggressive. The giant swirling soft-serve cone taunted me. *You know you want me,* it seemed to say. The pizza, french fries, onion rings—all of them filled me with guilt. It was so stupid. At Jezebel I had started to get comfortable with food; now here I was obsessing about it. Quitting the pageant hadn't made me feel any less ugly.

"It's just sugar," Milo argued. "Spun sugar." He held out his bag of blue cotton candy to me.

"Leave her alone," Owen said. "She's doing a great job. Look at the way her jeans are hanging off her." He said it like

I had agreed with him that I needed to lose weight, like I was trying.

"I only like the pink," I told Milo.

"Suit yourself." I liked the way they both said that. So little else about them was similar. I imagined life at their house back when Owen still lived there, the whole family shrugging and saying, "Suit yourself."

Owen led us to the carnival midway. The Ferris wheel loomed above. "A few years ago, some guy from Holyoke did a swan dive off that," he mused.

"Oh my God," I said. "Why?"

He shrugged. "Who knows? I know it's twisted, but I would have loved to have filmed it. Just that moment when the body was in the air—it could have been a beautiful image."

"In a movie, maybe," Milo said. "Not in real life."

"True," Owen conceded. He lifted his camera and did a pan of the midway. "Filler," he explained. A new plan for my autobiography was not yet clear, but Owen was still collecting film. He had officially taken over the project—barely even keeping me informed. I had stopped caring, and just let him get his kicks from it.

"Owen!" someone called out. We turned and saw a boy and two girls pushing toward us through the crowd. "Owen Moon, how have you been, man? You haven't been to any of the parties."

"I've been busy, Kyle."

"Sure you have," Kyle replied sarcastically.

One of the girls stared at me. I was pretty sure she was

high. Her red, glassy eyes gave her away, along with the way you could see each thought move across her face as she processed it. "Hey," she said. "Martha Washington."

"That's me."

"You're the girl that's doing Miss Hollis," she went on. "Martha Washington."

Was the town so small that word had already gotten around? "It's Dara, actually, and I'm not doing it," I told her.

"Shit," the girl sighed. "Someone's gonna take on Maddie Munson. That's gonna be awesome," she said as if she hadn't heard me say I wasn't doing it. Or was just too baked for it to register. She rubbed her eyes. "You know, I would've entered, but I don't have any talent."

"You've got talent, Shelly," Kyle said. He moved his hand back and forth in front of his mouth while pushing his tongue into his cheek. Shelly giggled. Next to me, Milo stiffened at the crassness of it.

"Seriously, it's time that bitch went down," the other girl said. She made a kind of punching motion toward Shelly. "You can totally take her. That skinny bitch don't stand a chance."

I kicked my toe into the dirt. "Yeah, well, someone else will have to do it," I said. "I'm out." They seemed to need to hear this a second time before it would sink in.

The girls shook their heads. "Still," Shelly said, "it'd be pretty cool if you beat her." It's like they had confused the pageant with a brawl.

"We were on our way to the Crystal Palace," Owen told them. News to me, but I was happy for the excuse to go.

"Cool," Kyle said. "Seriously, man, you need to show up at our killer parties—everyone's there, our whole class. I'll text you next time, all right?"

"All right," Owen said. We backed away from them into the throng.

"Friend of yours?" I asked.

"Not exactly," Owen answered.

Owen knew precisely where he was headed, and walked with more purpose than the average citizen. Milo and I had to trot to keep up.

The Crystal Palace was a squat, square building with a little turret slapped on the center of the roof.

"It's a maze," Owen explained. "Like a labyrinth. Let's race."

The two boys disappeared as soon as we stepped inside. Panels of clear plastic and mirrors created pathways and, more often, dead ends. I could hear voices drifting around, calling out names, but it was impossible to tell where they were coming from.

A few steps into the maze, I caught my startled reflection in a mirror, then smacked into a plastic pane. "Damn it," I whispered. I pivoted and went back the way I came. I was already lost. A child squeezed past me, giggling, followed by a second. I pressed my body against a mirror to let them pass.

It was way too hot in the Crystal Palace. I brushed my hair out of my face and started down another path. This one forked, and I went left and found myself at another dead end. I turned and went back to the fork and chose the right side this time. The long, narrow passage made a sharp right, almost doubling back. I could still hear voices, but I couldn't see any other people.

I eventually came into a small octagonal room of mirrors: the heart of the Crystal Palace. In the warped mirrors, my body was reflected back at me eight different ways. Thin me. Fat me. Short, wavy, tall me. I drew my breath in and looked at each version. I knew they were supposed to be twisted and funny, but they all just looked ugly.

My gaze fixed on a short squat version. My body was almost round, as wide as it was tall. I looked like a fantasy-movie dwarf, a troll. Small children would run away in fear. What the hell had I been thinking? How had I let Owen convince me to enter a beauty pageant? A *beauty* pageant. I could be the most talented, well-spoken girl in America, and still it would come down to my looks. My weight disqualified me before the contest even began. It was an exercise in self abuse. I had signed up to be ridiculed. The smartest thing I had ever done in my life was to quit Miss Hollis.

But I wanted it. I still wanted it, just like Mama Cass had wanted to be in the Mamas and the Papas. Unlike her, though, I had gotten the hint and backed down. She was crazy enough to take the scorn, and even make up some story about a pipe hitting her on the head, so she could go out there and perform.

I looked down at my body, my actual body, not the reflections. I felt trapped by it. What else had I had to give up? School dances, because no one asked me. Dating, for the same reason—and I wasn't going to risk certain rejection by asking. When I'd seen myself in the mirror at dance class, I'd seen how far my body was from the ideal dancer's body—lithe, lean—and gave up performing altogether. I'd decided I just wasn't meant to be onstage. I had let these things go as though they didn't matter to me, and dug into schoolwork because I was good at that. And the thing was, I'd thought these were the right, practical decisions at the time—that this was what people thought I should do—but now I realized I could have pushed back, just like Mama Cass had.

Milo appeared in the opening to the chamber. I saw his blurry reflection before I saw him. I wiped my eyes. "There you are," he said. "We've been waiting outside for like ten minutes." He looked at my face. "Are you okay? It's just a maze. It's not like you're going to be stuck in here forever."

"I know. I was just taking a breather." I smiled.

He stepped into the octagon. Behind him, I saw another reflection of me: the real me. There was one normal mirror, hanging crookedly, as if it had been put up to replace one that had broken—it was like the gift of the center—and it showed *me*, pink skinned from the heat, my eye makeup a little smudged. I looked at Milo. He smiled awkwardly and said, "It's quiet here."

I nodded and looked past Milo at my reflection—really looked at it. There I was: strong, healthy, and smart. Pretty. I had forgotten that.

If Mama Cass were stuck in the middle of the Crystal Palace with some cute boy, she wouldn't have just stood there. She would have taken a chance. This time, I wasn't going to give up the thing I wanted. I took three steps toward him, put my hands on his shoulders, and kissed him. A longer kiss than our first. He put his hands on my hips and pulled me against him. I pressed my tongue between his lips. He seemed surprised at first, then gingerly touched his tongue to mine. A shiver coursed through me.

When I stepped back, he looked at me intently. "What was that for?" he whispered. It was like he was echoing me in a flirtatious, sexy way.

As he'd done when he biked away from me, I just shrugged.

Milo finally broke his gaze, ending the moment. "Well, come on. Owen wants to go on the Tilt-a-Whirl."

I followed him out of the maze into the cool night air.

"Jesus, Dara, some kids went through there three times before you got out of there once," Owen said.

"Leave her alone," Milo told him.

"I found the center."

"Good for you. Unfortunately, the goal is to find the end."

"Not always," I said.

Owen turned from Milo to me and then back again. "Whatever. The Tilt-a-Whirl is this way."

Chapter Forty

I woke up on Thursday morning exhausted. We'd stayed at the fair until it shut down at midnight.

After Owen and I fed and milked, I drove him to the fairgrounds and helped him set up before leaving for my appointment. It was a beautiful day—cooler than the previous one—with a bright blue sky filled with puffy clouds. I left my windows open and sang along with pop songs on the radio as I drove to Dr. Eddington's office.

I got there early, but knocked anyway. I still couldn't bring myself to just walk inside her home. A few moments later, she opened the door. "Come on in, Dara. It's nice to see you early."

I smiled. I didn't dislike Dr. Eddington, and there was really nothing wrong with just mindlessly chatting with someone for an hour, even if her insights were less than inspired.

She took her yellow legal pad from her desk and sat down across from me. "So how are you doing today?" Before I could answer, she hopped back out of her chair. "I almost forgot." She rushed to her desk and picked up a folded newspaper, which she placed on the side table next to me. A quarter-page ad proclaimed: CELEBRATE THE END OF THE FAIR WITH THE MISS HOLLIS PAGEANT. AUGUST 14 AT 8:30 P.M. ON THE MAIN STAGE. Below the text were small pictures of each of the ten contestants.

"FYI—this is the type of thing my patients normally tell me about."

My picture made me cringe. Owen must have taken it, but when? He caught me laughing with my mouth wide open. Maddie's picture was a professional head shot. Her head was tilted, and there was a little glint from her lip gloss.

"I would have told you, but I'm not doing it anymore," I said. Of course, I could have told her weeks ago. "It was Owen's idea. For my autobiography project, but it wasn't working for me."

Dr. Eddington chewed on the end of her pencil. "You don't have to talk about it if you don't want to."

"There was something else I wanted to tell you about, actually," I said.

So I told her about getting stuck in the middle of the Crystal Palace and realizing what I wanted, and kissing Milo.

"Rewind," she said, standing up. "You kissed Milo because you were tired of not doing things you wanted to do because of your weight. And another thing you don't do anymore is perform. Right?"

"Right," I said slowly, sensing a trap.

"So why not be in the pageant? It's like kissing Milo."

"Yeah, well—" I started to protest, to explain why doing a pageant was nothing like kissing Milo. "Owen compared me to Mama Cass."

"Ouch," she replied.

"And this girl"—I pointed to Maddie's picture—"made me feel like the ugliest person ever to walk the face of the earth."

Dr. Eddington peered at the ad. "She looks like your classic Queen Bee." Maddie was slender and graceful, and every single strand of her hair was perfect—whereas I looked like I was exploding with laughter and girth. "You know," Dr. Eddington said, "I really love Mama Cass. Her version of 'Dream a Little Dream' is gorgeous." She looked off into space for a moment, seeming to let the song play in her head. "She was kind of a wild lady. I think she even sang a cover of that 'Wild Women Don't Get the Blues' song. She didn't take any doo-doo from anybody—at least, she never let it show that people had gotten to her."

This was a pretty big diversion, even for her.

"Owen may have made the comparison without thinking, but you don't have to take it in a bad way. In terms of force of will, she's not a bad person to emulate."

"But that's not the way he meant it."

"So what? Who's in charge, you or him? What do you know about Mama Cass?"

"She was a singer. She was big. And evidently, she was strong-willed."

"Well, there you go, two out of three ain't bad."

Chapter Forty-one

When my appointment was over, I should have gone back to the fair. But after the way Dr. Eddington talked about Mama Cass, I knew I had to hear the woman sing. I pulled my car into the parking lot at Pullman's Grocers, walked to the pay phone, and flipped through the yellow pages. There was only one music store listed in Hollis: Stan's Spins on Main Street.

I got back into my car and drove downtown, parked on Main Street in front of the Agway, and started walking up the block. And then I saw it: a glass door with a gold record painted on it. Bells jingled when I walked in.

The place was packed with crates of albums, only narrow paths cut between them. It smelled musty, like maybe no one had gone in or out in decades. Nina Simone crackled from a stereo.

"Hey there, sweetheart."

I looked up. In general, I'm against strange men calling me "sweetheart." This man, though, looked like he'd stepped out of some alternate universe, maybe one where calling girls "sweetheart" was okay. I assumed he was Stan. He had those thick-rimmed glasses that were popular in the fifties, boxy and black. His gray hair swirled up and fell in a slick curve across his forehead. He wore a floral button-down shirt that really should have had one or two more buttons done.

"Can I help you find something?"

"Mama Cass," was all I managed to say.

He nodded. "Cass Elliot. There was a fine lady. A fine lady." He said it like he knew her.

"She didn't choke on a sandwich," I told him.

"No, she didn't." He shook his head and smiled. "Come on over here."

I followed him toward the front corner of the store. "The voice on her," he said. "Like crystal."

"I've never heard her."

Stan stopped short and eyed me. "Well, then why do you want to buy her album?"

I rubbed my calf with my toe. "She's been coming up a lot lately."

The answer seemed to satisfy him. He took a few more steps and then leaned over a crate. The records were alphabetized by artist, though the crates also seemed to be color-coded, perhaps by genre. He pulled one out, and I expected him to hand it to me so I could go up and pay. Instead, he walked behind the counter to the stereo. He lifted the needle, cutting off Nina in the middle of "I Put a Spell on You," and replaced her with Mama Cass. "She hated being called Mama Cass, you know. She wanted to be known as Cass Elliot."

I could understand that. Mama was old. Mama was fat.

I thought she would sound like a hippie folksinger—pretty, a little raspy—but when she started singing, her voice blew me away. It was rich and bold, sultry like a lounge singer's.

I picked up the album cover to look at her. She held her shirt closed at the collar, and her feathered hair blew away from her face. Her eyes were deep brown and soulful, with long, thick lashes.

"She was usually a lot more flamboyant," Stan said. "You know, bright colors, big prints."

"Dream a Little Dream of Me" ended and the next song began; Stan reached for the needle. "Wait," I said. It started with a slow guitar and soft drumbeat. Then Cass's pure voice rose up through the accompaniment.

> *Nobody can tell ya*
> *There's only one song worth singing*
> *They may try and sell ya*
> *'Cause it hangs them up*
> *To see someone like you*

The tempo picked up and swung into the chorus. I felt like she was speaking directly to me, telling me to be myself and be proud of it.

275

When it was done, I said, "Play it again."

Stan grinned at me, lifted the needle, and started the song over again. I listened harder to the lyrics this time. The second verse caught me:

> *You're gonna be knowing*
> *The loneliest kind of lonely*
> *It may be rough goin'*
> *Just to do your thing's*
> *The hardest thing to do*

This was it. This was my song. "It's perfect," I said as it faded out. I wanted to sing that song. I wanted to perform it. I could picture myself standing on the open-air stage, microphone in hand. My voice would have soared and people would have seen me—they would have seen me the way Milo saw me. I pushed that thought away, the Milo thought. Instead I concentrated on her voice.

"Seems we've got a hooked one," Stan said.

"I was supposed to be in the Miss Hollis pageant," I answered, as if this explained it all.

"The Miss Hollis pageant, huh?" He considered the idea for a moment. "Cass would have liked that. Hold on, then, we'll have to get you the sheet music."

"But I'm not going to be in the pageant after all."

He didn't ask me why, thankfully. "Well, you ought to have it just the same." He emerged from behind the counter and went through a door to the left of it. He shut the door behind him, but I caught a glimpse of a room crammed with file cabinets.

276

Cass sang on, filling the dark store with her voice. How could the one thing people knew about her be that she had choked on a sandwich? And that wasn't even true. Here she was with this gorgeous voice, singing songs that cut right through you, and all anybody cared about was some stupid ham sandwich.

"There was a rumor she was carrying John Lennon's baby when she died," Stan said. I hadn't seen him come back.

"Do you believe it?"

"Who knows? Why not, right?" He stopped the record, slipped it back in its sleeve, and then put the record and the sheet music in a bag. "How much?" I asked.

"Forget about it."

"I can pay you."

He laughed. "I'm sure you can."

"So how much?"

"I told you, Cass would have liked this. When's that pageant? Week from Friday, right?"

"I'm sorry, but I already dropped out," I told him again.

"Just in case."

"You don't even know if I can sing."

"You can sing," Stan said.

"How—"

"I just know."

"Thank you," I said.

"Don't mention it."

I backed up, then turned for the door, feeling strangely giddy. Stan dropped on a Bob Dylan record, and the bells jingled as I walked out.

Chapter Forty-two

I couldn't wait to get back to the fair. As I drove, I thought about what Dr. Eddington had said about choosing how to interpret the comparison. Could I really do that? Being like Cass wasn't a bad thing, not when I thought about her voice and her strength. The sad thing was, she had made all this headway for big women, but then the revolution kind of ended. There hadn't been many more overweight pop stars, not like her, and her legacy was overshadowed by the stupid ham sandwich rumor.

Stan's words played in my head: *Cass would like that.* I knew what I had to do—what I wanted to do.

I brought the album with me to the cheese stand and placed it down on the counter. "I'll do it," I announced.

"I'll do the pageant, but I'm singing Mama Cass."

Owen looked a little embarrassed when I said her name. But then he grinned. "Cool," he said. "We've got a lot of work to do."

We stopped at Milo's house on the way home. Owen waited in the driveway while I went up to the door and rang the bell, my heart ricocheting in my chest. *Let Milo answer. Let Milo answer.*

He didn't. A petite, beautiful woman opened the door. "Hello?" she asked, confused.

I was wearing my Jezebel polo, so she must have known I had a connection to Owen. "I'm a friend of Milo's," I informed her. "Is he around?"

Her face softened. "A friend of Milo's?"

"Yes," I said. "I'm Dara." I held out my hand and she shook it. Her grip barely registered, and her hands were cold. She was the white half of the equation, and had given both sons her long eyelashes. Owen's angular cheeks came from her, and Milo had the same full lips.

She turned to call into the house, and I stole a quick glance at Owen. He was staring down at his lap. Mrs. Moon must have been able to see him, but her face hadn't shown it.

She turned back to me and gestured for me to come into the foyer. "Do you work at the farm?" she asked.

"Yes." I decided not to mention that I was Rachel's sister, figuring Rachel wasn't too high on Mrs. Moon's list of favorite people.

She ran the tips of her fingers through her hair, and I

fidgeted with my watch until Milo padded downstairs in his socks. "Oh, hey," he said.

"Hi," I replied.

"Mom, this is my friend Dara."

"So I've heard." She picked a lint ball from his T-shirt.

"Are you busy?" I asked Milo. "Can you come over?"

His mother stood between us like a wall.

"Sure," he answered, not looking at her. He bent over and picked up a pair of sneakers from a neat line of footwear by the door. No one said anything as he struggled to shove his feet into them without untying the laces. When he stood, Mrs. Moon said, "Remember what we talked about? Tell Owen, okay?"

Milo paused, but then he said, "Sure." He edged past her onto the front steps, and I followed him out.

"Be home by ten," she called after him.

"Bye, Mom," he replied without turning around.

"What does she want you to tell Owen?" I asked as we walked toward my car.

"That they're praying for him," he said. "And that they sent in the first payment for Williams."

It was so childish, I wanted to run back, fling the front door open, and tell her to stop hating Owen, and stop putting Milo in the middle. But I said, "How magnanimous of them."

"I guess." He shrugged.

"Dara's back in the pageant," Owen said as I pulled out of the driveway. "We need to go rehearse."

"You're going to sing?" Milo asked me. I nodded. "Cool," he said.

Back at the farm, we found Rachel in the barn and invited her to come listen. A few minutes later, she joined us in the parlor and flopped sideways into a wingback chair, her legs draped over the arm. I put the album on the record player so everyone could hear it.

"You have got to be kidding me," Owen said when the song ended. "That's so hokey."

"I love it," I told him.

He sighed loudly.

"I'm serious," I said. "This is the song I want to sing, and I'm singing it. It fits. It's about being yourself."

"It's about sixties free-love BS."

"I think it's pretty," Rachel chimed in. Owen rolled his eyes at her.

"It's nonnegotiable," I told him, and handed Milo the sheet music.

"This won't sound like the recording," he said. Obviously. The album version had a guitar and drums. There was even a horn section.

"I have a tambourine," Rachel offered.

"She cannot play the tambourine," Owen said. "We need to wow them, not make them feel like they're at a love-in."

"You don't even know what a love-in is," she told him.

Belinda walked into the room with her small, even steps, and sat down on the edge of the couch. Rachel sat up correctly in the chair.

Milo started to mess around on the piano, playing the song at different tempos. I sat down on the bench next to him. His long fingers hesitated over the keys, and then he

281

started playing again. It was amazing to watch his hands moving so skillfully. In other contexts, he never seemed completely comfortable in his body. At the piano, he was at ease and confident. "I don't know, Dara," he said. "This could be hard on just the piano."

"See?" Owen challenged. "May I please put in a plug for 'I Will Survive.'"

"This is my autobiography project. And this is my song."

"You have to do it your own way. I mean, that's the title, right? 'Make Your Own Kind of Music?' I think you have to find a way to make it your own," Rachel suggested.

Belinda stood up and put one hand on the piano. Then Sascha walked in with his dirty old Red Sox cap pulled tight on his head. When he saw Belinda, he pulled it off. "I thought I heard the piano," he said, nodding toward Milo. "What's going on?"

"Dara's back in the pageant," Owen told him.

"Good." He paused. "So, is this going to delay dinner?"

Rachel smiled. "Well, they don't want my tambourine—a noble instrument, I might add—so I'm not sure what else I can offer. I guess I can start cooking." She stood up, and they left the room. Belinda stayed with us.

"What if you slow it down a little and do more of a jazzy swing to it," I asked. "Almost like burlesque."

Milo tried to do what I asked, but it sounded more seedy than sexy. Belinda shook her head. She moved closer to the piano bench, pausing there for a moment until Milo and I stood up.

She tapped her foot on one of the pedals, setting the beat, and then began to play. She was rusty, and her knobbed, arthritic fingers often didn't reach the keys she meant, but the tempo and syncopation were almost what I had tried to describe. "Exactly," I said.

She stopped playing, and Milo sat down on the bench next to her. She nodded in approval as he played. When he got through the first verse and chorus, I told him to start over so I could sing my part.

Owen was smiling by the time I started on the second verse. "Okay," he said when we were done. "Okay, this can work."

Milo kept playing, experimenting with different chords and embellishments. Belinda turned around to face me, grinning, and I could see her younger self: the woman from the pictures. Her eyes blazed, and the hair around her face was escaping from her bun. I felt like I was giving her something—something back to the farm, and I think she was thanking me.

Chapter Forty-three

I didn't even bother to get in bed. I knew I wouldn't be able to fall asleep, I was so keyed up about rehearsing and being back in the pageant. My chances of victory, I knew, were slim, but that didn't matter as much to me now. I still wanted to win and knew I'd feel humiliated when I didn't. But it was worse to give up. I wasn't going to do that anymore.

I flipped through the pages, automatically scanning for Rachel's name. When I found it, I took out a stack and snuck downstairs to the back porch. It was a warm night, and a breeze pushed through the screens.

```
a reason to go back. All of them did, I
suppose. All of them, even Bette, had
```

something that made Jezebel not quite home. A
person, a memory, the way the sun slanted
across the front steps: part of their hearts
would always be in the place that made them
leave. Rachel, though, was tempestuous about
it. Guilt-ridden and torn up for days at a
time. She hadn't yet been here six months
when she threw her first fit. She said she
was going back to Maine. She said she was
going to see her baby sister. "They can't
keep me from seeing her!" she cried. "I'm not
going to hurt her, I just want to see her!"
Bette took her by the arm and led her
upstairs. I heard a crash, but didn't go
check on it. Bette knew her business, and I
knew my place. Bette would figure out what
was really bothering her.

I felt a fluttery feeling in my stomach. It was like the
moment before I found Rachel's birth certificate—I was
about to discover something and wasn't sure I was ready.

The next morning, before the other girls were
awake, she called home. I listened, though I
knew I shouldn't have. She was crying, and
her words came between sobs—she was pleading,
then angry. Then she hung up the phone,
silent tears streaming down her face.
Without her fierce makeup she looked young

285

```
and childlike. I went into the kitchen to
comfort her, but she stood up and pushed past
me and wouldn't come out of her room. Her
mother called once, a few days later, but
Rachel wouldn't talk to her.
```

I felt sick to my stomach. What had happened? I wondered if my parents really did have reason to be afraid of Rachel, beyond just her general rebellion. But then, they hadn't told me the truth—they said she hadn't wanted to come home, and she had. Only that one time. That *one time* they called, and she wouldn't answer. They should have tried harder. If they had tried, they would know her as I knew her. Not dangerous, but wonderful.

```
Eventually Bette told me what had happened,
why Rachel had left home and come to Jezebel.
My heart ached when I heard. It's simple to
tell myself that I, who have taken all these
girls in, would have had more forgiveness
than her mother. Perhaps. Perhaps not. When
Bette and Rachel left the farm, I knew who I
blamed, even though it was Rachel who came
```

I put the paper down on my lap. I couldn't learn more about Rachel from Belinda. This was my family's story, and there was only one person who could tell me the truth. But I wasn't sure I wanted to hear it.

Chapter Forty-four

I slept poorly and woke with dark circles under my eyes. Owen noticed. "You look like crap, Cohen. Raccoon eyes aren't acceptable for Miss Hollis," he told me as we walked out to the goats.

"Screw you," I said.

"Easy, tiger."

I sidestepped a pile of goat shit. The day was humid already, which meant it would be oppressively hot and unbearable.

Owen tried to make me smile. *"Nein!"* he yelled at the goats. *"Sprechen sie Deutsch!"*

I snapped leads onto two of the goats and led them into the milking barn.

On the way back out to the field for the second round, Owen asked me, "All right, what's going on?"

"I'm just thinking about things."

"What kind of things?"

"Home, I guess." We each grabbed our second pair of goats and hooked them up. Owen started the milker.

"Yeah? About going home?"

"It's going to be complicated," I said. "Everything's different now."

"It's okay to be nervous. I'd be nervous about going home or seeing my parents again. I mean, yesterday I thought I was going to have a heart attack. I almost hoped my mom would come running out to the car, crying, and tell me she was sorry, and then we'd hug and go inside. But at the same time, I just never want to see her again."

"Yeah," I said. I was only half listening. I watched the goats being milked and tried to put myself in my parents' place. How bad would it have to be for me to disown a daughter? Could she have been violent? I couldn't imagine Rachel trying to physically hurt anyone.

Owen walked to the milking machine and switched it off. "These guys are done," he said. We let them out of their stands and gathered the next set.

Once we were finished, I took my time getting ready for breakfast, hoping Rachel would be in her office by the time I came downstairs. Instead she was in the kitchen serving eggs. "Morning," she said. I didn't make eye contact. It was like I knew a secret about her that changed things between us. But I *didn't* know the secret, and that made it worse. I was starting to wish I hadn't read those pages.

I put my fork into the eggs, but didn't eat.

"Not hungry?" Rachel asked.

"Not really," I replied.

Owen checked his watch. "We're running late. We've got to get going." He shoveled a few last bites into his mouth.

Rachel took a sip of her coffee. "Listen, I should have mentioned this last night, but we really need to trim the goats' hooves. Can one of you stay and help me?"

Owen grimaced. I knew I couldn't run the stand by myself—Owen was the salesperson. "I'll do it," I conceded.

"If you get kicked, Dara, it's all over," Owen said.

"I don't hear you volunteering," I retorted.

"Snippy, snippy. Watch out, Rachel, she's in a mood."

Rachel raised her eyebrows at me. "Everything okay?"

"I didn't sleep well," I replied. Which was the truth, just not all of it.

After breakfast, Rachel and I led the goats back into the milkers and clipped their heads into the stands. "It's easier when they're hooked in," she told me. She explained how the sidewalls of the hooves grow too quickly to be worn down when they live on the farm. In the wild they're fine, but in captivity you have to trim them. She showed me how to hold the hoof, to scrape out the dirt, and then to cut. "Once you see pink, stop. You don't want to make them bleed," she said, then handed me her orange-handled clippers. She stood over me to watch my first attempt.

"Good, just go slowly, and only cut down until the sides are even with the frog—that's like the sole of the goat's foot."

I nodded. She watched until I finished the first hoof, then picked up another set of clippers and started on the next goat down the line. My goat kept nipping and nuzzling at my neck as I worked. I batted her away with my left hand while trying to hold the clippers and her leg in my right.

"Rachel?" I asked. I had to know.

"Yeah?"

"Can you tell me why you left? The whole story?"

Rachel stopped working. "I told you I just needed to get out."

I started to feel shaky, but didn't give up. "There has to be more than that."

She finished her goat and moved on to the next one, putting a little more distance between us. Finally she said, "You know when you were younger and you'd practice kissing with your friends?"

I nodded even though I had never done it.

"My friend Liza was over at our house. It was her idea to try it so we'd know what we were doing when we actually got to kiss boys. But you know, I liked it more than I was supposed to." She laughed nervously and looked down at the floor. "We did it a lot. No, not a lot, a few times. I told her we needed more practice. Just to be sure. Maybe she felt the same way? I don't know. One time Mom came in. . . . She freaked out and sent Liza home and made me promise never to do it again. I was so embarrassed. And the next morning Dad could barely look at me."

"How old were you?" I asked.

"Eleven," she said. "Something changed after that. It's like they were watching me, questioning everything I did. I had to leave the door open when my friends were over. Every time we rented a movie, she'd read the description twice, making sure there was nothing deviant. It was all so humiliating for me."

I knew exactly what she meant. My throat was starting to ache.

"Eventually I just started ignoring them and doing whatever I wanted. I drank, I smoked pot, I stayed out way too late and sometimes never came home at all. I cut class and shoplifted." She shook her head. "But I never broke that one rule. I still felt guilty and perverted for kissing Liza. I dated all sorts of jerks, like Ricky, but never kissed another girl. Not until Georgia." She just stared at the floor for a moment. "It was the summer before my senior year, and we were both scooping ice cream at Beal's. Right from the start she came after me. I tried to blow her off and would run for the door as soon as I got off work. I held out for almost the whole summer. Then one day Georgia cornered me in the supply room and said, 'You know, this hard-to-get act is really getting old.'" She smiled at the memory. "So I kissed her, and it was like a thousand times better than kissing Ricky or any of the stupid guys I dated. Better than Liza.

"After that I was kind of obsessed with her. You know what it's like when you first fall in love?" I didn't, but again I nodded. "I wanted to spend all my time with her, and share every possible experience with her, and for her to be obsessed with me too. I wanted to impress her. So I convinced her to climb this water tower with me. I know how stupid it sounds, but I thought it would be so sexy and exhilarating. We would be able to see the whole city and the ocean. . . . I knew she didn't want to. She was scared, but she didn't want to let me down."

My heart started to hammer.

"I started to climb first. I was almost to the top. She didn't even scream or gasp. I just heard a clanging sound, and then . . . When I got down and saw her, I threw up. I didn't know what to do. I couldn't just leave her, but I had to get help. We'd been drinking, just a few beers, but I really, really don't think that mattered. I stayed with her. She couldn't say anything. I think she was in shock. Finally I drove and got help."

"Was she okay?" I asked.

"She broke a lot of bones. Mom and Dad wouldn't let me go see her, and her parents didn't want me to see her either. I couldn't even call her. They came over and screamed at Mom and Dad and accused them of raising a psychopath, and all these other nasty things. Afterward I was crying in my room, and Mom came in, and I thought she was going to comfort me. But instead she told me she and Dad were too ashamed to even know what to do with me anymore.

"That night they went out, to get away from me. They didn't come in to say good-bye or anything. I was so pissed. I went and got all of our photo albums and pulled out every picture of me. From when I was a baby right up until then. I had this huge pile, and I dumped them in the bathtub. I tried to light them on fire with my lighter, but they wouldn't catch. So I went down to the basement and got some kerosene, and *that* made a fire."

What had she been thinking? She could have burned the whole house down!

"I remember staring at those flames, almost hoping they would start climbing up the walls, and realizing that nothing was ever going to change. So I left. When the flames started to die down, I packed a bag and walked out the door and started hitchhiking. I got a ride with this lady who told me never to hitchhike." She laughed. "And she dropped me off in Hampton Beach, and I found this seedy motel, the Stardust Motor Court, and I got a job there cleaning people's rooms. It was disgusting. I kept thinking that any minute Mom and Dad would show up and get me. Or maybe it would be even more dramatic and the police would show up, and it would all be part of this huge hunt for me."

Rachel cleared her throat. "No one ever came. After a few months, I convinced myself that things weren't as bad as I remembered them, and I decided to go home. I'd go back to school. I'd be a good kid. Everything was going to change." She laughed sadly. "I got home, and no one was there, and I didn't have my key. I don't know what happened to it. And then it started to rain, like, a huge thunderstorm. I guess I could have gone to one of the neighbors, but I just really wanted to get inside. I was tired and cold and dirty. So I went around back and broke one of the panes of glass in the back door. I was going to patch it up and pay for it. Then I reached in, unlocked the door, and let myself in."

I pictured her breaking into our house, carefully reaching

through the broken pane of glass so she wouldn't cut herself.

"I went upstairs to the bathroom and it had been completely remodeled—and that's when I realized I had done something really stupid. I was lucky it hadn't been worse. Then I went to my room. Except—" She stopped talking. She didn't move. "It was painted all pink and there was a crib."

That was how she found out about me?

"I didn't know what to do. And as I was sitting there on the floor of the room, this alarm started to go off. So I panicked, I guess. I don't know. I knew I had to get out of there. I knew where Mom and Dad kept a stash of money, so I went and grabbed it, and I grabbed some of Mom's clothes out of her closet, since I didn't know where mine were. I filled my backpack with her stuff." She paused.

"I ran down the stairs, and when I got to the first floor, there she was. Pregnant. She didn't seem surprised to see me. She disarmed the alarm. Then she looked at me and said, 'Just go.' So I did."

My mind reeled. I couldn't say anything.

After a minute, Rachel stood up. "Excuse me," she said, and walked out.

I watched her go. I should have said something. Hands shaking, I picked up my clippers and finished trimming the goat hooves on my own.

Chapter Forty-five

The next few days were a whirlwind of cheese and pageant-related distractions. Owen got us on a rigorous schedule: feed and milk, work the fair, pick up Milo and rehearse before dinner, rehearse more after dinner, bed. Repeat, repeat, repeat. By the end of each day I was so tired I fell asleep immediately.

Rachel and I avoided being alone together. And really, even when we were in the same room, we hardly talked. No one noticed because Owen was so full of energy about the pageant, he talked enough for both of us.

Wednesday was our last day at the fair. The pageant was in two nights, and Owen decided we'd need those days for final preparations. As it was, I had to leave our stand by

11:30 for pageant orientation. We unloaded the cheese into the mini refrigerator, then I took out a slab and began spreading it onto crackers. Owen sat on his stool and watched me. "Sun-dried tomato," he said. "Bold choice."

"Uh-huh."

"Are you even in there?" he asked. "You can't let whatever's bugging you get in the way of the pageant." He switched to a terrible French accent. "Vee have vorked too hard for zis, my dahlink." He hopped down from the stool and stepped over next to me. "Seriously, what's bothering you? I don't think it's just nerves."

I wanted to tell Owen, but I couldn't. It was still too new, too close. Rachel's story—the fire—had shocked me. I didn't know how to talk to her now, and I didn't know how to explain that to Owen. "I'm fine," I told him.

"Is this about going home?"

I shrugged. "It's complicated."

"Are you sure you don't want to talk about it?"

"I'm sure," I answered. I didn't want him to know what I knew about Rachel.

"When I have a problem, I like to talk about it."

"You just like to talk." I put the last cracker down on the tray.

"True enough," he admitted. "So talk to me."

I gave him a smile for that. "I don't have to indulge your every whim."

"Just most of them. And the other day you wouldn't speak German to the goats with me. So I think you owe me a whim. For example, you should go out with my brother."

"He hasn't asked me out." Unless the haunted house thing counted.

"So you would if he asked you?"

"It's not even on the table."

"I see. So it's under consideration. Good to know."

"Owen." I slapped his arm.

"There's a smile! Hey, are you going to put Vaseline on your teeth? I read that your mouth gets dry during these things, and the Vaseline keeps your lips from sticking to your teeth."

"I hadn't thought about it."

"We should add Vaseline to the prep list," he said. "What do you feel is the most challenging issue facing teenagers today and why?"

"Wow, where was the segue there?"

"We're practicing your interview questions. So, what do you feel is the most challenging issue facing teenagers today, and why?"

I tried to relax. I couldn't get ready for the pageant with my mind all twisted.

"Say drugs," Owen prompted.

I took a deep breath. "Okay, the pressure to do drugs is the most challenging issue facing teenagers today. We see it all around us—in the movies, on television, and, unfortunately, in our schools. It takes a really strong person to resist. As Miss Hollis, I would serve as a model to other teenagers that you can not do drugs, that you should not do drugs."

"Good, I liked that last part. What is the best advice you've ever been given?"

I started to sing "Make Your Own Kind of Music."

"Dara, this is serious."

"I am serious. 'Be yourself' is the best advice I have ever received. You can't be someone else. Our differences are what make America the best country on earth."

Owen snickered.

"Too much?" I asked.

"A little. How about, what is your favorite color, and how do you feel when you wear it?"

"Where did you get these questions?"

"I had Milo go on some pageant Web sites."

I cleared my throat and sat up straight. "My favorite color is red. When I wear it, I feel strong, confident, and dramatic."

"Bravo! Bravo!" He clapped his hands together. "Our film is going to be awesome. And then you can go back to school, and everyone will think you're all badass, and you'll be the star of the senior class. Plus you'll get into Williams and go to college with me."

He made it sound like it was easy, but aside from the pageant, everything else was so messed up. As for school, I wasn't so sure they'd consider me a badass. More like a nut job.

I arranged the crackers in concentric circles on the plate. *Focus on the pageant*, I told myself. Suddenly it seemed like the only thing I had any control over.

Chapter Forty-six

"A pageant is like the simultaneous blooming of a bouquet of roses." Mrs. Pelletier, the pageant coordinator, looked around at all of us, the blooms of her bouquet, and frowned.

I shifted in my metal folding chair. When I had arrived, the few girls that were already there gave me looks, but none said anything. I had introduced myself to Mrs. Pelletier and then chosen a seat in the second row. A moment later Maddie had come in and sat right behind me.

I tucked my feet under me, crossed my hands on my lap, and sat up straight, prim and proper. Mrs. Pelletier explained the order of events from the front of a room inside the fair offices. She was in the middle of the promenade part. "As you reach the head of the stage, pause for two beats, then move on with your escort. Once you get off the stage, you must wait silently for the introductions. Each contestant will be announced." On the dry-erase board beside her, she drew a dotted line on the diagram of the stage.

My attention wandered to the other girls—all cute and skinny. Big surprise. Maddie was the one to beat, though; she was the prettiest, the most intimidating.

Mrs. Pelletier chirped on, "Your name will be called. You and your escort shall walk the perimeter of the stage, like so." She indicated her dotted line on the board. "Then you will introduce yourself to the audience. 'Hello. My name is Nancy Pelletier, and I am escorted tonight by Mr. Les Pelletier.' Got it?" We nodded. "Dara, why don't you be our example? Come up here." I took a deep breath, then slid out of my chair and walked up to the front. "Now, we obviously do not have the full stage space here, because it seems the beer-keg-tossing competition took precedence over our rehearsal, so we will have to use our imaginations. So walk, walk, walk, pause, and introduce yourself."

I straightened my back and took five gliding steps toward the other girls. "Hello, my name is Dara Cohen." I focused on Maddie. "I am escorted tonight by Owen Moon." I paused a moment longer, pivoted gently, and walk, walk, walked away.

"Lovely," Mrs. Pelletier said. "It's so wonderful to have someone with pageant experience among us." Owen had put it on my application, of course. I got the impression that Mrs. Pelletier was not that wowed by the Miss Hollis pageant. When she had begun the orientation earlier that day, she made a point to remind us that it was a local pageant. "That is, there is no advancement to a higher level. It is merely a one-shot deal." Being runner-up in such a pageant was nothing to be proud of.

Mrs. Pelletier went over the format of the interview section, then the order for the talent showcase. We didn't rehearse our acts, which was too bad, because I was curious to see what the other girls were going to do, and how well they could do it.

"Now let's talk about the finale." She described the dance number that closed the show—it didn't count in the competition, but gave the judges a chance to tally their scores. Five of us would enter from each side. Then we were supposed to fan out and weave among one another. One by one, we would spin out to center stage and bow. All of this to the tune of "Isn't She Lovely."

She split us into groups, and we moved to opposite sides of the small room. "Take teeny steps," she said. "When we get on the real stage, we can expand." She shook her head, still miffed about the keg-tossing competition.

Next to me, a blond girl chewed on the edge of her thumb. "She's making this way more complicated than it needs to be," she whispered to me.

"You've been in this before?"

She shook her head. "Nah. My older sister won a few years ago. She talks about it. All the time." She grinned.

"I'm Dara," I said.

"Shannon," she replied.

I watched Mrs. Pelletier demonstrate the finale. I wasn't too excited about this part. It had been years since I had danced.

At one time I had been good. My teacher had said I had "extra-ordinary promise." Now I'd just be clumsy and jiggly, and I could already hear Maddie snickering.

Mrs. Pelletier started the music, and we moved toward each other with our teeny steps. Our spacing was off, and there were some collisions. Mrs. Pelletier gave a heavy sigh and restarted the music. We tried again. And again. And again. Until we got it close to right. The most amazing thing was I still was a good dancer. In dance class we had always focused on our core—the torso—and I used that to control my body. I wasn't as strong as I used to be, but I didn't jiggle.

At 6:30, Mrs. Pelletier stopped the music and gathered us in a semicircle around her. "I guess that's the most we can hope for," she said. It wasn't exactly a pep talk. "Be at the stage by four thirty on Friday."

And that was that. I didn't feel particularly oriented.

Maddie walked out in front of me, with a petite girl by her side. A secondary minion, I figured. Her regular girls wouldn't dare challenge her in the pageant. "It's so gorgeous," Maddie was saying. "But I had to have it taken in. Wait until you see it!" She looked back over her shoulder, "Nice job today," she said to me, her voice dripping with fake enthusiasm.

"Thanks," I said cheerfully. "See you Friday!"

Maddie turned back to her friend. As soon as she was around the corner, I squealed, "Wait until you see it!" and mimicked her obnoxious hair toss. Next to me, Shannon giggled. I smiled back.

Shannon was wearing a pair of 1950s-style short shorts with suspenders over a white short-sleeve shirt with a Peter

Pan collar. I liked her style. She looked too hip for Miss Hollis. "Please don't take this the wrong way, but this whole scene doesn't seem like your, you know, thing," I said.

I suppose she might have said the same to me. But she didn't. "Well, it's a funny story. My sister is almost as bad as Maddie, and she talks about her victory two years ago like it's the crowning achievement of her life, no pun intended. So my dad, who has a totally twisted sense of humor, dared me to win this thing just so she would shut up."

"That's hilarious!" I said. "So what do you think so far?"

"I've had a good laugh or two," she said. "Of course, I've yet to get up in front of the whole town and play the banjo, a skill which I learned, oh, last month." She grinned. I must have looked surprised, because she said, "Well, I already played the guitar."

"Cool," I said. "So I'll see you Friday."

"Sure will," she replied. She waved good-bye to me as I headed back to Owen.

Mrs. Pelletier had told us to rest up, but that night Owen, Milo, and I went out on the roof. The moon hung low in the sky, its swirls and valleys visible. Somewhere above us an owl screeched.

"Friday," Owen said, "Dara will take back the crown."

"Hardly," I said.

"That's really not a good attitude," Owen said, tapping his feet on the shingles.

There were nine other girls in the pageant—all of them, not surprisingly, thinner than I was. They had good skin, pretty smiles. I wasn't sure how talented they were, but in a pageant like this, looks probably trumped talent.

I pulled the strings of my hood so it tightened around my face.

"It might be better if you don't win," Milo said. "I think that would be the real compliment."

"That's not very helpful, Milo," Owen said. But I thanked him.

"The two of you," Owen said. He slapped his hands against his corduroys: one-two-three, one-two-three, over and over again. "I can't be the only one taking this seriously. I can't be the only one on board here."

"I'm on board," I said. "I'm doing it, aren't I?" I didn't look at him. The truth was, I still wasn't sure if I was on board or not. I wanted to win, it's true, but I wasn't sure why. I guess I was trying to get something back—a simpler time, and all that. But that wasn't all of it. And I didn't think, if I was being honest, that I was on some sort of fat-girls-are-pretty-too crusade. I wasn't doing it to prove a point.

"Yeah, but you're ready to jump ship at any time," Owen said. "Again."

He picked up his camera and started filming the sky and the trees across the street. Then he turned it on me. "Quit it," I said.

"This is for the dark and introspective portion."

"I thought we weren't doing dark and introspective," I said.

He shrugged and turned away from me to the side fields. The moon cast a pale light on the shed and the worn-out fence. I pulled my hands up into the sleeves of my sweatshirt. Milo shifted, moved a little bit closer to me. "Cold?" he asked. He smelled different from Owen. Owen had a spicy, almost cinnamon smell, but Milo smelled like honey. I tried not to read too much into the distinction.

"Uh-huh," I said.

Milo didn't do anything. Didn't put his arm around me, or slide over more so our sides touched. He hadn't kissed me since the Crystal Palace. Owen was wrong—Milo had no interest in me.

Not that I cared.

"Okay, forget dark and introspective. Say something positive," Owen instructed. He had the camera trained on me again. "Say something positive about the pageant. You know, like on a reality show. Explain that it's two days until the pageant and how you're feeling about it."

I looked down at my knees for a moment, and then back up at the camera. "It's two nights before the pageant, and I feel like barfing."

Owen pulled the camera to the side. "Come on, Dara, be serious. And take your hood down."

"Shouldn't it be real?"

"Sure it should. But it should be a positive version of real."

I sighed and pulled off my hood. "It's two nights before the pageant, and I'm feeling anxious, but also excited. There are a lot of really pretty girls—really nice girls—and so it's hard to predict how it's all going to work out. But I'm going to go out there and do my best."

Owen held the camera on me for three seconds, and then

snapped it shut. "Good," he said. "A little canned, but good enough."

I rolled my eyes. "I should go to bed."

"That's right. You need your sleep."

I crawled backward through the window, hoping neither of them was paying attention. "Good night, guys," I said, waving from inside. Owen said good night, but Milo just waved, with a little smile. Was it a flirtatious smile? Damn it. When he accompanied me, it felt right. Like we had something. But that wasn't anything definite, and I didn't know if he was feeling it too.

I didn't even know what I was feeling. In the Crystal Palace, I had kissed him like I really liked him. And then I had acted all coy about it, leaving it to him to make the next move. Maybe that had pissed him off? But if he was pissed, would he still have spent so much time rehearsing with me?

I got into my bed. It was nicer thinking about Milo, confusing as he was, than worrying about Rachel. I let myself remember the kiss, the way his lips felt against mine, until I started to get that quivering feeling. I relived it over and over again until I fell asleep.

Chapter Forty-seven

Owen had the forty-eight hours leading up to the pageant planned down to the minute. He made spreadsheets at the library and gave one to each of us, with our responsibilities highlighted. Mine was awash in pink.

One of my main tasks for the day was a pedicure. With my feet still soft and damp from an Epsom salt bath, I slipped on a pair of terry cloth flip-flops and walked back to my room to paint my toenails. Of course I had painted them many times before, but this was the first time I had a purpose. Until now, toenail painting had always been an end in itself; it was just something to do. Melissa and I would sit on the floor of my room, passing the bottle back and forth between us. Now I had all sorts of pressing decisions. Did I leave the flip-flops on or take them off? Dusty Sienna or Ramblin' Rose? Square or rounded? I should have worn closed-toed shoes.

I started with my left foot, on the pinky toe, so small I barely touched the brush to the nail and it was done. I moved along my left foot. I got some on the skin of my middle toe, wiped it off with my thumb, and then reached for a tissue. I moved on to the right foot. Big toe first, smooth strokes to fill in the whole surface, then on to the smaller ones. I surveyed. Decent. I should have done a second coat, but I didn't. I twisted the brush back into the bottle and went downstairs to get Owen's opinion of my color choice.

They were silent in the parlor, so I almost walked right past them: Belinda and my parents. I stopped in the doorway, keeping my toes curled up because the polish was still tacky. "What are you doing here?"

Mom stood up, a nervous smile frozen on her face. She walked toward me, as if to give me a hug.

"Toes," I said, pointing to my feet.

She stopped. "Owen called and told us about the pageant. We would never miss your big day, honey."

Her hands were clasped in front of her hips, and she was still smiling tentatively.

Dad stood up, stuck his hands in his pockets, and then took them out. "So . . . another pageant, huh?"

"Yep." If I didn't talk to them, maybe they would go away.

Belinda took a sip of her tea and watched us. Mom looked down at her hands, unclasped them, and smoothed her palms along the front of her pants: a nervous habit. I did the same thing. So did Rachel.

"You came for the pageant?" I asked. I was still trying to come to terms with the fact that they were there, sitting in Belinda's ancient parlor, sipping tea with her.

My parents exchanged a concerned look. "Yes, we came for the pageant," Mom said. "Owen said you were doing well." She was wearing a pair of white capri pants and a blue short-sleeved sweater. She looked like she was about to go for a sail.

"I *am* doing well," I said.

Dad rolled back on his heels. "Well, that's good news." His fingers drummed against his leg.

"It's not news," I shot back.

"It's good to hear all the same," Mom said.

I felt the anger rising. How could she stand there, in my world? How was she able to take it over and crowd out everything else? I knew how Rachel felt when she had burned her pictures and left—the suffocation, the shame she must have believed would never go away. "Is Rachel here?" I asked.

Another exchanged look. "We haven't seen her."

Crap. I felt like I had betrayed her somehow, implied that she was irresponsible or something. "I see," I said.

What had Owen been thinking to invite them? They were the last people I wanted here. He had to know that.

"You look good," Mom said. "You've lost weight."

I looked down at my body. I had lost some from farm-work and Rachel's balanced meals. "I'm healthier," I answered.

"Well, that's wonderful," Mom said. "I'm proud of you."

"I didn't do it for you."

Mom clenched her jaw. I wondered what they were thinking. What they were planning.

I wasn't ashamed of the remark. It was the truth. I crossed my arms over my chest. Belinda put her pink teacup back in its saucer with a clink. I shifted my weight from my left heel to my right. "I have a lot to do to get ready," I told them.

"Of course," Mom said.

"I wasn't expecting you."

"Don't let us get in your way."

We all looked at each other for a moment more before I backed out of the parlor and went into the kitchen, hoping that Rachel was hiding out there, but it was empty. I leaned against the counter, picked up an apple, rolled it in my palm, and put it back in the bowl. I had a huge lump in my throat, and my eyes burned. It was all too much.

Through the window, I caught a glimpse of Owen walking past the picnic table. I rushed out of the kitchen and through the side door. I grabbed him by the shirtsleeve and pulled him into the barn. "Why the hell did you invite my parents?"

Owen's grin faltered. "I thought you'd want them here."

"Why?" I asked.

"You've been so nervous about going home. I thought that if they came out to see you first, it would be easier," he said.

I shook my head. Owen was the one who wanted reconciliation. He was the one who fantasized about his mother embracing him and welcoming him home. I still hadn't decided what I wanted. "Does Rachel know?"

Owen avoided my eyes. "No," he admitted.

"Shit, Owen, she's going to freak out." I looked over my shoulder. "Where is she? You have to warn her. She hasn't seen them since she was seventeen."

Owen's face grew pale as he started to realize what he had done, not to me but to Rachel. "I'm sorry," he said.

My whole back was tense. All the stress was balling up between my shoulder blades. I tried to relax, but then Owen said, "Shit."

I turned and saw Rachel opening the door to the mudroom.

We chased after her, but we knew we were too late. We found them all in the kitchen, looking at each other. No one had spoken yet. Belinda hovered in the doorway to the parlor.

Rachel's face was white. Mom wore a cold and appraising smile. Dad looked around the room. "Nice kitchen," he said. That was the first thing he chose to say to her?

Rachel picked up a dish towel and began wiping down one of the counters. "I suppose you should stay for dinner," she said.

A terrible idea. I looked at my mother, sure she would refuse.

"That would be nice," Mom replied.

The clock ticked out the seconds.

Rachel wiped harder at the counter, at a spot that only she could see. "It won't be much. We're all in a flurry here because of the pageant."

"That's fine," Mom said.

I could hear Owen breathing next to me. He should say something. This was his mistake; he should fix it.

Mom didn't give him a chance. "I know you all have lots of work to do. We'll go back into the parlor. Let us know when dinner is ready."

"Yeah, sure," Rachel replied.

My parents followed Belinda out of the kitchen.

"I'm sorry," Owen said to Rachel.

"It's fine," she replied. And then she picked up the phone and dialed a number from memory. "Hello. I'd like to place an order for delivery."

Chapter Forty-eight

When the Chinese food came, Owen and I spooned it from the plastic and cardboard containers into serving bowls. We set the table with forks and knives, as well as the paper-wrapped chopsticks that came from the restaurant. Owen went to the parlor to get my parents and Belinda. I went upstairs and knocked on Rachel's door. "Dinner's here," I called through the wood.

"Okay," she replied, but I didn't hear her moving. I thought about going in but wasn't sure if I'd be welcome.

When I got back downstairs, Sascha was in the kitchen, along with Milo, who had come over to rehearse and had no idea what he was getting into. "Hey," I said to him.

"Hey." He nodded back.

Rachel appeared a moment after the rest of us sat down. The big table felt crowded: Mom, Dad, Sascha, Belinda, Owen, Milo, Rachel, and me.

We passed the dishes around and served ourselves, and that was good for a few minutes. But then the food was on our plates, and we could either talk or eat in silence. Silence won out at first. Mom held her fork but didn't eat. Dad shifted in his seat and cleared his throat several times before he finally said something. "You look great." It wasn't clear if he was talking to Rachel or me. Neither of us said anything.

Mom put her hands flat on the table. "How were your exams, Dara?"

"Fine."

"Have you started your applications?"

"No." I couldn't believe that after all this time, we were still talking about the same things.

"So what's farm life like?" Dad boomed.

I looked at Rachel, but she wouldn't catch my eye.

"Good," I said. "I like making cheese."

"Well, that's great," Dad said. "And you've made new friends." He nodded at Owen and Milo.

"Uh-huh."

"Well, that's great," he said again. "Plus, I can see you've lost a lot of weight."

I bit my lip, humiliated. *Thank you, Dad, for pointing that out in front of said new friends.*

"Have you signed up for your classes for next year?" Mom asked.

"Yes." Registration had happened well before the debacle. She knew that.

At the end of the table Belinda ate slowly. She chewed her food in her methodical way as her eyes flitted from my mother to my father. Maybe she would say something.

Sascha and Milo were as silent as Belinda. Their plates were nearly clean, but the rest of us, with our meaningless chitchat, had barely touched the food.

"Tell us about this pageant," Dad said.

"It's small—just ten girls. I'm going to sing."

"Great! What song?" Dad asked.

I had a mouthful of shrimp fried rice. Before I could swallow and answer, Mom pushed her plate away. "How's therapy, Dara?" It was like we had been driving along a slow country road, and then she took a sharp right into oncoming traffic.

"Fine."

"Making progress?"

"I suppose." I picked up my fork and pierced a shrimp.

"We've been worried about you," she went on.

I snapped my head up. "I'm sure," I said. Under the table, Milo reached over and took my hand in his. It felt good. *If things really go bad*, he seemed to be saying, *I'm ready*.

"When you had your little breakdown," Mom began—so that's what she was calling it, *Dara's little breakdown*. I could hear her talking to her friends. *Oh yes, Dara just had a little breakdown. All that pressure. She'll be just fine, though. We've sent her to convalesce in the Berkshires.* "Well, we were upset."

Rachel snorted.

Mom turned to her. "Something wrong?" It was the first time Mom had acknowledged Rachel during dinner.

"Dara didn't have a breakdown," Rachel said.

"You weren't there, Rachel," Mom said.

Rachel looked at her plate. "No, Mom, I wasn't. But I'm here now. And there's nothing wrong with Dara."

My stomach tightened. Milo squeezed my hand. He was used to this. The tension. The awkwardness.

"Rachel, this really isn't any of your business," Mom said. Everyone at the table flinched.

Rachel sat rigidly in her chair.

"I'm fine," I said. "I'm doing fine." I disengaged my hand from Milo's so I could eat more of my rice. Eating meant not talking. Eating meant we would be done sooner, and my parents could get out of the house.

Mom cleared her throat. "I have to say I'm a little confused."

Everyone at the table looked up, not sure at whom the comment was directed. "About what?" Sascha replied finally.

"About you, Owen. You live here?"

He sat up and glanced at me before answering, "Yes."

"But why?"

I watched his face—he looked wary, afraid to say the wrong thing. "My parents and I have some fundamental differences of opinion."

"About what?"

Milo was nervously twisting his napkin.

Owen looked across the table at me then back at my mom. "I'm gay," he said.

"And?" she pushed. What the hell was wrong with my mother? Why was she messing with him like that?

"Our parents can't accept it," Milo said. "They didn't accept him, and so he came here, where he knew he'd be welcomed."

"That's ridiculous. Do you need someone to talk to them?"

She was sitting right there, with the daughter she had pushed away for the very same reason, and pretended she was outraged. My mouth tasted of metal. I hated her in that moment.

"It won't do any good," Owen said.

"I think that if your mother knew how you were living, she'd be willing to talk to—"

Owen interrupted. "How I'm living?"

Mom blushed, as if she realized she had pushed it too far. But I was pretty sure this was where she had wanted the conversation to go the whole evening. "You have to admit it's an odd setup here."

Rachel, Owen, Sascha, and I looked around the table, wondering what my mother could think was odd. At the head of the table, Belinda sat tall and still.

"I mean you have a middle-aged man, a silent matriarch, and . . ." She paused. "It's an odd environment for adolescents."

"I thought even you were more open-minded than this," Rachel said, so soft it was almost a whisper.

Mom folded her hands and leaned forward. She was trying to look sympathetic, but she reeked of condescension. "Rachel, I'm not here to question the choices you have made. I'm here for Dara."

Rachel put her hand up to her face, covering her eyes. I knew she was trying not to cry, and I could feel tears forming in my own eyes. I desperately wished my mom hadn't brought me into this fight.

Sascha folded his napkin and stood up. With a nod, he left the room. I could tell he was leaving to keep himself from telling my mother exactly what he thought of her assessment of life on Jezebel Farm.

Mom ignored the gesture and kept barreling over us. "Dara, we've had a lot of time to think, your father and I, and we've decided it's time for you to come home. This has gone on too long. It's ridiculous."

"You have no idea what it's like here," I said. My voice wavered with anger.

"We know you belong at home with your family," Mom said.

"Rachel *is* my family," I snapped.

"Well, of course," Mom said, waving her hand in the air, like it was nothing.

"No, not 'of course,'" Rachel said. Her voice shook a little, but her eyes were fierce. "I would never have met her—"

"Rachel, *please*," Mom said, her calm demeanor cracking.

"Rachel," Dad cut in, "I think it's perfectly understandable that we weren't comfortable having you in our home. And I think you'd agree that you would not have been a good sister to her."

"That's not true!" I said. "Rachel is a great sister." She had messed up, true, but that didn't matter anymore. "From the minute I walked through the door, she's made me feel at home. Everyone here welcomed me, and I've felt like I'm part of a family." Mom tried to interrupt me, but I kept going, my cheeks growing warm. "Rachel didn't have to take me in—and after the way you treated her, I'm not sure why she did—but she did."

Mom looked like I had slapped her. "The way I treated her?"

"I know what happened," I said.

Mom shot Rachel an accusing look. "You don't know everything, Dara."

Maybe not. Maybe there was yet another side to the story of why my parents had cut Rachel out of their lives, but I had seen enough tonight to know that my parents were incapable of the forgiveness Rachel needed.

I knew, too, that I couldn't leave, not yet. "I'm not going back," I said. I looked at Rachel. I think she knew what I was going to say next, what I had decided right then. She smiled and wiped her eyes. "I don't want to go back at all. I don't want to go back to Portland Academy. I want to stay here and go to school in Hollis."

Mom frowned at me, still reacting like I was a little girl. "Dara, that's really not a decision for you to make."

"Why not?"

Dad closed his eyes and squeezed the bridge of his nose, like he was the big victim here.

"You're still our daughter," Mom said. "And you will live by our rules." She followed the script, but she looked exhausted.

Dad coughed and put his hands flat on the table, steadying

himself. "I think what your mother is getting at is that it's a big decision, and you shouldn't rush into it. Why don't we take some time to think it over, and we can all talk about it tomorrow."

I looked across the table at Owen. He nodded at me and gave me a little smile.

"We can't talk about it tomorrow, because I have the pageant," I said. "Anyway, I don't need to think about it anymore. I know what I want, and I want to stay here."

"Fine. If that's what you want," Mom said. She looked off to the side, as if she couldn't be bothered to look at—or think about—me anymore.

"That's what I want," I said again.

"Well then," Mom said. "I think we should be leaving." She pushed her chair back from the table with a loud screeching sound. Dad grimaced at the noise, but then he stood up too.

"Good night, Dara," he said to me. "It was nice to meet you all. Good night, Rachel. Thank you for dinner."

Rachel stared at him. "You're welcome," she said coldly.

We all watched them go out the side door. The car's headlights shone into the kitchen, then faded as they pulled away. Rachel stared out the window while Owen, Milo, and I began clearing the dishes. As I reached past Belinda to pick up her plate, she wrapped her leathery hand around my forearm. Her hand was warm and soft. She smiled up at me, and I knew I had made the right choice.

Chapter Forty-nine

I found Rachel on the back porch. She sat in a creaking glider, her knees drawn up to her chest. Next to the glider, there was an old rocking chair, and I lowered myself into it. I started to rock slowly.

The moonlight fell in patches on the grass. The pastures were empty; the goats had all gone into the small open barn to sleep.

"I thought your coming here was a sign that things were better. Or could be better. I thought it was a first step." She looked out over the pastures as she spoke, not at me. It felt like I had walked in on a conversation she was having with herself.

I kept rocking the chair with my foot: flat to point, flat to point. I heard a car drive by, going too fast down our street.

Maybe that was all she was going to say. Her attention was focused so far in the distance, I wasn't sure if she even wanted me to be out there with her.

She leaned back in the glider and looked up at the ceiling. My gaze followed hers. Curls of paint hung down, and it looked like there was some mold, though it was too dark to tell.

"I guess we should take better care of this porch," she said.

"Uh-huh."

"I'm glad you're staying."

"Me too."

"You don't have to, though. I mean, I understand how Mom can make you say things sometimes, and if you don't really want to stay . . . I know you have friends back home."

I did. Melissa would probably wail and beg when she heard I wasn't coming back. Or maybe she wouldn't. The truth was, I really wasn't all that excited about going back to Portland Academy. Being "that girl who was Little Miss Maine and then got fat" was bad enough. Being "that girl who was Little Miss Maine and then got fat and then got pulled out of school" would be too much. Hollis High would be a fresh start.

Rachel and I looked at each other in the fading light. She reached across and took my hands in hers. Her hands were warm and rough, the hands of a woman who had done a lot of work to get where she was. She pressed my palms together with hers around them, like we were praying together.

"You're going to need my help once Owen goes to school," I said. "Plus, you're my sister and I want to be here."

She smiled. "It's kind of nice to finally have someone to turn to and say, 'Holy hell.' All my life, I don't think anyone else ever really got it."

"It is," I agreed. I thought of all the diary entries I had written to her. And now here we were together. It was hard to believe. I wrapped my hands around the arms of the rocker. "Are you okay?"

"Yeah. I mean, no. But I guess I'm no worse off than I was this morning. I just don't have my illusions anymore." She paused. "Listen, this is going to sound really odd, considering what just happened, but you shouldn't let things get to where they are with me and Mom."

I picked at the paint on the rocker. "I think that depends on her."

"You can't do it that way. It sucks, but you've got to be the one to make it happen."

It was exhausting to think about—the idea of salvaging my relationship with my mother seemed too much to take on.

Rachel smiled at me. "Don't worry about it tonight. You've got a big day tomorrow," she said.

I nodded. "Thanks for everything."

She shrugged. "Don't worry about it."

I was glad she didn't say something hokey, like "That's what sisters are for."

"Good night, then." I walked to the door and held it open for her. "Coming?"

"No, I think I'll stay out here a bit longer."

I stepped into the warm, bright house and let the door slowly swing closed behind me.

In bed I thought about what I had done. I wasn't going home. I had given up my friends and my school to stay in Hollis. I thought I should feel sad or scared, but I didn't. This felt like home. Maybe everybody has a place where they are meant to be. For Rachel it's surely Jezebel, and for me, too, maybe.

I wanted to win the pageant for Jezebel—for Belinda and Rachel, and Owen and Sascha, too. So there would be something new to add to the history of the farm—something new and exciting.

My thoughts weren't making sense. I knew that. I knew that winning the pageant wouldn't bring all the liveliness back to the farm. But still. I yawned and looked out the window. Owen would kill me if he knew I was still awake, losing my chance at a good night's sleep. I closed my eyes and settled back into my pillow, waiting for sleep to overtake me.

Chapter Fifty

In his slim-fitting tux, Owen looked like a model or a
European playboy. Except he couldn't stop fidgeting with his
tie. "It's fine," I whispered. We were waiting in line for our
turn to be introduced.

I had forgotten the jitters, the sweat, the dread and anticipation that came before a pageant began. With my free
hand, I tapped my thumb against my middle, index, ring finger, pinky, over and over again to keep from touching my
dress or hair.

The other girls were wearing prom dresses, bright and
gaudy, in my opinion. One girl, I think her name was Niki,
was wearing a dress with a low-cut bodice that reached
almost to her navel. It was filled in with that skin-colored

sheer fabric, but her breasts were small, so it hung loosely and puckered.

In front of us, Shannon and her Mohawked escort stepped closer to the stairs. I heard a girl behind me hiss, "Really, Brian, was deodorant too much to ask?"

Then Maddie came down the stairs with a cute, slightly puffy boy with wide-set eyes and freckles. She wiggled her fingers at us. When they passed I turned to Owen to comment, but he had suddenly grown somber. "Hey," I whispered. "Hey, what's wrong?"

"Oh my God," Owen replied, almost laughing.

"What?"

"That's him," Owen hissed. "That's Andy Temple."

I looked over my shoulder to get a better look, but they were too far away for me to see much.

"Forget the freshman fifteen, he's gained the freshman fifty. Holy crap, did you see how big his ass is?"

I gritted my teeth and didn't say anything.

Shannon and her escort walked up the stairs and then out onto the stage. She was wearing this great vintage flapper dress that sparkled in the spotlight. The stagehand, a girl of about thirteen wearing overalls and a high ponytail, let the curtain drop.

Owen giggled. "Boy's got junk in the trunk. Oh my God, this is so crazy!"

"Enough, Owen. Okay?"

"Sorry," he whispered. "But boys aren't supposed to have hips."

I flicked him hard in the arm, just as the stagehand beckoned to us to ascend to the stage. We glided into the bright lights, his arm linked through mine and his other hand on my elbow. Owen let my arm free, and I stepped up to the microphone. "Hello. My name is Dara Cohen, and I am escorted tonight by Owen Moon."

The faces and bodies in the audience were eclipsed by the spotlight. I gave my two-beat smile. From the bleachers, an explosion of applause. My smile widened so much that my cheeks started to hurt. I waited a beat longer than I should have, basking in the stage lights and the cheers. Mrs. Pelletier was probably having a conniption fit, but these people were clapping for me, and it had been a long time since that had happened.

I stepped back and took Owen's arm again. We walked around the other half of the stage and back to the exit. Maybe the applause wasn't for me, exactly. Maybe they clapped for everyone that way. And probably some of the applause was for Owen. Still, that clapping felt good. My heart raced. I had forgotten how it felt to be up onstage with people watching me, enjoying me. I was giddy. Giddy! When was the last time I had felt this way? I gripped the sleeves of Owen's tux and kissed him on the cheek. "Thank you," I said.

Arm in arm, we walked through the backstage area to the open-air changing room, sectioned off by fabric partitions. He hugged me close to him. "Good luck, superstar," he whispered in my ear.

The changing area was a girl frenzy. Contestants were slipping out of evening gowns and pulling on their outfits for the interview portion. I reached around to unzip my dress.

"Let me help you."

I couldn't tell whether Mom had just come in, or if she had been waiting for me. My body tensed. So they were here. They had stayed, even though I told them I wasn't going back with them. That said something. Hopefully the message was *We support you no matter what*, not *We're not leaving until you come with us*.

"Okay," I said. Was she going to cause a scene? Was she going to ruin this for me?

I turned and she unzipped the evening gown straight down my back. I held the front up against my chest. "Which one's yours?" She indicated the rack of dresses a few yards away.

"The black one. On the red hanger." Owen had purchased red satin-padded hangers for all of my outfits.

Mom nodded and went to get the dress. She seemed to have grown smaller. She slipped the black dress off the hanger and brought it back to me. I carefully stepped out of the evening gown and handed it to her. "This is gorgeous," she said.

"We found it in Rachel's attic."

"You looked beautiful in it. You looked . . ." She didn't finish. I took the black dress from her and pulled it on like a jacket, wrapped it around me, and tied the belt off to the side, as Owen had insisted.

"You're a little . . ." Mom began. She looked flustered as she tugged at the dress around my breasts, her fingers skimming my skin. "You were uneven."

328

"Thanks," I said. The skin on her face looked tight and thin. I expected her to say something, but she didn't. So I said, "I need to fix my makeup."

She followed me to a vanity with a mirror bordered by lights. I grabbed my makeup bag and pulled out the eye shadow.

Mom stood behind me. Our faces were both framed in the mirror. With the heavy stage makeup, my features were clear and distinct. Hers were less defined.

She said, "I'm proud of you, Dara. Those are empty words, I know. People say that all the time and don't even consider the full meaning." She touched the tips of her fingers to her hair, watching herself in the mirror. She smoothed down a flyaway. "Since you've been away, I've given a good deal of thought to what happened. I don't know if we over-reacted. I don't know what your autobiography project really meant, or what you meant by it."

I picked up a tube of shiny red lip gloss and smoothed it across my lips before blotting on a tissue. Looking at my own reflection, I could not ignore Mom's. She put a hand on my shoulder.

"Dara, when you decided to be in this pageant, you made a choice to be in the world again, and that's what makes me proud."

I wanted to laugh. It was ridiculous, what she'd said. And condescending. She watched me hopefully. I said, "Thank you."

"I don't understand your choice to stay here." She looked back over her shoulder, then at my reflection in the mirror.

"I don't understand what it is that you're trying to find, or what, perhaps, you're running away from."

I was sick of people thinking I was running away.

"But it's time for me to allow you to make your own choices." She put both hands on my shoulders, and I looked up at her reflection. "If this is what you want, what you really want, then I suppose we can make it work."

"I do," I said.

Her face fell a little, as if she had expected me to change my mind, or at least to think about it a moment.

Then she nodded. "Okay, then." Now that she'd lost, her body seemed to relax. "You're beautiful. You always have been."

We should hug, I thought, turning from the mirror. But she didn't hug me. She smiled and stepped aside to let me pass.

We were on to the interview portion. I shifted from foot to foot and listened to the other girls' answers. Maddie got: "What's the one thing you would change in this world if you could?" A total puff question.

"I would ask us all not to put aside our differences, but to celebrate them. I'd want the whole world to recognize and appreciate how varied and how very unique each one of us is. It's a simple thing, but if we can love each other for our differences, imagine the ripples throughout the world."

Blech. It was a total vanilla answer, plus there was no such thing as "very unique."

When they asked Niki what value was most important to her, she answered, "Virginity. My virginity is a gift from God, and it's my job to protect it."

I could picture Owen rolling his eyes at that, and I did too. But who were we to talk? We weren't trying to protect our virginity, and we still couldn't give it up.

Shannon gave me a wink before she walked onstage. Her question: "What is the greatest challenge facing teenagers today?"

Drugs! I thought. *Say drugs!* But she said, "The greatest challenge facing teenagers today is the same as it has been for every generation: self-definition. We each have to figure out who we are, and then fight to be that person, often in the face of overwhelming pressure to be like everyone else. It would be easy to give in, to wear the clothes the stores tell us to wear, to listen to the music the advertisers tell us to listen to, and to have the ideals that our teachers and our parents teach. The challenge is to filter all of that and to come into our own as real individuals."

It was a pretty great answer, I thought. She passed backstage, and I stepped up to take her place. With the spotlight centered on me, I waited for my question.

"Dara, why do you want to be Miss Hollis?"

This wasn't a question we'd rehearsed. What kind of question was it, anyway? Why did anyone want to be Miss Hollis? *The fame, the glory, the tiara.* I took a breath and tilted my head to the side, as though I were giving the issue careful consideration. "I want to be Miss Hollis because . . ." And then, nothing. Silence from me. Silence from the audience.

My heart was racing again, this time not with giddiness.

I took another breath. "As you know, I'm new to Hollis. At the end of the summer I was supposed to go back to Portland, where, quite frankly, no one has ever heard of Hollis, let alone the Miss Hollis pageant. So asking me why I want to win is a good question."

I wished I could make out faces in the audience—any faces. I saw a few tiny green lights, which I knew were the lights of video cameras. I picked one and decided it was Milo filming me, even though I knew that Owen had gone into the audience and taken over so that Milo could come backstage to meet me for the talent portion. Still, I said to myself, *That light is Milo.*

"Truth be told, I didn't even sign myself up for this. Owen Moon did. You see, I'm here because I got in some trouble at my old school, and I have to do this autobiography project as part of my punishment. It's a redo. Owen thought this would be a good way to frame the project." As I spoke, I turned my head, addressing the entire audience.

"I say that I was *supposed* to go back to Portland, because I've decided to stay here in Hollis. That means, I think, that I don't need to do the project anymore. But I decided to stay in the pageant and complete the project because now that I'm in the contest, I do want to win. This summer, I've lived and worked on Jezebel Goat Farm. As many of you know, the farm has served as a safe place for lesbians. A place where they could work and live, and have a family when their own didn't want them anymore. Hollis has made a place for Jezebel Goat Farm. Perhaps begrudgingly, it's true, but the farm is now a part of the town. Now I'm part of this town too. I would be proud to represent my new home as Miss Hollis."

Seventy-five percent truth, twenty percent bullshit, and five percent finesse. I didn't think it was quite as good as Shannon's answer, but it was good enough to keep me in the running.

Once again, the crowd applauded. Loudly. Happily. Or at least they seemed happy to me.

"Thank you," I said into the microphone. I smiled with my chin tilted forward, my hips at an angle. Then I left the stage.

I went back into the changing area to get ready for the talent portion. I was going to wear a white sixties-style sheath dress that I had brought with me from home. Owen had found a pair of red platform shoes up in the attic, and I pulled those on too.

About half the girls were still waiting to do their interviews when I came out of the changing room. Mrs. Pelletier had expressly forbidden going anywhere near the audience, but I didn't care. I slipped out and sneaked up to the edge of the bleachers.

Rachel sat with my parents on one side, Belinda and Sascha on the other. Their faces were cast in shadows. No bloodshed yet. They didn't have their arms around each other or anything, but at least they were sitting near each other and hadn't erupted into an argument.

When Rachel saw me, she smiled and waved. I waved back.

"Hey," someone whispered behind me. "Shouldn't we be backstage?" It was Milo.

I turned around and looked at him. He was wearing a gray suit with a red tie, crooked of course. I reached out and straightened it for him. "Sure," I said.

As I followed him backstage, I saw Rachel still watching me, still smiling.

Chapter Fifty-one

Milo air-keyed the accompaniment as we waited. His fingers were mesmerizing. Onstage, a girl delivered Juliet's balcony speech in a horrendous British accent. Shannon was next, waiting offstage, gripping her banjo tightly by its neck. Maddie stood by the stairs behind Shannon. She looked back at us and smiled, completely relaxed, like she already had the whole thing wrapped up.

The Shakespeare girl exited the stage, and Shannon went on. "Hello, people." Her voice echoed back to us. "I was going to do 'Dueling Banjos,' but I couldn't find anyone to fight me." The crowd laughed. "So I'm going to do the next most popular banjo song. Now, I'm not a singer, so I'm not going to sing, but you all should feel free to sing along." While the crowd was still laughing she launched into "Rainbow Connection." She played the song in this hauntingly beautiful way that made it even sadder. I thought it would be really cool for us to sing and play together at coffee shops or something.

When she came offstage, I met her at the bottom of the stairs. "That was awesome," I said.

"Thanks," she replied. "And now the Wicked Witch of the West."

She watched with Milo and me as Maddie strutted to the microphone. She adjusted the stand and said, "Hello. You all know I'm Maddie. Tonight I'm going to sing one of my favorite songs for you." She cleared her throat, the prerecorded accompaniment began, and she started to sing.

I let out my breath. Maddie's voice was pretty, but weak, and she had picked a bad song: one of those pop-country crossovers that had a big long note in the middle that she couldn't hit and couldn't hold. Milo grimaced as she tilted her head back and tried to reach up another third. I just smiled. She might beat me in this whole pageant, but at least I knew I was more talented than she was.

As the applause died down, I took deep breaths, preparing myself.

"Knock 'em dead," Shannon whispered.

Milo went up the stairs and held open the curtain for me. Its velvet brushed my skin as I walked onto the darkened stage. I took my place near the front, then checked to make sure Milo was in place at the piano.

The spotlight turned on and cast a bluish light over my face. Owen had given a specific and detailed lighting plan to the AV kids who were running the tech for the show. I replanted my feet, one in front of the other, a little bit sexier, I thought.

The beam widened to encompass my whole body as Milo began playing. I removed the microphone from the stand and walked to the edge of the stage, singing the first few lines in pure Cass Elliott style—strong but wistful.

Owen had warned me not to get too close to the edge of the stage or else people could look up my skirt. I stepped back and then crossed to stage right.

I heard my voice rush out of me and echo toward the bleachers. I dipped down into the sorrow and anger I'd felt that summer and turned it around into something more powerful than anger. Something like pride.

I walked back toward Milo and stood by him as I sang the next verse, my hand on his shoulder. This was a silly little bit, choreographed by Owen. It was all rehearsed—every step, every inflection—but singing under the stars and the lights had a different feeling entirely from our rehearsals in the parlor. The song felt new, even more alive than it had when I'd first heard it in Stan's record shop.

I walked back up to the front of the stage for the big ending. This was me singing now. I wasn't channeling Cass. The voice was mine—strong like hers, but more hopeful. I held on to the last note for two aching measures before gently decrescendoing out. Milo and I stopped at exactly the same time. I lowered the microphone. There was a moment of silence. I thought maybe something had gone terribly wrong. Then the audience thundered with applause. It felt like heat waves coming at me. "Thank you," I said softly.

Symone Lyons, last year's winner, clapped enthusiastically as she crossed the stage toward me. She was tall, with impossibly blond hair, and the lights glinted off her tiara and her shiny white teeth. I passed her the microphone.

"Give it up for Ms. Dara Cohen," she said, leaning in to give me a hug. "Good work," she said into my hair.

I met Milo by the piano. He had the biggest smile I had ever seen on him. I wanted to hug him, but he took my hand and we walked offstage together.

"Come here," he said. Still holding my hand, he led me to the left of the changing area, into a field behind the stage.

"I have to go change, Milo. For the finale."

"Look up," he insisted.

The moon was still a crescent, surrounded by a spattering of stars. "What?" I didn't see anything spectacular.

"Wait."

We stood like that in silence, his hand warm and damp against mine. I tapped my foot. I needed to get back, to change into my evening gown and finish this thing. I needed to see how I measured up.

"Wait," he said again. The moon cast an uneven glow on his face.

I looked up at the sky. The stars seemed to pulse for a second—they actually twinkled. And then one star fell across the sky, followed by a second.

"How did you know?"

"It happens every year during the waning gibbous in August."

"Waning gibbous?"

"Moon phase."

"What's the star thing called?"

He shook his head. "It doesn't have a name. I saw it one year, and then it happened again the next year. So now I watch for it. When it didn't come last night, I knew it would be tonight."

"You're the only one who knows about it?"

"Probably there are other people, but I'm the only one who really cares about it. And you, maybe." He looked from the sky to me, I could feel it, but I kept looking up. "I don't want to have one of those big conversations, you know, about us. I mean, since you're staying I guess we should, but I don't really see the point in putting a name on something."

I watched the sky, wondering if more stars would fall, thinking about what he had said. From any other boy it would have been a rejection. Any other boy would have meant, *Can I just keep kissing you, and really, can we start doing more, when it's convenient for me, and the rest of the time you can just stay out of my way?* But I knew Milo didn't mean it that way. He was scared, I could hear it in his voice. Like if we had the conversation, I might say no.

"You know, I've heard that when there's a shooting star, you're supposed to make a wish. So that's one wish for each of us."

I turned from the sky to look at his big brown eyes. He closed them to make his wish, and I leaned in and pressed my lips against his.

Chapter Fifty-two

The final dance was an unmitigated disaster. We fanned okay, but the weaving caused two near head-on collisions. During the spin out, Maddie had her foot on the hem of Niki's dress. Instead of twirling, Niki stumbled forward. She righted herself and gave a small curtsy.

By the time the whole thing was over, we stood in a line, flushed and hot. A bead of sweat dripped down my back.

Mrs. Pelletier and Symone walked onto the stage, arm in arm. I straightened my back. Symone had the kind of posture I wanted to emulate. We all did.

Mrs. Pelletier stepped to the microphone. "Let's give all of the girls a round of applause for a glorious evening." She held her hands away from the microphone and clapped heartily.

Symone smiled and gave us a wink.

"Miss Hollis is a small pageant, it's true. But these girls all have big hearts and big hopes. No matter if they win, or are among the losers, it's clear that these girls are stars. Only ten girls are up on this stage tonight. Ten girls out of how many in Hollis?"

Beside me, Shannon whispered, "We're spe-ci-al."

Mrs. Pelletier kept on, "Many people think pageants are silly or frivolous. Some even argue that pageants are demeaning. Do these girls look demeaned?"

We should have held still and maintained our smiles, but we all looked at each other, in search of signs of debasement.

"No. These girls are strong, powerful, and proud. These are the girls who will make a difference in the world."

The audience was silent for a moment before realizing that the hole was meant to be filled with applause. So clap they did, and Mrs. Pelletier beamed back at them.

When the applause died down she said, "Now, I would like to announce our three finalists." She cleared her throat. "Miss Shannon Pierce." Shannon looked stunned. She turned to me, and I wrapped my arms around her. "You're supposed to shriek and be all excited," I whispered.

"Whoops," she whispered back. She stepped out of line in front of the rest of us. I was glad for Shannon. She was cool, and I could really picture us as friends.

"Miss Madeline Munson."

Of course.

She slinked from the line and positioned herself a step in front of Shannon, a bitchy move. I started wishing for

Shannon to win. Concentrated all my energy on it. *Shannon. Shannon. Shannon.* As though my thoughts could change the outcome. I didn't need to win, but I couldn't bear it if Maddie did.

"And our third finalist, Miss Dara Cohen."

My stomach dropped. My hands shook. "Oh my God," I whispered. The girl next to me grabbed me and squeezed me to her. "Congratulations," she said. "I hope to God you beat Maddie." It was loud enough for everyone onstage to hear. Another girl in line snickered, and Maddie pursed her lips for one second before slapping her smile back on.

I went to the front of the stage with Maddie and Shannon. The other seven girls stepped back into the shadows at the far end of the stage.

"All three of these girls deserve the title of Miss Hollis, and Hollis should be proud to have any of these three," Mrs. Pelletier said. She looked at us for a moment, remembering, I'm sure, her own pageant days.

A few flashbulbs gleamed from the audience. Somewhere out there Owen was filming the whole thing. Here was the end of my autobiography project, unfolding in front of him.

I wanted that crown. I still hadn't figured out exactly why. The farm was part of it: I wanted there to be something for the farm to celebrate. And I knew I wanted to beat Maddie.

I wanted to win for me too. I wanted someone to tell me I had the right to feel good about myself. That I might have gained weight, but I was still me. I still had talent. I was still beautiful. Owen had told me, and Rachel too, but I needed someone outside to tell me as well. Dr. Eddington would love to hear about that.

Shannon reached down and squeezed my hand. Her palms were warm. The light caught some sequins in Maddie's dress and sparkled up at us.

An ego stroke wasn't all I wanted, though. As Mrs. Pelletier lifted the microphone to her lips, I realized what it was: I wanted something that was mine. Not my parents' goals for me, not Melissa's causes, not Rachel's cheese, and not Owen's film. I wanted something that I did, that I won.

Mrs. Pelletier lifted the microphone to her lips. "I will now announce the second runner-up, followed by the first runner-up. Then we will crown our winner." She smiled at us. "Our second runner-up is Miss Shannon Pierce."

Shannon gave me a wink, and then she squealed, "Oh my God!" When she gave me another hug, she said, "Was that better?"

"Much," I replied.

She stepped forward and Symone presented her with a bouquet of white roses.

It was a perfect ending to my autobiography project: Maddie and me. My nemesis, both of us connected to Owen. Of course, none of the background tension would be in there. When people saw it, Maddie would just be some girl.

This autobiography was all wrong. It didn't tell my story. I couldn't tell that story myself. I'd need my parents, Melissa, Rachel, Owen, and Milo. Sascha and Belinda and even Maddie should be a part of it. It's not like we exist in bubbles. The things we do may describe us, but not define us. It's other people, our relationships with them that make us who we are.

Mrs. Pelletier said, "And now our first runner-up."

Mr. Fitz would get his video. I'd mail it to him along with a note that said I wouldn't be returning to Portland Academy. He'd get this little capsule that fit his guidelines, but he still wouldn't know me. I thought of Belinda typing up everything that happened to her from day one to the present, and even then she left things out. There are always things left out; things you forget, and things you choose not to include.

"Miss Maddie Munson."

Next to me, Maddie slumped. "Freak," she whispered before she plastered her grin back on and stepped forward. It was that word, *Freak*, that made me realize I had won. Shannon tugged on my arm. "Holy crap, you beat Maddie," she said.

I suppose I ought to have felt elated, but calm swept over me. The lights faded. The applause slowed down.

Mrs. Pelletier made the pronouncement: "And may I now present to you Miss Dara Cohen, our new Miss Hollis."

Shannon let go of my arm, and I floated over to Symone and Mrs. Pelletier.

This was the way Owen had planned it. How wonderful, how divine to have someone like that watching over me.

Symone lifted the tiara from her head and placed it on top of mine. "Thank you," I said.

That's how a pageant ends. The winner is announced. Clapping. Tears. Stylized waves to the audience. Someone gets on the microphone and says, "Thank you for coming.

See you next year." No victory laps. No concession speeches. It just ends.

Before all the girls had left the stage, the audience began to move out of the bleacher seats. Lights came on over them, eliminating the boundary between stage and audience.

I felt hands on me, whispers of congratulations.

In the audience, Belinda had the faintest of smiles on her lips. Would this make it into her pages of memories? Or would I be one of the things she left out? Someone snapped a picture of me, flashbulbs went off all around me. I imagined hanging the pageant photo on the stairs, along with Owen's graduation photo and the one of me and Rachel on the Ferris wheel—adding to the memories and the history of the place.

Sascha helped Belinda to her feet. There was a smiling woman standing with him, almost as tall as he, and rail thin. I knew it was Sylvie Hansen from the gourmet market.

Next to them, Rachel stood with a blond woman, laughing. The woman turned to me, and I realized it was the beautiful piano player from the Hollis Village Inn. So *she* was the woman Rachel loved! Rachel put her hand on the woman's arm and climbed the three stairs of the stage. She hugged me, and I squeezed back. "Congratulations," she said, her eyes shining. "I'm so happy for you."

"Thanks," I replied. "For everything."

"It's what I do," she said.

I glanced over to my parents. They stood separate from the crowd, looking awkward. They waved at me and smiled, and then they turned and left.

Beyond them, Dr. Eddington was talking to a man in a suit. Her boyfriend? She waved at me, and I waved back. Right now she was just happy for me, not analyzing my motivations. Now that I wasn't going back to Portland, I wouldn't have to see her anymore, and that almost made me miss her.

A little girl wrapped her arms around my thighs. Her mother whispered, "Careful of her dress, Clio." I shook my head and smiled to let her know it was okay. In the middle of the stream of people heading back toward the fair stood Stan. He placed his hand flat across his heart and then flashed a peace sign at me. So he had come after all, to hear me sing Cass Elliot.

Milo hopped up the steps to the stage and took my hand in his, and I squeezed back. No conversations needed. A grin stretched across his wide face. I pulled him to me and wrapped my arms around him. He stumbled back a little, surprised by my sudden embrace, but then he reached around me with his arms and squeezed me closer.

When I looked over Milo's shoulder, I saw Owen flirting with Andy Temple. He gave me an exaggerated wink, and I almost felt bad for his prey.

Yes, this was the ending Owen wanted: everyone pairing off, making up. It was impossible, but it appeared to be happening.

It wasn't going to be easy, of course. Owen was leaving. I was going to start a new school as a senior—attached in some unnamed way to a sophomore. We would have to have a conversation sometime, and I knew that it would be awkward.

I needed to pick colleges and write my essays. At least I knew what I was looking for—someplace strong in English with a good performing arts program. Williams, maybe. I'd get my tour from the biggest heartbreaker in the freshman class.

Rachel and I had years to make up for. We still needed to figure each other out, and build more of our sisterhood. Living together for real would be different from visiting for a summer.

And, of course, my relationship with my parents needed mending. We'd have to talk and actually be honest, which could be as hard for me as it was for them.

All of that was to come. But I'll stop the story here because, just like Owen, I want a happy ending.

Acknowledgments

Thank you to my early readers and advisers: Larissa Crockett, Manda Goltz, and the Boston Writers' Workshop, especially Kate Racculia.

Thank you to my amazing agent, Sara Crowe, and my incredible and insightful editor, Emily Schultz. Thanks also to Donna Bray and everyone at Disney•Hyperion Books.

Thank you to my mother, for being an amazing role model, and to my father, for teaching me that hard work bears rewards.

Finally, of course, thank you to Nathan.